SIDEARM

BOB HERZBERG

WOLFPACK PUBLISHING
— EST 2013 —

Sidearm

Paperback Edition
© Copyright 2020 Bob Herzberg

Wolfpack Publishing
6032 Wheat Penny Avenue
Las Vegas, NV 89122

wolfpackpublishing.com

Paperback ISBN 978-1-64119-684-0
eBook ISBN 978-1-62918-215-5

*The beginning of a new series can tax the patience of a saint!
And yet my first-line editor, my faithful wife of fifty three plus
years, has lovingly and patiently put up with my many efforts
of bouncing new ideas and characters around in our
conversations. But most importantly, when I get that faraway
look in my eyes and have deaf ears for anything of the present,
she simply smiles and goes on with her tasks of lovingly taking
care of this old man. So, once again, I dedicate this work to her
and her illimitable patience and love, without which it would
never happen.
And to the many readers that have asked about this series, here
'tis! I hope you enjoy it, and if you do, leave a review. If you
don't, shhhh, don't tell anybody, but you can drop me a message,
and I'll try harder to please you next time! Thanks to each and
every one who makes it possible for me to do this, my publisher,
Mike Bray, and his wonderful staff, most importantly, Rachel
Del Grosso, and the many readers and friends. Thank you!*

SIDEARM

CHAPTER ONE

Shadows grew longer across the cluster of trees and shrubbery in the woods east of Lawrence. The sun was now in his eyes, glinting off the barrel as he was trying to aim. Zeke speculated that perhaps getting behind a tree and out of the sun might give him a clearer view. He knew, though, that if he so much as lifted a finger, the quarry would run or at least hop away.

His hat was off, but his perspiration only grew in the late August heat, staining his shirt and freely running down his face until it stung his right eye. Zeke knew that to even lift his hand to wipe it away would be like shouting his presence. His legs were cramped from the prolonged crouching position and his patience was getting thin.

But come what may, he had to get used to it.

He had made sure that the Henry rifle was cleaned and ready to fire long before his quarry made its appearance. Unfortunately, the stinging in his right eye couldn't be so easily remedied.

The furry little creature wiggled its nose adorably and was facing west when Zeke now decided that this would be the moment for the kill.

Absently he cocked the hammer and a split second later knew he had made a huge mistake. The hare shot off into the brush with no more notice than a quick breath. The bush rustled loudly in its wake and it seemed quite possible the little creature was now crossing the Missouri border.

Zeke uttered the curses he was not allowed to utter at home and got up, clicking the hammer back into the guard. He put his hat back on and faced the horizon, pointing the gun at the ground. Another fifteen minutes or so it wouldn't make a difference anyway.

All the forest creatures came out after dark, but he would not be able to see them—something he was sure they knew. He had always admired forest creatures for their cunning, a kind of native intelligence that allowed them to see in the dark and instantly sense the presence of man—that is, unless man learned to play the game their way.

He was a lanky young man and the thinness of his frame was emphasized more by the fact that he was already over six feet tall. Had his hat been off, his sandy hair would have glistened in the sun.

Damn, he thought. *This is slow going.* If he was to join up, he had to improve his aim. And even then, he knew that would only be the beginning.

When Zeke heard the horse's approach sound on the path above, he knew that hunting time was over. He heard the animal stop and someone dismount.

His foray into adulthood would have to be postponed —for now.

The voice calling to him from above was affectionate yet jeering.

"Hah! Look at the Great Hunter! Just wasting shells again, if you ask me."

Zeke's little sister, Ruth, stood there with her hands on her hips and peered down the hill. She was frowning, but her eyes held something playful behind them.

He looked up at her. "You got someplace else to go?"

"Yeah, home. And you're going too."

"Says who, bunny-head?"

"I say, Ezekiel. Supper isn't going to be held for you all night."

Zeke slowly climbed up the hill, occasionally using the rifle as a staff, the barrel pointed skyward.

"I was coming along anyway," he announced in a surly tone. "As soon as you showed up, all the animals heard you and high-tailed it to Texas by now."

"Yeah? Well, if those animals want to be Ribs, they can stay there. We won't miss 'em."

Zeke looked away from Ruth and grinned at that. For thirteen years old, she already had the stubborn Tyler streak.

When Ruth turned to climb up on her horse, Zeke playfully bumped her across the rear with the rifle butt, careful that the barrel was pointed skyward and his hands were not near the trigger.

"Hey!" she yelled. "You stop that, Ezekiel! I'll tell Ma!"

"You just climb up on Red and keep your squealing to yourself, bunny-head."

Zeke walked over to a large tree a few yards away and untied his palomino. He slid the Henry into the scabbard on his saddle and climbed up. Then he walked the horse over to his sister's and looked at her seriously. Ruth saw the look.

"What's wrong?" she asked. It was the first time she sounded concerned since she found him.

"Nothing's wrong," Zeke said, moving his horse down the trail. Ruth urged her horse onward, keeping pace with him. "I was just thinking," he continued, "this is going to be the last time or about near it, that you'll be coming out here to fetch me."

"Why?" She knew why and was afraid of his answer.

"Next Tuesday I'm joining up."

Ruth suddenly looked sad and cast her eyes to her saddle horn for a moment. Then she said, with hope in her voice, "You're lying now, Zeke. You're not joining up."

He looked at her earnestly. "I *am*. I swear—"

"Hush! Mama said you shouldn't use the Lord's name like that."

"I didn't get a chance to…Huh, I can see when you're married, telling your husband what to do and when. You'd make some poor man a great wife."

Ruth frowned at him. Then she watched the trail and said, "You've been talking about joining up since Fort Sumter."

"I wasn't about to turn nineteen around the time of Fort Sumter. I think it's high time I got into it. I should've done it a year ago. I kept letting Ma talk me out of it. Not this time…"

Ruth said nothing then.

They rode on for a while, the small house near the edge of town with the newly thatched roof was coming into view.

Ruth was unhappy and he knew it. Otherwise she'd be gabbing all the time about the folks in town or their children or just about anything. He hated to wave it in her face, but she had to get used to his decision sooner or later. Pa finally said that was the day he could do it, when he turned nineteen (though he always suspected his parents were hoping the war would be over by then). And being a good Kansan, he was going to hold his father to it.

As they passed the house next to theirs, a middle-aged woman waved at them from the kitchen window. They both waved back.

"It is a hot day, children," the woman called. "Would you like something to drink?"

Ruth answered, "No, thank you, Missus Klausen. We have dinner waiting."

"All right then."

Zeke smiled politely. He was irked by the *children* remark, but he realized Mrs. Klausen was just a nice European lady who meant no harm. Raising Victor on her own must have been hard enough after her husband's death.

After they turned the horses into the barn and gave them feed, they entered the house.

Their parents were already seated at the table and both looked up when they entered.

Luke Tyler looked across the table at his wife and remarked, "Dan's Boone's arrived, time to eat."

Sarah Tyler had a dignity and a forbearance that shone through the hot August evening, and her blue eyes shot her husband a stern look.

"Those are your ideas, Luke…"

"Sure, they're my ideas!" he thundered. "Blame me for everything!"

"Don't try to avoid this, Lucas. You bought him that Henry, and now he's never home." She then gave her son a withering look. "He's out huntin' *Rebs*."

Ruth was still quiet. Luke noticed immediately.

"What's wrong. Kitten?" he asked tenderly. "You're kind of… less noisy."

"Nothing, Pa." She absently went over to the chair at the side of the table and sat down, her father watching her all the time.

"You two have a fight?" he asked her. "Did Zeke hit you?"

She shook her blonde head sullenly. Like her brother, she was tall for her age, and the gentle face held the same firm chin and blue eyes of her sibling, now set in a grim expression no one could miss.

"What is this, a graveyard?" Luke asked wryly. "Someone tell me what's wrong."

Zeke threw his hat down on a shelf and sat down.

Sarah turned to him. "What do you think you're about to do?"

"Eat."

"Not until you get the smell of the forest out of your hands. Now go out back and wash up."

"Soldiers don't wash up," Zeke answered glibly. "They have to fight whether they're dirty or not."

"General Grant, isn't he?" said Luke. "Boy does have a point though."

Sarah said irritably, "In *my* house, he washes before dinner! That clear, Ezekiel?"

"Yes, Ma..." Zeke sullenly got up and disappeared out back.

After he left the room, Ruth said, "He said he's joining up come Tuesday..."

Sarah stared accusingly at her husband, but he quickly averted her gaze. "You gave him that idea, Luke."

Luke raised his eyes to her finally and said, "What's wrong with a boy wanting to fight for his country? I did it in Mexico. Knew Grant when he was the supply clerk. I've got a bum leg today because of my service down there, but I felt proud doing it. Grandpa did his tour in 1812. Why not Zeke getting his turn?" Then he decisively stuck his fork into a slab of meat and took a mouthful.

Sarah watched him eat and glared at him even more. *They didn't even say Grace yet.* He saw her look, then quickly dropped the fork onto his plate and said a prayer. Sarah did also, then Ruth.

"Wait for him," Sarah ordered. The others stopped praying in mid-sentence.

When Zeke returned, he almost showed his hands to his mother, but then felt that soldiers don't show their now-washed hands to their moms.

"You clean?" she demanded to know.

"Yes!" Zeke said resentfully, after sitting down. He muttered the prayer, then started in on his food.

They all ate in silence for a few minutes. Then Sarah eyed her husband as she chewed her meal. After a swallow, she said, "You going to get around to mentioning that letter, or do I?"

"Like to digest first," her husband answered.

She turned to Zeke and said, "Your pa got a letter from Aunt Agnes. Timothy broke his leg. Fell off his horse, they say."

"Drunk," muttered Luke, avoiding Sarah's eyes.

"*Anyway*, he broke it," Sarah continued defiantly. "They're a couple miles outside town and we're the closest relations. Farm-house needs some work. There's a hole in the roof that needs fixing, taking care of the stock, things like that. Until they can get hold of some youngster in town to help them, they want us to send you."

Zeke looked down at his plate and picked at the food. He was seething. "They're not my favorite people," he said.

"Did I ask you that?"

"No, ma'am."

"Olathe isn't far, it wouldn't be a long ride. Help them for a couple days, then come back here—and I do mean *come back*!"

"What's the matter? Afraid I'll hit a recruiting station on the way back?"

Suddenly Sarah threw her fork down on the plate and said angrily, "Don't be insolent with me! You're not joining up! You're just a boy."

"And when is a boy supposed to become a man?"

"When he's still alive to do so!"

"The South isn't going to fold up by itself. They've got to be beaten."

Luke said, "Boy's got a point, Sarah."

"There isn't going to be any war after the summer," Sarah said glibly. "The two sides will see it isn't getting them anywhere and they'll talk peace. You'll see." She then turned her attention back to her meal.

"Excuse your mother, Zeke," said Luke playfully. "It's just that she's too modest to tell you that she knows all this 'cause of her meeting with Lincoln the other day." He then started to laugh and its annoying rasp infuriated Sarah the longer she heard it.

She cut through the noise by saying, "Go ahead and laugh! You think young boys shooting each other somewhere off in the woods is funny!"

Luke stopped and looked at her seriously. "I went through it, Sarah…You know I don't…"

"I can do it, Pa," said Zeke. "I'll be a good soldier. I want you to be proud."

Luke reached over and put his hand on his son's shoulder affectionately. "I *am* proud. You don't have to prove anything to me."

"But I want to do it. Come Tuesday, I'll be fighting for the Union."

Ruth suddenly got up from the table and ran to her room, trying to hide tears as she fled.

"Some people will miss you," Sarah said grimly. "Did you think of that?"

Zeke looked down at his plate, no longer hungry.

"And those other boys butchering each other," his mother continued, as if Ruth had never existed, "they're all way past twenty." Both father and son stared at her, knowing full well she didn't know what she was talking about.

"A man's age isn't what's important," Zeke replied. His parents noticed that he said 'a *man's* age', not a boy's. "It's his wanting to fight. Ask Pa. Out in the woods, I hit everything I aim at. And Pa was the best marksman in the infantry."

Luke looked down sheepishly.

"Phony fighting," said Sarah, with barely concealed contempt. "Hiding up in trees and just over hills waiting for some poor man to show up and then you shoot him from a distance...You call that fair fighting?"

Luke's face clouded over angrily. "No, Sarah," he said, "it's called war." He then got up from the table and walked outside to get some air.

After a moment, Zeke excused himself and also got up from the table.

Sarah watched him leave, then looked down at her plate listlessly. She felt martyred, all alone at the table. Not an unpleasant feeling...

Zeke thought he should go out and talk to his father, but instead turned to his left and went to his sister's room. When he got to her door, he heard her crying. Well, she was a kid, what did he expect? She wasn't going to hear that her brother was going off to war and just take it in stride. He knocked on the door.

He heard her stop crying abruptly and she sniffed back tears. "Come in," she said meekly.

Zeke entered and closed the door. He sat down on the bed and looked at his little sister. Her eyes were red, and her cheeks stained with tears. Zeke loathed himself at that moment, but he knew there was nothing he could change; the decision had been made.

Zeke reached up and pushed back her hair. "Well," he said off-handedly, "you didn't think I was going to stay here forever, did you?" He was trying to make it all sound so cheerful and failed miserably.

Ruth wiped her eyes and looked up at him. Her brother was her closest friend, her playmate, her babysitter and her protector. Through the years, he had fought several bigger boys who were pushing her around—and won every fight. And though her attitude towards him grew more insolent as they got older, Ruth never forgot what her brother went through for her. She was loath to say that she loved her brother, but she was terrified at the thought of him getting shot up by a Secesh in some far-off valley in Virginia.

"You'll get along," Zeke said gently. "You've got to take care of ma and pa while I'm gone."

"You going to come back, Zeke?" Ruth asked, tears starting to come again.

"'Course I will! What a fool thing to say! I'll be back and no different."

Tears came then and Ruth freely cried into her hands.

Zeke suddenly felt angry with himself. What right did he have to put her through this? And what guarantee did he have that he *was* coming back—and be 'no different'?

He lifted her up and they embraced, her tears soaking his shirt. "Promise me you'll come back," she implored.

"I promise…" Zeke said earnestly.

Outside the door, his mother called.

"Ezekiel! You go to bed early, you hear me! You're riding to Olathe in the morning."

Great, he thought. Before he becomes a soldier, he's got to be his hated uncle's ranch hand.

He continued to hug his little sister even as the riders crossed the Kansas borderline and headed southwest, skirting Union patrols and then cutting towards Spring Hill. Soon they would turn north to Gardner and then take the trail up to Lawrence.

That night, Zeke tossed in his sleep.

He never understood why he dreamt it, but he was having a nightmare about horned demons taking over his home...

The morning of August 21st was hot. Even that early, the sun was beating down on him as he took the trail to Olathe. The thick branches of cottonwoods hung over the trail, but they provided no shade for him, for he was moving fast. The palomino's hoofs thundered down the road, urged on mercilessly by its rider.

Zeke had left home without breakfast and was hoping to make Olathe in good time before hunger started to set in. He was usually sullen and ornery at this time of day and left early in order to get this silly task over with as soon as possible.

Zeke didn't like the Trevinses, as his mom well knew. Timothy was her brother and a more wasteful man never existed. He started out in life fixing saddles and ended up shoveling the filth out of pigpens—someone else's, of course. If not for his mom's generosity, Aunt Agnes would have left Timothy long ago and he would have taken up residence not far from the spittle jar of the nearest saloon. *A couple of days with them, no more,* he decided.

Then a couple days after that, he would be Private Tyler of the Something Kansas Infantry. On his leave, he'd parade around town in his Union blue, all the girls kicking about, giving him the eye and a big smile as he walked past. *Girls love a uniform.* He smiled at the thought and almost forgot the misery he was riding towards.

He saw a buckboard approaching in the distance and instantly recognized the black man driving it. As it came closer, he slowed his horse to a trot, then stopped as the buckboard pulled up to him.

The man pulled on the reins and stopped also.

Turning in his seat, he said, "You're moving fast, Zeke. Riding off to Virginia to help Grant and Sheridan?"

"Quit your funnin', Tobe Johnson. I'm in no mood."

"Testy this morning, aren't you, Ezekiel?" At times, Tobe would call him Ezekiel just to annoy him further.

Tobe Johnson was pushing fifty. His skin was weathered from years past when he worked long hours in the sun, and though his hair was already turning gray, behind his eyes the twinkle of youth remained.

He had always gotten along well with the Tylers, especially Zeke. Sometimes he would go out hunting with Zeke and his father. There wasn't a safe animal anywhere in the forest, it seemed, not with two former infantrymen and one would-be infantryman on the prowl.

"You seeing those awful relations of yours?"

"Yeah," said Zeke, eyeing the ground.

"You've got more than that on your mind," Tobe observed.

"I'm joining up Tuesday. Ruth is real broken up by it."

"Well, she's your sister. What do you expect, a celebration?"

"Yeah, but..." His voice trailed off before he could begin his meager explanation.

Tobe tried to look under that downcast face. "What else? I know that's not it."

Zeke finally looked at him. "Tobe, what does it take to be a man? I mean, you know...real grown up and being your own man."

"'Course you're a man! What'd you think you were?"

"You know what I'm getting at," Zeke began lamely. "I want

my own things. And I want to get them my own way too...Want to settle down one day..."

Tobe looked sharply at him. "Settle down? You've been watching the girls in town, haven't you?"

"Like to do more than watch..."

"Now you stop that talk, Zeke Tyler!...Least till you talk to your pa."

Zeke looked at him mischievously. "You once told me you were quite a ladies' man yourself and you were just fifteen."

Tobe cleared his throat. "Well, I talk a lot...Maybe too much sometimes..."

Zeke looked over and noticed boxes piled in the back of the buckboard. "More printing?"

"The cause won't be successful unless people know about it."

"Yeah, I guess so..."

"Don't worry, Zeke. With you kicking Johnny Reb from one end and my group printing our literature from the other end, I might actually live to see slavery dead in my lifetime! There's a lot of folks who will benefit...Yep, lots of folks..." Tobe then looked off briefly, his eyes far away. Zeke detected something like tears behind them, but he wasn't sure. In the past he had heard snatches of conversation between Tobe and his father about a family that Tobe still had back in South Carolina. Zeke didn't think much of it then.

Then Tobe realized how he looked and suddenly burst out laughing.

"Thought I went sentimental on you, huh?" He laughed again, a bit too forced this time, Zeke noticed. Then he reached out to shake Zeke's hand and said cheerfully, "Take care of yourself, Mister Tyler! And good luck to you!"

Zeke clasped the hand tightly and said, "And good luck to you, sir!"

And then Tobe did something that startled Zeke. He looked at the young man earnestly, then raised his hand to his temple and saluted him.

For a moment, Zeke felt a catch in his throat and swallowed noticeably. After a pause, he raised his own right hand and saluted the black man in return.

Tobe nodded at him then and with a shout to the horses, shook the reins and headed straight down the trail to Lawrence.

Zeke turned around to watch him go. After the buckboard disappeared over a rise, Zeke turned his mount back toward Olathe. He was ashamed to hear himself complain after thinking of all the troubles Tobe had been through. *Lord, if that man wasn't up north...*

Zeke picked up speed and shot through the trees as he headed towards the blasted place.

The riders pulled out of Franklin a couple hours before and their horses were brought up Mount Oread at a trot. The sun rose slowly, revealing close to four hundred men on horseback. Many of them were tied to their saddles to prevent them from falling off if they slept.

Those men now threw the ties off. They wanted freedom in the saddle and the ability to dismount and attack quickly. Weapons were checked again.

The column stopped then, and many of them were able to see the town from the vantage point of Mount Oread. A five-man team had already been sent down to look over the town.

There were complaints, of course; with some in the group shouting that this was madness and that perhaps they were going too far—especially since their opponents would now be able to see them in the coming dawn.

Their leaders, however, reminded them of the results of their intelligence work, which began days before. All weapons were locked up in the armory at the other end of town. The Union garrison consisted mostly of green recruits, boys really, not much older than they were themselves. Only tents stood in their path. The Second Colored Regiment was camped close by, also under-manned and outgunned.

As they waited for the five men to return, Charlie Morse of Tennessee, stood up in his stirrups and tried to see what was going on down in front.

"What's the hassle now?" The twang in his voice carried and was heard down the line. A few men turned back to look at him in the gray silence of the dawn.

Greg Tilton, formerly of Charleston, South Carolina, looked at him and said, "What's your hurry, Charlie? Time enough to clean 'em out. Hell. we'll have all day." As punctuation, he spat some awful tobacco juice on the ground.

"Let's get to it then," said Charlie, sitting tautly in the saddle. "Where are those five boys they sent down? Don't like this waitin'."

"I want to get going too. Got me a new navy and I want to put it to some use."

"Why are you fellows so nervous?" asked Jean Beaucaire, his French cadence sounding strange among the southern and Midwestern voices. "No one's going to warn them. That family back there in the farmhouse won't trouble us--"

"The ones in front did that!" Morse said resentfully. "What'd all the rest of us do but eat their trail dust?"

Tom and Mart Janey sat their horses nearby and laughed. They were identical twins, recently of Kentucky; both had short blond hair and bristling mustaches. They were both huge men, wide in the shoulders and big in the belly; and being twins they had long ago decided to dress alike; old calico shirts, gray pants with suspenders and dirty slouch hats. Their eyes always showed amusement and they both laughed loudly at the drop of a hat—especially if the joke was at someone else's expense.

All of them were young men, already rough and battle-hardened. They were excellent horsemen, riding the finest horses that could be stolen within a fifty-mile radius. Most of them were armed with six to eight navy colts each, all stuffed into waistbands or extra pockets. The extra guns were to save the time of reloading untrustworthy percussion cap weapons.

Those in front of the column wore captured Union army shirts and hats in order to lull the town's defenders into thinking they were just a patrol.

Mart Janey grinned and said, "I got a special hankering for some of them Kansas women."

Al Roster, a tall, strapping former grocery clerk from Independence, Missouri, listened to Janey's comment about the women of Kansas with something close to exhilaration. The smile on his face was huge and twisted and made the pimples at either side of his mouth more prominent.

He looked at Janey and said, without any sincerity, "Now, now! The colonel said no women are to be molested."

Tom Janey replied through stained teeth, "Our daddy said to us more than once, rules are made to be broken. And me and Mart are nothing if not obedient sons..."

All of the men within earshot laughed so loudly at that remark that those riders further down front had to turn around and tell them to shut up.

Nothing was going to interfere with this day's work...

CHAPTER TWO

THE HEAT OF THE PAST SEVERAL DAYS DID NOT LET UP ON THE morning of the 23rd.

Zeke held his horse to a trot as he rode the trail back from Olathe. His sleeves were rolled up and his hat was on the saddle horn as he took in the forest around him. He had ridden this trail many times, but now for some reason it felt different.

He had slept terribly over the past few days thanks to the nightmares. The devils of Hell were dancing everywhere and conquering all in their path. He never had dreams like that before and quickly attributed them to his anxiety over leaving his family and going off to war. That or perhaps too many fiery sermons from Reverend Cordley.

For Zeke, he had repaired his last Trevins roof, fixed his last Trevins fence and poured his last scalding cup of coffee down Uncle Trevins' throat while the old fool tried to sing some filthy song about naked women cavorting in Topeka. Soon Zeke would be an enlisted man and all that "helpful youngster" stuff would be gone forever.

Aunt Agnes' eggs and beef stuck to his ribs like wet plaster and he couldn't wait to get back to town and eat plainer food.

Armies traveled on their stomachs; that meant all home cooking was out. He had spoken to the soldiers from the garrison in town and picked up a great deal of information. For instance, he found it intriguing that the usually inadequate food a patrol would get was almost always supplemented by a little farmyard shooting. He was sorry there would have to be butchering of live-stock, but he also realized the greater need to keep the patrols on their feet and ready to fight.

Ready to fight...

In his mind, he was already seeing the torn bodies and choking on the smell of blood. As he rode, he shivered involuntarily.

Well, this war won't end by itself. Not until all folks are free.

Just then, it seemed that the air became thinner around him. He started to wipe his forehead several times in the last half mile, as if the day's heat had suddenly increased by twenty degrees. Then it hit him in a sudden wave; the foulest smell he ever experienced. To Zeke, it was like the combination of burning meat and burning chicken feathers or—

Something in town was on fire.

Zeke spurred the horse brutally and hit the road at a gallop. As he drew closer and closer, the stench picked up and his nostrils filled with the monstrous odor of dozens of burning houses off in the distance. The sweat poured off him now in what seemed to him like buckets; his mouth choking with the taste of ashes he saw floating above the trail like macabre snowflakes.

Somewhere beyond the woods and the trail, in the middle of an already stifling summer day, under a smoke and soot-filled sky, sat the charred remnants of his hometown...

Zeke took the back trail from Olathe and rode in from the other end of Massachusetts Street, at the far end of town from the Tyler property. His horse galloped into a wide street already filled with crowds of people putting out the still smoldering blazes of blackened homes. Buildings, houses, cottages, hotels, none seemed as intact as before he left. When they were not smoldering skeletons of wood pilings, they were broken and ripped apart; windows smashed, and bullet holes riddled the walls.

Charred corpses littered the streets, some under sheets laid out on any platform or piece of ground that was available; some without covering at all.

The sight of them and the relentless odor repelled Zeke. The horror he felt was reflected by that of the people he found on the street. Some were crying, some were putting out now dying fires, but most were wandering, lost and alone, their eyes red and hollow, their walk aimless.

Many in town were hard at work clearing away the damage, seeking loved ones—or their remains—lost or buried beneath still smoldering rubble.

On the sidewalks and in the street, dried blood could be seen.

He saw Union volunteers helping clear away the mess and collect the bodies. And then it struck him like a shot. The Union soldiers, whom he saw were not from the Lawrence garrison, were the only men on the street. Only teary-eyed women seemed to mill about; not one man from town came within sight.

Zeke climbed off the palomino and tied her to one of the few hitching rails available. After he dismounted, he turned and noticed eyes were on him. Some women were openly glaring at him. In seconds, they had drifted towards him; and as they came closer, he saw the hatred in their eyes, but didn't understand why it was directed at him.

Then one middle-aged woman approached him. The bun in

her hair was pulled down and her hair disheveled, her clothes blackened with dirt.

Grimacing at him, she gave him a stinging slap across the face.

He quickly grabbed hold of both her wrists and shouted, "What's wrong with you! Have you gone crazy!"

"That one!" screamed another woman, her shawl falling off her shoulders as she trembled with rage. "Where was *he*!?"

Zeke stared at her, his head spinning. Bewilderment showed on his face as he saw the crowd of women, some young, some older, gradually surrounding him.

He pushed the woman's wrists away from him and she staggered back slightly, still glaring at him.

She spat at him. "He's one of them!"

"Look at him!" shouted a woman in the crowd. "Fresh and clean as a daisy! Not burned to a crisp like my David!"

Somewhere off to the side, two women saw the confusion on Zeke's face and shouted at the circling crowd.

"Leave him alone! He's just a boy!" cried one of them.

The one with the disheveled hair screamed at her. "And what do you think *they* were? They were all boys! Stinking animals so young they didn't have any beards."

The other of the two spoke up, her Irish brogue sharp in their ears. "Can't any of you see he just rode into town? He's not one of them! Do you think they'd have the sand to come back after this?"

At that point the crowd was tired of words; suddenly they started their attack. They closed in on Zeke and started beating him. He tried vainly to block their assault, but there were too many. As the attack continued, the two women who tried to save him attempted to push their way through but were roughly shoved back.

Immediately behind the crowd, deeper voices were heard, and some women glanced back. By this time, Zeke was on the ground and worn shoes were kicking his sides and his back as he was doubled over in pain. That's when he heard the firing of a Dragoon Colt.

Instantly frightened by what they thought might be a repeat of the violence they had suffered, the crowd parted like the Red Sea and staggered back, some falling to the ground and others tripping over them.

A Union sergeant stood there with his pistol pointing skyward, smoke drifting out of the barrel. He was a tough Irishman from the east with a black handlebar mustache and thinning hair under a crooked Union cap. His stern gaze took in the women and then looked past them to the object of their hate. With a slight movement of his other hand, he gestured for his men to take action. They moved in then, using their rifles to keep the crowd back. Seeing the odds against them, the women gradually retreated and soon drifted away.

The sergeant came forward and looked down at Zeke sprawled on the ground. Holding out his hand, the sergeant asked gently, "You all right, son?"

Zeke reached up with one hand and let the sergeant lift him up as he wiped a trickle of blood off his mouth. With the Dragoon pistol still in his other hand, the sergeant watched the crowd warily.

"I have precious little tolerance for lynch mobs," he said grimly.

"Didn't care much for this one either..." said Zeke quietly, the side of his face throbbing.

The sergeant turned to Zeke and put his hand on the younger man's face. "I'd suggest our doctor, but he's kind of busy right now..."

"What happened here?"

"You don't know, do you?"

Zeke looked all around him and said, "This town looks like it was hit with cannon fire...Reb army do this?"

"Worse. Bushwhackers. They rode in on the morning of the twenty-first. The usual crew. Quantrill, Anderson, Todd. They wiped out the tow—"

"The twenty-first, you say?"

The sergeant nodded.

"I was with my kin in Olathe."

The sergeant looked at him sympathetically. "You were lucky. Strapping young fella like you, they would've shot you dead in two seconds...They've murdered all the men."

Zeke turned to him, shocked. *"What?"*

"And all the young ones too. Little boys, youngsters."

"What kind of madman would do such a thing?"

"You said it, lad. A madman. They've murdered all the males. Only some angry and devastated women left...Oh, some men got away. They hid, they ran. Especially that chicken-eatin' senator and self-appointed town protector we've got, Jim Lane. He always breathed fire where the crimes of the South were concerned, but when it got down to the thick of it, they found him sniveling and quaking in a cornfield with the rest of the women and children." He then spat on the ground as punctuation.

Zeke looked at him suddenly. "Did they get *everyone?*"

"Just about. We're trying to identify folks, but it's not easy. Many of the bodies were burned to a crisp. Some were shot so full of holes, it's hard for their wives and sisters to recognize them...'Course being Quantrill's men, most of the victims were shot in the back, indicating they were either running or minding their own business when they were attacked." He looked at the ruins around him in disgust. "This whole thing was a planned massacre, pure and simple."

"But why?"

"This is an abolitionist stronghold, that's why...We even had a Negro garrison here. Some were smart enough to hightail it to the hills. The ones who stayed were strung up to the nearest tree or crossbeam...The ones that lit out, I can't say I blame them too much. A bunch of coloreds falling into the hands of four hundred white trash—"

Zeke grabbed his arm suddenly. "Did they find any free-staters?"

"Plenty!" he said, freeing his arm from Zeke's grip. "Some woman in town was supposed to have furnished Quantrill with a list of names. They fired the Free State Hotel and all the Lawrence newspaper buildings...Listen, I've got to go."

"How do I find out who got killed?"

"Look around you, boy. There's rows of bodies everywhere. I'm afraid you'll have to find out on your own, until we get organized here...I'm sorry."

The sergeant walked away as Zeke wandered down the street. The women still watched him but were afraid to touch him now because of the soldiers. He moved further away from them, walking stiffly and dabbing his mouth with a handkerchief. Wagons full of the dead and dying, rolled past him as he moved further up the block. He was drowning in the awful stench around him, but he had to find out.

Several blocks further, somewhere outside the charred hulk of the building that was once the LAWRENCE STAR, he found a row of men piled on a blood-soaked stretch of ground in front of what was once the building's alley. He slowly walked over and looked at the faces.

Since most of them were white, it took him just a few moments to find Tobe Johnson. He was near the end of the row, the rough noose still around his neck, two bullet holes in the back of his head.

Zeke was suddenly dazed by it all. A couple days ago he was alive.

Absently, he removed the noose from around Tobe's neck. He looked at it and angrily tossed it into the rubble. Sadly, he looked at Tobe again and started to reach out to him when two soldiers with cots shouldered him aside. One barked at him to keep back, though Zeke barely heard him. Zeke looked at him again, then reluctantly backed away. The men laid the cots on the ground, then started to pile bodies. He noticed that the cots had originally been the doors of now-destroyed houses.

Zeke eventually returned to get his horse. At first, he rode slowly down the street, trying to avoid people, but it was impossible. Finally, he cut down a side street and headed for the outskirts of town. The level of destruction was no different there either, just crying widows and burned-out homes.

Zeke rode fast through backyards with no homes and alleys with no buildings around them. He was punishing his horse, but he was more frightened than ever now. With each stride, his terror increased. Since the guerrillas had struck the main streets and business district, he was praying that they had missed the house at the edge of town, near Mount Oread.

When he rode up the hill overlooking his house, he expected to see the thatched roof over the rise. But when he reached the top, he saw nothing. Nothing at all. Only a clear patch of sky where a thatched roof used to be. When he gazed down the hill, his heart sank.

His home was burned to the ground. Only charred piles of wood remained, the stench rising above it in the already stifling air. The walls, what were left of them, had fallen in. Zeke could see the blackened floor of the kitchen he used to have meals in just a couple of days ago.

He rode in a panic, nearly toppling from his horse as he made his way down the side of the hill.

Two Union men were searching through the wreckage. Their faces were lean and all too young and their expressions showed boredom and a general contempt for their menial task. Their mounts were tied to a pair of trees a short distance away.

Zeke rode up to the two men and stopped suddenly, almost hitting them. Then he jumped off the palomino and ran over to the rubble, searching frantically.

Turning back to the soldiers, he shouted at them. "Where are they?"

The two young men glanced at each other, then one of them walked over to a patch of ground a few yards away and just stood there.

The other soldier walked up and put his hand on Zeke's shoulder. He said quietly, "I'm sorry, fella."

Throwing the arm off, Zeke turned and advanced on the other soldier. He could see that the man was blocking his view of something on the ground.

"Now listen, boy—"

With strength he didn't know he had, Zeke reached out and threw the man aside. He then looked at the ground.

What he saw brought tears to his eyes and sickened him all at once. He threw his hand to his mouth and ran off into a cluster of trees. His knees buckled and he fell, one arm grasping the nearest trunk and the other steadying his body as the dizziness almost overwhelmed him. It was sudden and down to the pit of his stomach, taking a little while before it passed.

The two young soldiers watched him grimly, as they forced themselves to look unconcerned.

After a few moments, Zeke's breathing was back to normal and he rose, steadying himself on the tree. He turned back to them.

"Your folks?" one of them asked.

Zeke nodded.   Then, choking back tears, he said, "I almost didn't recognize them."

"Yeah," the first soldier said. "Tough break..."

"Where's the girl?" Zeke demanded.

The two men looked confused and glanced at each other.

"Who?" asked the second one, looking as dumb as Zeke had ever seen anyone look.

"The little girl," Zeke repeated, his voice rising. "Where is she?"

They both hesitated.

Finally, Zeke shouted at them. "The girl, you fools! Where is she?!"

"What girl? We were just—"

With frightening speed, Zeke went up to the first soldier and grabbed him by his blue coat. The second one tried to remove Zeke's hands and said helplessly, "Now listen here! You can't—"

Almost by reflex, Zeke back-handed him across the face. The weak-jawed fellow collapsed onto a pile of rubble a few feet away, out cold.

Still glaring at the first soldier, Zeke shook the helpless man and shouted in his face. "Did you find her? Did she die in the fire? Tell me!"

Scared, the young soldier spoke fast. "We didn't find anyone! Just the old couple. Our patrol rode up here and found the wreckage just the other day. We looked the place over from top to bottom. These folks were the only ones we found." He even raised his hand. "Honest!"

Suddenly a broken voice came from behind them.

"Ezekiel..."

Zeke turned around and saw young Victor Klausen standing there. Absently he pushed the soldier away and stared at Victor.

The boy was thirteen and much shorter than Zeke. His clothes were torn and blackened by the fire. A huge gash creased the top of his skull and his scalp was singed. His full head of wavy blond hair was burnt almost to the stubble. Zeke was horrified by his appearance.

"My God..." Zeke said. He ran back to his horse and returned with a canteen. Carefully he fed the water into Victor's mouth. The boy's lips were cracked and dehydrated, and though he drank the water gratefully, somehow the boy realized the rejuvenating effect was only temporary.

Victor pushed the canteen away and spoke. The words came out fast.

"They killed my mother..." He swallowed quickly, then continued. "She tried to save me and they shot her. They kept shouting that we were Dutch and that we deserved to die...We are not Dutch, we are German! Who would want to kill us because we're German? Who?"

"Sit on the ground, Victor."

"They struck me on the head with a pistol! One of them did. While they were stealing our furniture, I revived and ducked out the door. By the time I ran out to warn your folks, two men fired your house. I'll never forget them—or the others! The two men who burned your house were—they looked exactly alike...yes, that's it! When they heard my accent, they threw me into the burning house and shot at the windows when I tried to escape...Your parents were already dead, they shot them both. The other men who were burning our house joined them and shot at the back way to make sure I didn't get out..."

"How'd you make it out?"

"Found a crawlspace in your basement."

Zeke almost smiled; he remembered playing there as a kid.

The first soldier grabbed Zeke by the arm. "You better come with us."

Zeke yanked his arm away and said tautly, "Forget about me. Get him a doctor."

Then Zeke felt the small figure's weight go dead in his hand. He gently lowered the boy to the ground

"You hold on, Victor. I'll get a doc."

The young German looked up and Zeke saw the anguish on his face.

"They took her, Zeke…"

Zeke's face became very still. Then he said, "Ruth?"

The youngster nodded. "She screamed and put up a fight, but I saw them. Some man they called Morse. He tied her to his saddle and rode off yelling and whooping…like after a celebration. The twins followed him and then two…no! Three more! They looked like they were headed away from town…like maybe south, down the back trail to Spring Hill. Ruth was crying, Zeke. I heard her screams from down the road."

"Names, Victor," Zeke insisted. "Did you hear them call each other by any names? Besides Morse?"

Victor's eyes were slowly rolling back in his head. Against his better judgment, Zeke shook the youngster roughly.

"Hey now!" cried one of the soldiers.

Zeke shouted back at them. "Shut up and get a doctor, will you!"

He was about to try the canteen again, until the boy's eyes came into focus again. "A man with a French accent…I heard him shout, 'Roster, get the wagon!'" The boy then swallowed painfully.

Zeke picked up the canteen again. "Come on, Victor. Drink up."

But the face that stared back didn't see him. Zeke gently set him down and then put his head to the boy's chest. Slowly he rose and looked at the soldiers.

"Maybe you should come with us," one of them said.

Zeke didn't hear him; he just looked off down the road. "You got a patrol out looking for the men who did this?"

"They're probably across the border and back in Missouri by now. What's the sense?"

Zeke stared at him his eyes narrowed.

"We know how you feel, but the ones that done this are gone."

"Yeah!" echoed the second one, feeling his jaw.

Zeke went over to his horse and put away his canteen. Then he pulled the Henry rifle out of the scabbard. When he returned to them, the rifle was brought up and pointed at their heads.

"Hey, what do you think you're do—"

"The Dragoons!" Zeke said tautly. "Pull them out of your holsters and hand them to me."

"You're crazy!"

Zeke jacked a shell into the chamber, then pointed the rifle inches from the first soldier's head.

"That dead immigrant on the ground understood English better than you. Now hand it over! Butts first."

Carefully the young man pulled the Dragoon pistol out of his holster and handed it over to Zeke, who stuffed it into his back waistband. Then he grabbed the other Dragoon out of the second soldier's slow-moving hand and stuffed it under his belt.

"The holster too."

The second soldier glanced at his friend, then slowly took off his holster and handed it to Zeke. He took it and stepped back several feet.

"Ammo in your saddlebags?"

"Where else?"

"Get on the ground, face down."

"What kind of robbery is this?"

"Hal," said the second one. "Do what he says. I don't like what's behind his eyes."

They did as Zeke ordered. Quickly he went through their saddlebags and brought out spare shells for the Colts. With the two soldiers still tasting Kansas sod, he swung up on the palomino and turned him south.

Then Zeke spurred the animal down the road as fast as he could.

At that point, Zeke wasn't sure of his destination or what he would find. But one thing was certain: wherever he was going, he would stop at nothing to get there...

CHAPTER THREE

His horse was spent, and he knew it.

For over an hour he spurred his mount down the road, watching for signs of which direction they were headed. It wasn't very hard. Horse and wagon wheel tracks were all over the road.

The fact that they had brought wagons with them galled him further.

Mass murder was bad enough, but they took every piece of property not too heavy or not tied down and left the survivors with literally nothing to rebuild their lives with, just corpses and memories of happier times before they rode in.

As Zeke rode, he thought of his parents and the tears came, angry tears, stinging his cheeks and falling onto the pommel. He wiped his eyes periodically and sniffed back the tears. He wanted to stop, to get off his horse and just shed tears till the end of Creation, but he couldn't; there wasn't any time. God knew how much of a start the guerillas had. Two days, he figured. The tracks looked fresh. And if Zeke had bothered to look, he would have seen items tossed haphazardly off into the forest on both sides of the road--children's toys, clothing, cigar butts, empty liquor bottles, and particularly tools which were only for folks who worked for a living.

Zeke was now wearing the holster; one of the Dragoons was in it, the other stuffed in his back waistband out of sight. He had never worn guns before, and at first, he felt strange with a holster around his waist. And then he realized something: From now on, nothing was going to be like it was before.

Nothing.

No sooner had Zeke realized this, it was then that he saw it. Columns of black smoke to the south, rising over the treetops in the distance. Again, he felt the summer wind carry the heat and the stench of burning homes miles away.

They weren't hard to find, were they...

Zeke spurred his mount even more now, but he knew he was pushing it. He felt the sweat and foam on the palomino's neck. Zeke had not given him water since they left Olathe and the only rest he'd gotten was the few minutes he stopped in Lawrence. Miles ahead of him was the village of Brooklyn, for all he knew, possibly burning to the ground as Lawrence had.

Zeke was contemplating this when he looked ahead and saw two horses standing off to one side of the trail with two men near them. Strangely, one of the men seemed to be standing too close to a cottonwood, as if he were vainly trying to hide behind it.

The other man freely stepped into the trail in front of Zeke and signaled for him to stop. At first, Zeke thought they had been waylaid by the guerillas, until he realized that they still had their horses. Gangs who grabbed furniture wouldn't let two men still keep their horses. To Zeke, something smelled funny and it wasn't the burning homes of Brooklyn.

Zeke yanked the reins and his horse gratefully slowed down, finally coming to a stop directly in front of the man. He was a grimy-looking man in a dirty shirt and well-worn pants. His face was bearded and sweaty, the eyes beneath his black hat small and piercing. The smile he gave Zeke tried to widen with the appearance of being friendly and amiable, but he didn't quite make it. The small eyes stayed on Zeke, never once glancing over to the horses or the man who, just seconds ago, scurried out of sight to hide behind a tree.

"Glad you came down this trail! Did you hear what happened?"

The voice was too southern for that region and as soon as he finished his sentence, the man seemed to realize it. His right hand was getting too close to his holster.

"Yeah," said Zeke, his face very still. "I heard."

"Damnedest thing I ever saw! They burned the whole town! I had just enough time to clear out and then, wouldn't you know it, my horse goes lame. Damnedest thing!"

"Yeah," said Zeke, completely deadpan, "the damnedest."

The man's expression got less cheerful and in his narrow eyes was a nagging suspicion that Zeke was no fool. Time to end the playacting.

"So, I'll give it to you plain: I'd like *your* horse."

Zeke replied, "I see two horses back there, mister. Why don't you ride the other one?"

"'Cause that's mine!" said the other man, coming out quickly and holding a gun. He was shorter than the first man and wore a checked shirt pulled up at the sleeves, showing muscular arms. He was chewing tobacco and quickly spat some of it in the grass. His eyes laced into Zeke, watching his hands closely.

"Take his gun, Teddy," said the man in the road.

"Like hell I will!" said Teddy. "He takes it off! I'm not gettin' near him. He looks big enough and young enough to jump both of us."

Teddy didn't look older than twenty-two himself.

"You heard 'em," said the man in the road. "Take it off."

Zeke eyed Teddy warily, seeing the Navy Colt in his hand.

"Slow, boy," said Teddy. "One move and you get blasted off that horse and we'll take what we want anyway. No law to help you out here. Right, George?"

"That's right," said George cheerfully, as Zeke was unbuckling his holster. "*We* are the law! And the law is Quantrill!"

Zeke shot him a look and the man saw it.

"That's right," he repeated, taking the holster from Zeke. "We took a piece out of Lawrence, what're you going to do about it?"

"Look at him, George. I can't figure if he's riding from trouble or right to it. Which is it, boy?"

"I'm riding to it," said Zeke, without expression.

"I'd say so," replied George. Then he balanced the holster in his hands and looked at it appraisingly. "Union hog-leg! He pulled this off a Yankee!" Then he looked up at him, gesturing with the holster. "What were you going to do with these? Go after Quantrill all by yourself?"

Zeke said nothing. He just glared at George, then Teddy. He was purposely trying to give the impression that he was just giving them angry looks, when in reality he was measuring distance, isolating exactly where they stood at that moment.

George's face lost all its cheer and his mouth became a grim little slit.

"All right, enough gab. Get off *my* horse."

Zeke's hands were resting on the saddle horn. As he watched them, he pulled his feet out of the stirrups and slowly threw his right leg over the horse's other side, hoping the dragoon colt behind his back wouldn't be seen as he turned. He figured after he dismounted, the horse would be between him and the robbers.

"Hey, get off on *this* side!" shouted George, too late.

Teddy cursed and aimed his gun.

Zeke realized Teddy had spotted the Dragoon. With his right hand already hovering behind his back, Zeke quickly drew the gun, thumbing the hammer back at the same time. He fired straight at Teddy as he cleared the saddle. He saw Teddy fire a shot and then grab his chest. Staggering to his left, he went head-first into the side of a cottonwood and collapsed.

George dropped the Union holster and quickly drew his own gun, which turned out to be a fatal move. Had he pulled the Dragoon Colt from the holster in his hands, he would have won.

By this time, however, Zeke had hit the ground and was firing up at him from just a few feet away. The ball pierced George's throat and neatly severed his windpipe before he had a chance to fire.

Suddenly a shadow loomed over Zeke and in that split second, he realized that his palomino was hit. He threw himself out of the way as the fatally wounded animal toppled and fell heavily to the ground.

Zeke rose carefully and surveyed the scene. George was dead, with his face in the dirt. So was Teddy. Turning back, he saw that his horse was laid across the trail, blood coming out of his side.

Zeke looked down at her sadly.

"I'm sorry..."

He thumbed back the hammer of the dragoon and pointed the gun at the palomino's head. Then he fired one shot.

There was a rumble of hoofs in the distance and Zeke looked down the trail from Lawrence. He didn't know who the riders were, and he wasn't about to take a chance. The woods were probably full of robbers and his two pistols and one saddle gun were no match for them.

Zeke grabbed the holster off the ground and strapped it on again. With some effort he untied and pulled the saddle off the dead horse. He then went over to the other horses and searched them for anything he could use. He found a bedroll, coffee, two loaves of hard bread, some currency and a coffee pot. After combining the various articles, he tied his saddle to the horse that wasn't lame and then mounted him.

By this time the rumbling in the distance was growing louder and he hurriedly spurred the horse out of there. He now had some supplies at least. Despite the carnage up ahead, he figured the guerillas wouldn't stick around and take in the damage. The Union army was alerted to Lawrence by now and they had to be on Quantrill's trail. Maybe the riders he heard in the distance were a Union column, but he couldn't take a chance.

Zeke thought about the money he found in the saddlebags—a few hundred dollars in Union currency, probably stolen from Lawrence. He felt funny about having it in his possession. The people who had that money were probably dead, but he knew he had to do some serious traveling and would need it to survive.

He tried not to think of the word *ghoul*.

It was a good horse and it took to the road easily, almost as if it were bred for the chase. A perfect horse for a raider, and quite possibly stolen as well.

Zeke didn't know who was behind him and didn't slow down or look back. All he knew was that the gang that took his sister was probably headed south. He thought of Missouri. There were some folks in the bigger towns who were against slavery, and that meant they were also against Quantrill, but he wasn't sure.

What would the south's reaction be to the massacre? Or the reaction of folks from Missouri? Considering all the hardships they were taking from the Union army would the people of Missouri cheer the massacre? Or recoil in disgust as decent folks would?

The smell of burning houses suddenly hit Zeke, and then all thoughts of decent folks disappeared...

Zeke rode into the town of Brooklyn and instantly saw heaps of rubble on either side of the town's main street. It was a lot smaller than Lawrence, he noticed. Most of the fires were out, with just a few homes still smoldering. It was obvious some men had put up a fight, yet the destruction didn't seem as bad as in Lawrence. He didn't know whether it was because Quantrill was now in a hurry, having lost the element of surprise, or whether he didn't have the belly for a fair fight. Either way, the scene was heartbreaking.

Zeke pulled up in front of an aged sycamore and tied the horse's reins to it. Then he walked down the street, surveying the damage, grateful that, so far, a crowd of women weren't attacking him. In fact, unlike Lawrence, Zeke spotted several men still alive to do the cleaning up.

He saw an old man sitting in a chair against what used to be a thriving general store. The rear of the structure was a charred mess and the front display window was broken out, glass littering the sidewalk. Blankets and sheets were pulled out through the window and some cans of food were scattered near the entrance. The roof had caved in.

The old man took a deep breath, then got up and took the broom that leaned against the wall. Tiredly, he continued to sweep the glass shards off the sidewalk. Then, sensing that someone was watching him, he looked up and saw Zeke.

"Why aren't you cleaning up?" he drawled. "You on furlough or somethin'?"

"I just rode in," Zeke replied. "Quantrill do this?"

"Nah, the whole town just blowed up by itself!" The old fellow shook his head and started to sweep again.

Zeke asked earnestly, "How many dead?"

"Don't know yet. Some men are dead, some cleaning up, and a

whole pack of them lit out after Quantrill along with some soldiers." He eyed him closely. "Where you from?"

"Lawrence."

The old man looked down for a moment and seemed to be examining the glass slivers at his feet. When he looked again at Zeke, his expression was sympathetic.

"I'm sorry...Lose any kin?"

"Both my folks. And they got my little sister."

The old man's eyes seemed to moisten quickly, then he said, "I've got a son fighting in Tennessee. Got another son and his wife trying to make a go of it on the Plains." Sarcastically he said, "All they've got to worry about is the Indians." He looked at the ground for a moment and said, "I heard Quantrill's gang doesn't harm womenfolk."

Without emotion, Zeke said, "Guess Quantrill didn't hear it..."

He looked up at Zeke and said, "They'll let your sister go. They have to. What're they going to do with her?"

When the old man saw Zeke's face grow tense, he realized he'd said the wrong thing. He quickly changed the subject. "One of our boys got wounded in a skirmish between Quantrill's bunch and the Federals somewhere along the Fort Scott cut-off. They just brought him back. He said they took the Santa Fe Trail around Paola and turned back up north again."

"North?"

"Well, northeast anyway. They weren't about to go back the way they came, not with half the Union Army tracking 'em. Everyone says they're heading for Missouri."

Absently, Zeke looked off to the east. He had caught snatches of conversation at his parents' dinner table. They were discussing the war and one of the topics concerned that of southern renegades who grabbed northern women, both white and black, to sell into slavery down south. However, those times he appeared for dinner, usually late, his parents mysteriously dropped the subject.

His expression must have been macabre, for the old man then said, "Take it easy, son. The army will get 'em."

Zeke looked at him and said nothing. After a moment, he asked, "Got a shortcut to the border?"

The old man studied Zeke. "You're heading into trouble. If those folks find out you're from Kansas—"

"I'd like to think not everyone in Missouri sides with Quantrill."

"No, just most of 'em. Maybe you should just go—"

"What road do I take to the border?"

The old man sighed and pointed to the end of the block.

"Make a left turn and take Judson Street. Go down for maybe a half mile or so, you'll hit a wide stretch of road heading northeast. I heard that once you pass the border and keep straight, you'll hit either Lone Jack or Warrensburg, I'm not sure which. You won't get to it in the next hour. It's a few days' ride."

"Thanks."

Zeke turned and headed back to his horse as the old man watched him sadly.

As Zeke rode down Judson Street, he passed several people digging through the rubble. On both sides of the street there were ruins of once proud homes, now just burnt lumber casting crooked shadows on the ground. *Were these people abolitionists too? Was that the excuse this time?*

Because of these people, Zeke slowed his horse to a trot, until he could get out of town. He looked at them sadly. Again, his nostrils were full of the smell of burning lumber, and a hot breeze carried the floating ashes through the air.

Preoccupied with their own troubles, the townsfolk mostly ignored him. And as he continued down the road, even these

groups got smaller until they were now mostly behind him. He
still had a way to go before he left town and now with less people
on the street, he decided to spur the horse faster.

And it was then that he spotted the house.

It was a fairly-new home, a simple one-story structure behind
a whitewashed fence. It was further up the block on the left-hand
side and ordinarily he would have ignored it except for two things;
one was that it sat among devastated homes with hardly a scratch
on it.

Another was that Ruth's horse, Red, was tied to the fence.

Zeke stopped before the charred remains of a home across the
street. The house was still standing, but Zeke noticed it had been
gutted. He dismounted and tied his horse to a tree slightly off the
road.

Zeke watched the house across the road, seeing old Red tied in
front, and tried not to show the rage growing within him. Then,
looking around and seeing no one close by, he slipped the spare
Dragoon pistol into his saddlebag, still keeping the other one in his
holster. He wanted to go up and see Red again, to calm the horse
down, to reassure him that he would be back home again. Then
he realized what a useless dream that was.

All he had was Ruth. He hoped to God that she was inside and
all right. He didn't want to think beyond that.

As Zeke approached the house, he glanced both ways to see if
anyone was watching him. No one was on that part of the street.
He watched the house and then the rear yard. Seeing no movement anywhere, he then turned left and cut down an alleyway
adjacent to the house. He moved silently, as if he were back
hunting in the woods near his home.

When Zeke got to the rear of the house, he spotted a door.
Then he stopped suddenly and saw an open window a few feet
away. The door was slightly open, yet he knew more than anyone

that doors on frame houses tend to creak. His ma had tried to get his father to fix theirs for the longest time. A lot of good that would have done now.

Being over six feet, he had no trouble reaching up to the open window and putting his hands on the sill. There was just enough room to squeeze through without him opening it. As quietly as he could, he lifted himself up and scrambled through the opening.

When Zeke stood up, he found himself in a small kitchen. The sun streaked in through the window, but as he looked beyond the kitchen's archway, he saw darkness.

Then he noticed the kitchen table was set for two. There were plates of food half-eaten, with utensils out of position, as if they were dropped suddenly. He wondered about this, and when he reached the end of the table and looked down, he had his answer.

A man in his thirties was lying spread-eagled across a toppled chair, blood seeping out of his forehead. Tensing up, Zeke looked towards the archway and drew the Dragoon Colt. Holding it before him, he quietly walked around the dead man and approached the arch. Two curtains were hung over it but were drawn back so that Zeke could see the living room.

Zeke expected an attack of some kind, so he quickly moved through the arch and then turned back to point his gun at the curtains. There was no one hiding behind them. In the partial darkness, he looked around and noticed many bare spots around the living room. Obviously, someone had taken furniture which looked especially good to them. He looked down and saw that the rug was bunched up and pushed aside. Something was pulled across it and he was wondering whether it was just furniture.

Zeke looked to his right and noticed another archway which led into a hall. Again, he advanced carefully deeper into the house, moving through the archway and seemingly ready for anything.

He knew someone was still there. Red's presence outside pretty much verified that.

In the darkness, he suddenly came upon an open bedroom door to his left. He looked inside and the first thing he noticed was the window with its curtains drawn, sunlight peeking in through the edges. Still, Zeke could make out a bed against the wall with some rolled up blankets on it.

Curiously he went over to the curtain and pulled it back with one hand. Sunlight shot into the room, and Zeke blinked his eyes adjusting to it. Then he turned around.

The woman was lying under blankets already darkened with blood, her arms spread out across the mattress. Her blue eyes were open, staring in a frightened gaze at the ceiling, redness around the sockets. She had once been a beautiful woman, with her long brown hair now pulled down about her shoulders. Bruises were on her face and arms.

Zeke was breathing fast. He was starting to feel dizzy, the gun becoming heavy in his hand. Leaning against the wall, Zeke caught his breath and made himself look at the woman.

Slowly he pushed himself off the wall and stood over her. Then he hesitantly reached over and pulled the blanket back. He saw the huge gash, the blood-stained dress torn around her, and then thought of the way she must have fought.

Yeah, Quantrill's boys never harmed women.

Angrily Zeke threw the blanket back over her, cursing the man responsible. As soon as he said it, he realized his mistake. A noise came from the direction of the living room, like someone moving fast over the carpet.

Raising the Dragoon, he turned to the doorway and carefully went out into the hall. Just then he heard a movement from the other end. He froze and watched the archway.

Again, he moved in cautiously, but this time, as he cleared the archway and entered the living room, he immediately heard the click of a hammer pulled back. He started to turn to the sound when a voice in the darkness barked an order.

"Drop it!"

Zeke dropped the Colt to the floor. He slowly turned to his left and saw a tall fellow wearing a partly buttoned calico shirt over trousers marked with soot. He was also barefoot. Al Roster had left his vest containing extra Navy Colts piled with his hat in a corner of the dead woman's bedroom. Had Zeke not been distracted by her corpse, he also would have seen where Roster had left his boots.

Al Roster, the former grocery clerk from Independence, smiled wryly and said, "Seems a man can't be left alone nowadays even to do his business." He pointed the Colt at Zeke's chest and stopped smiling. "Who're you? Kinfolk?"

Zeke, who had his hands raised slightly, just stared at him.

"Don't like talkin', huh? Maybe you like dyin'..."

"With all those folks out on the streets, I wouldn't chance a gunshot if I were you."

Roster seemed to think about what Zeke said. He stepped back slightly so he got a good look at him. His eyes were amused.

"Tall cuss, aren't you? They raise 'em that big where you come from?"

Zeke stared at him with malevolence. "You mean Lawrence?"

Roster's eyes widened, and he stepped back even more. In the light from the window, Zeke saw a thin and youthful face, with brown peach fuzz growing around the chin. His eyes were already hooded and far away, with bags under them. He had ridden hard and was living pretty fast for his own good. Behind the eyes, Zeke saw very little except hate and a rat's will to survive.

Then it was Roster's turn to spot something in Zeke's eyes; without thinking, he raised the pistol higher. "You put those ideas out of your head, sodbuster.   Big as you are, you couldn't take me..."

Zeke stared back and said nothing. *But I'd sure like to try.*

Then the questions came. "How'd you get here? You got more men with you? You better talk, you haven't got much time."

Seeing the look in his eyes, Zeke figured it wouldn't matter if he raised the stakes a little.

"Which one are you?" he asked. "Morse or Roster?"

Roster's mouth dropped, and he stepped back again, staring at the Kansan.

When he didn't reply immediately, Zeke ventured, "Roster?"

"Where'd you get my name?"

"You have my sister's horse out front."

"Your *sister's?*"   Roster thought for a moment, then looked close into Zeke's face. "That little girl is your sister?"

Zeke tried to keep still and suppress the rage he felt, but it was hard. He nodded without saying anything, but Roster could tell he was tense.

A little grin then came to his face and his eyes gleamed.

"Pretty soon ol' Charlie Morse will put her up for sale."

Zeke was furious but held his ground. His eyes quickly took in the floor at Roster's feet, then raised again.

Keep him talking. He's the kind who likes to crow.

"You and those twins fired the Germans' house."

Now Roster dropped his grin and his eyes narrowed in the faded light.

"How do you know? We didn't see you there."

"There were witnesses..."

"That doesn't matter none.   They're halfway to Lone Jack by now.

Let 'em run. I always had more nerve than any of 'em."

"How's that?"

"When I saw that filly through the back window, I knew I was going to have her. The town's so preoccupied with their burned up homes, I knew they wouldn't bother us…"

"So, you stayed the night."

"But only one of us got up this morning."

Roster started to laugh, but never got to finish it. Zeke's left hand grabbed his gun wrist and yanked it hard. At the same time, Roster stumbled on the bunched-up rug Zeke had steered him to. Then, as he started to fall, the pulled back hammer of the Navy Colt was released and it fired loudly in the small room.

Zeke threw himself backwards and fell against a wall, unaware the bullet had already gone into the ceiling. Roster raised himself up and saw that his gun was now on the floor within Zeke's reach.

And that's when he ran. A desperate run through the hallway and, after throwing open the front door, threw himself forward toward the street. Running from a man with a gun was one thing, Roster knew; running from a man with a gun whose family you've killed made even more sense.

Instead of the Navy Colt, Zeke grabbed the discarded Dragoon pistol and ran for the front door. He rushed outside just in time to see Roster put his hands on Red's saddle and try to mount him, but the nervous horse kept pulling away. Apparently, Roster was so desperate to get away, he forgot to untie the reins.

Zeke cocked the hammer of his pistol and aimed it at Roster, but the skittering horse kept getting in the way.

At that point, shouts came from up the street and Zeke saw a crowd of people forming and looking in his direction. *They must have heard the shot.*

Seeing that his attempts to mount Red were useless and having already spotted Zeke across the way with a Yankee Dragoon in his fist, Roster turned and ran into the burnt shell of the frame house across the street. By this time, the killer's feet were scraped and bleeding, but he kept running into the cavernous house and beyond.

Zeke had wanted to fire at the bushwhacker, but instead decided to take him alive and make him tell exactly where Ruth was being held.

He was not happy about taking him alive.

Zeke made it across the street and practically dove through the open front door. He looked around and found himself in the blackened skeleton of what was once a fine home. Ashes and rubble surrounded him, and the air was thick with the odor of burnt wood. The house was still standing, but Zeke figured this was largely an illusion. The only reason the walls and ceiling had not fallen down during the fire was due to a few strategically placed wooden posts holding the works up. His father had actually served under Lee in the Engineers Corps during his service in Mexico. He had told Zeke about buildings and structural supports and what it took to maintain them. He told him that houses and buildings weren't just built, they had to be maintained as well, like a mine tunnel or a bridge, and how little it would take to bring any of these structures down if they were weakened enough.

Sure enough, as Zeke advanced, he saw a devastated living room with four wooden posts, now definitely weakened, reaching up to blackened crossbeams. The ceiling, once made of the finest lumber, now had gaping holes in it. Sunlight streaked in, revealing damaged furniture and torn upholstery.

Zeke looked at the ceiling, then the devastated living quarters.

"This is not a good place to be..." he said worriedly.

With his eyes on a pair of damaged chairs, Zeke didn't see the shadow flying at him from the far left. As soon as he cleared the arch, Roster threw himself on the young Kansan, knocking the Dragoon off into a corner. The lunge was quick and caught Zeke totally by surprise, the momentum causing both of them to fall against the nearest post and crash through it.

Now Zeke knew just how weak the posts were.

As they fell heavily to the floor, the top part of the broken post swung dangerously back and forth, its splintered edge hung over them. Zeke's hat fell off, and as he was on the ground with Roster, a glance told him that the splintered end of the post was lower than it was before. His eyes glimpsed the ceiling and just, as he suspected, a portion of it had dropped down by a couple of feet, held back only by weakened crossbeams.

Then as if by some signal, both men grappled more intensely, their hate mounting as they fought. Both men's fingers gripped each other's throats as they rolled across the broken wooden floor. They continued to roll savagely across the living room until they stopped at another post.

By this time, Zeke had totally given up the idea of taking him alive...

Both men gradually struggled to their feet, grunting painfully as they kept punching each other, sweat burning its way into their bruises. Still, Zeke didn't look as badly as his opponent, who was now sporting a black eye.

Roster held Zeke against the post, putting his hands up and closing his fingers around Zeke's throat. Zeke was straining to push him off, but Roster wasn't merely boasting before; he was strong. For all the fights Zeke had ever been in, none of his opponents had ever tried to strangle him. He gritted his teeth and his eyes were wide with terror as he stared at the bushwhacker. His efforts to pull Roster's hands off his hurting throat were useless, and the man's fingers were only tightening more.

Desperately, Zeke pulled his hand off Roster's forearm and shot his fist into the killer's already blackened eye. Roster cried out shortly and pulled one of his hands off Zeke's throat to cover the eye. That's when Zeke punched the eye again, through Roster's fingers, only harder this time. Roster yelled again and this time staggered back.

Zeke leaned against the post and felt his throat, inhaling deeply. Then he stared at Roster, who was shaking his head and holding onto his eye. Suddenly, in a rage, Zeke bent his head low and dove into Roster's stomach, wrapping his arms tightly around his body as he did so. But as soon as he had made the dive, Zeke realized what he'd done. He was too mad to notice another weakened post behind Roster and directly in the path of his lunge.

Before he could stop himself, he plowed into Roster and the two of them struck the post hard. To Zeke the moment was all a blur; he remembered the impact of striking the post, the splintering crash and then the two young men slamming into the floor a few feet from the archway.

A second or two after they hit the floor, Zeke heard something else—a loud snap. Then the sound of wood splintering from above and a final sudden break. Zeke had landed on top of Roster and saw that the killer was too stunned by the attack to push him off.

In the second it took Zeke to raise himself up and look down at Roster, his eyes spotted the black shadow of something huge plummeting towards him.

In the blink of an eye, Zeke leapt off Roster and dove under the hallway arch. After he hit the floor beneath the arch, Zeke heard an immense crash which he thought might get him as well. A cloud of dust flew up in the living room and Zeke quickly threw his arms up over his head. In this awkward position he glimpsed what looked like the left wing of the house falling in. The debris fell quickly and before anyone knew it, what had once been a living room was now buried beneath what was once a heavy wooden roof.

Zeke coughed loudly as the dirt and soot rose up in dark, angry clouds, threatening to choke the life out of him. The rotted walls of the right side then had their turn and they fell in with an awful finality. On the ground under the archway, Zeke had rolled himself into a cowering ball, his arms covering his head as he called out to Jesus, Mary, or anyone else who happened to be available.

Eventually the tearing and crashing sounds ended and the billowing dust settled into an odor of broken and charred lumber, never to rise again.

When Zeke cautiously pulled his arms away and looked up, he saw the sun shining overhead, almost blinding him now that most of three walls and the ceiling were not in the way. He slowly rose to his feet and saw that only the archway and the front of the house were still standing. His shirt was completely torn apart, revealing a muscular chest now blackened with soot. His face was also covered with dirt and his pants were filthy. Blood ran down his chin and his forehead was bruised on the left side. He wiped the side of his mouth with a torn sleeve and cautiously looked inside.

The roof of the house was now literally in the living room. He glanced around quickly and, wiping the dirt from his eyes, finally spotted him—or at least his bare right foot anyway. The rest of Al Roster lay beneath several tons of mortar and heavy wooden crossbeams.

Zeke wiped his bleeding mouth again and stared at the body. His thoughts were suddenly interrupted by shouts from outside.

"Hey, anyone in there?"

"Good Lord, you all right?"

Zeke turned around and staggered over to the front door. When he reached for the knob, the door suddenly fell off its last hinge and toppled into the front yard. He walked through the doorway and immediately saw a crowd surrounding the yard, but at a safe distance. They were shocked when they saw him. Some women had grateful tears in their eyes when they saw how young he was and that he was still alive. Others were plainly horrified at his appearance.

Looking to the front of the crowd, Zeke recognized the old man he had spoken to before. He was shouting at Zeke.

He cocked his head to listen to what the old man was shouting, but his ears were too full of soot to catch it. He looked to the others and saw them excitedly gesturing at him. Straining to hear, he then caught the words, "…gonna fall!" and knew immediately.

Zeke dove forward, leaping past the yard and ramming into two men in the front of the crowd.

Seconds after he hit the crowd, the hallway arch collapsed and with it, the front of the house. The two men Zeke had plowed into pulled him back as the crowd retreated across the street. Clouds of dust shot up from under the collapsed structure as it hit the ground. Soon all was silent and just the clouds remained.

The big man who held Zeke asked, "You all right, son?"

The old man chastised him immediately. "What do you think, Hank? Look at him! You think he's all right?"

Another man said to Zeke, "We went to the Swensons' house after we saw you chasing that fella. We found both of them inside and figured you were settlin' a score for them." The man looked up at the fallen structure and said, "Looks like he paid real good."

Zeke's eyes were starting to go far back in his head. He said harshly, "For my folks too!"

Then his head fell back, and he gave way to the dizziness and the exhaustion, knocking him out for the rest of the day and the coming night as well.

Still tied to the sycamore several feet away, Red looked at the crowd and wondered why, with so many people around, he still wasn't being fed…

CHAPTER FOUR

THAT NIGHT, FOR THE FIRST TIME IN MANY NIGHTS, ZEKE SLEPT IN a decent bed. It was not as good as his bed in Lawrence, but it was far better than the bed "out back" that the Trevinses had always given him. He slept deeply, but not very restfully. Once again, he dreamt of demons coming to his home. He was shooting at them with his Dragoon pistol, but there were too many. Suddenly his home became a crumbling house, with debris falling all around him. Finally, when the ceiling plummeted toward him, he cried out his sister's name.

When he opened his eyes, he looked at the ceiling and realized he was in someone's bedroom. The air still told of the fires of the other day, yet it seemed clearer now. This might be in the country or at least outside the town. The singing of the birds outside was deafening.

Zeke was lying on a feathered pillow and had a blanket near him, which he had just thrown off. When he turned to his right, he saw a woman in her forties seated in a wooden chair near the bed. Gradually he inched the blanket back over his body.

The woman smiled wanly at him, as if she didn't know what

his reaction would be to his surroundings. She had dark brown hair in a bun and quiet blue eyes that made one relax instantly in her presence. Yet they also had a spark behind them which implied something not so quiet and gentle should the need arise. She was tall and generally pleasant-looking and wore a dress she had worn many times around the house, an apron tied around it. On a stool near his pillow sat a tray with a plate of eggs, warm bread and sausages.

She saw his eyes watching her and then knew that he was fully alert.

"We were checking up on you ever since the sun came up," she said, in a Midwestern drawl. "When I saw you starting to toss and turn, I figured you'd be up soon. I timed it perfectly." She gave that quiet smile of hers again and gestured to the plate. "Got your breakfast."

Zeke glanced at the plate, then at her. The food smelled wonderful after twenty-four hours without eating a thing. He smiled back at her.

When she saw the smile, something changed about her and the quiet, blue eyes became deep and far away. Zeke suspected there were even tears behind them.

"Something wrong, ma'am?"

She shook her head quickly and said, "Eat or your sausages will get cold."

Sausages! He had died and gone to Heaven—and then slowly he came back to earth.

"Who are you, ma'am?"

"My name's Helen Dawson. My husband was one of the two men who pulled you away from the falling house."

"I'm obliged to him."

"Listen, that's not important now." She gestured at the plate.

"It's getting cold." The tone was gently scolding, as a mother's might be. She rose. "I'll be back with the juice."

"Do you have any coffee? Please."

Helen smiled at him again, then said quietly, "Yes, you're a man now, aren't you? Yes, I'll bring you coffee." She turned to go, then stopped and earnestly looked at him. "Was Ruth your little sister?"

Zeke hesitated before he answered. "Yes, she is. How did you—"

"We heard you call her name…She's the one they took, isn't she?"

Zeke nodded uncomfortably.

Again, the tears seemed to appear, but she turned quickly and said, "Eat first. We'll all talk later." Then she vanished out the door, leaving it slightly ajar.

Later, Zeke was lying back on the bed and still digesting his meal when two precocious angels appeared. The little girls both had twinkling blue eyes and they shined mischievously as they looked in on him through the open doorway. Zeke raised his eyebrows and stared back from his pillow curiously.

Finally, one of them said loudly, "You're handsome!"

Then they both giggled and ran away.

Zeke grinned and raised his eyes to the ceiling. *Well, things could be worse.* In the back of his mind, he tried not to think of another little girl, far away from where he was and probably not even half as comfortable.

That's when she appeared in the doorway. His eyes widened in shock and he raised himself up on an elbow.

"Hello?" she said. "Can I come in?"

"Yes!" he answered, a bit excitedly.

"Thank you." She looked at him strangely, and as soon as she entered, she saw his crestfallen look. She was about twelve years old and had brown hair and quiet blue eyes. He guessed she was

Helen's daughter. She seemed more serious than the other two girls and stared at Zeke with some curiosity. She was wearing a blue dress that was simple yet presentable, as if someone had prodded her to dress a little better, at least for today.

"You're the one who killed a bushwhacker?"

Zeke paused, a little surprised at the question. Then he answered, "No, honey. It was an accident."

"That's not the way I heard it."

He looked at her and asked, "What did you hear?"

"That you settled the score for the Swensons..."

Zeke took his time before he explained, "I meant to take him alive."

"The whole town knows about what you've done. They say you're a hero."

Zeke eyed the covers briefly, then turned away.

"That's nothing to be embarrassed about."

He looked back at her. "Were those two little girls your friends?"

"Yes," she sighed. "But they're not as mature as I am. They go mushy and giggly pretty easy."

"Oh," he said, smiling. "And what's your name?"

"Louisa Dawson."

"You're a pretty girl, Louisa."

She sighed again. "I know."

"I have a sister around your age."

Louisa just blinked her eyes innocently.

Zeke then started to sit up. He looked at himself, noticing he was all cleaned up. His bare chest was cleaned of soot and his face, though marked by a couple bruises, was no longer bleeding. He was even clean shaven.

Feeling his bare chin, he asked, "Who did all this?"

"My folks. Mostly my pa. He carried you all the way here all by himself."

"Really?" That must've been some task. Who is her father, a circus strongman?

A heavy knock was heard on the door.

Louisa looked at him expectantly.

"Uh, come in," Zeke said.

"Heard you were up," said the man entering the room.

He was a big man, with dark brown hair graying at the sides. He had broad shoulders and a sturdy chest. The face was tanned from working outdoors and his brown eyes were alert. Had this man been sick a day in his life, Zeke would have been shocked. He recognized him as the man who pulled him back from the falling house.

The voice was deep and rich, with more than a trace of the deep south.

He put his huge hands on his daughter's shoulders. "This one here has a curiosity that won't let up. She's real bright too."

"Pa," Louisa said, with a little embarrassment.

"She says she wants to be a doctor or something in science." He shook his head good-naturedly and his hearty laugh filled the room. "That's some ambition for a young lady, eh?"

Louisa said stubbornly, "And I'll do it too!"

Her father held her in front of him and looked her in the eyes. "And you know something? I really think you'll do it too." He laughed again and embraced her. Then he walked her to the door and said, "Okay, come on now. I want to talk to this fella."

"All right," Louisa said, a little disappointed. She turned to Zeke. "Bye. See you later." She left, closing the door.

Then the man stood over Zeke and said, "I'm Hank Dawson." He held out his hand and Zeke shook it, feeling some pain as he did.

Zeke glanced briefly at his fingers, then said, "Thanks for pulling me back from that falling house."

"Don't thank me," Hank said. "We should be thanking you. Not everyone would have the sand to go after a killer by himself. Some folks recognized him as one of the gang that torched houses and shot up the town. And wherever the Swensons are, you done 'em a favor."

Zeke looked at him sadly. "I done 'em a favor too late...Seems I'm always too late..."

"Whatever happened to your folks wasn't your fault."

"How do you know what happened to my folks?"

Hank sat in the chair opposite the bed. "My pa told me."

"Your pa?"

"That was the old man you spoke to who was sweeping up outside the store and he was with me when the house almost clipped ya."

Zeke remembered what the old man had said before. "You have a brother traveling with his wife on the Plains?"

"That's right. I was out there myself briefly."

"Were you with the army?"

"I was...Tried to join again, but when they fired on Fort Sumter, I wasn't a young man anymore. Anyway, the recruiters told me if I wanted to help the Union, I should keep freightin'. I run freight over the counties."

"That's pretty dangerous."

Dawson shrugged. "I keep on my side of the border. And my service with Winfield Scott down in Mexico taught me to hit anything I aim at...And some of those border rats know it too."

"My name is Zeke Tyler."

"Nice to meet you, Zeke Tyler."

"Excuse me for asking this, sir, but...are you from the South?"

Hank eyed his big hands briefly, then he said, "Yes, I am."

"Uh, don't you find it kind of uncomfortable up here?"

"I'm originally from Texas…Fort Dallas. I was married before and we lived pretty well for a while. Then one day Kiowas raided us and killed my wife."

"I'm sorry."

"Thanks, but…I guess it was partly my fault for staying in such a dangerous place."

"That wasn't your fault. A decent man shouldn't have to leave his home because someone else makes it a bad place to live. He should stay and fight for it—" Then he realized how he sounded, and stopped.

Hank didn't take any offense. "No, you're right…And I'll never forget that again. My family and I moved up north and I married Helen. She gave birth to our kids and by God, these border scum aren't going to run us out. We're lucky, we know that, but so far, we stuck. And we'll keep doing it that way."

"You didn't join the Confederacy?"

"I don't go along with slavery and I never have. The Good Lord said we're all His children, not only the white ones. I don't recall anyone bein' left out…Anyway, a man can't get strong when someone else is doing his work for him…So now we all ended up in the Abolitionist State. And we like it up here. We just wish the South would come to its senses and see how wrong they are. I just hope they can set themselves straight one day and we can all be proud of our country again."

Zeke looked at him sheepishly for a moment and said, "I'm obliged to you and your family, sir. Your wife's cooking is really something. I'll probably be full for a week."

Hank smiled.

"But one thing bothers me though. If you'll excuse me for asking. Why does she look so sad when she looks at me?"

"Our son was killed at Manassas."

Zeke stared at him, then looked down sadly. "Maybe I'd better leave."

"We know about your sister, Zeke."

Zeke looked at him and already knew what he was going to say.

"Don't do it, son. Don't go after them."

Zeke said tautly, "I'm not your son. I don't have a father anymore."

"I'm truly sorry about that...But you are your parents' only living offspring—"

"You have no proof of that! She's still alive, I know she is!"

"Then let the army rescue her. You shouldn't have to throw away your life."

Zeke sat up and looked sharply at Hank. "Did your son throw away his life?"

Hank's face grew hard and he replied, "That's not the same thing and you know it! He was doing his job for his country. You're not a soldier."

Zeke said passionately, "Look around you, Mister Dawson. We're *all* soldiers now. They won't give us a choice."

For the first time, Zeke noticed the deep voice breaking. "If you go to Missoura, you haven't got a chance!"

Zeke replied, "If I don't find her, neither does she."

Hank Dawson rose quickly and went to the door. After opening it, he stopped and stood there for a minute or two, Zeke watching him all the time. His back was still turned when he said, "In an hour or so, I'll be running freight to Olathe...You think hard about what you want to do. Real hard. If you're still of a mind to head into Missoura, I can save you some ridin' and drop you a mile or so from the border..."

"You don't have to do that."

Hank finally turned to him. His grim expression almost made

Zeke recoil. "I'm not doing you any favors," Dawson said. "My boy used to have your streak. He was as pig-headed as they come...Anyway, a man's got to find things out for himself. You deserve that chance..."

An hour and a half later, Zeke had bathed and was now wearing a clean shirt and trousers. He also had a new Stetson and a pair of decent boots. The clothes fit almost too well. They had once belonged to Hank Dawson Jr., late of Manassas.

At the front gate, Zeke waved goodbye to Helen and Louisa, but before he turned to get on the wagon, Helen said, "We pray that you find her."

He was turning back to the wagon when Helen suddenly grasped his hand and said, her voice full of emotion, "And, Zeke... Whether you find her or not...come back to us..."

Zeke stared at her sadly, not knowing what to say. He then looked down and nodded faintly.

Quickly he jumped on the wagon and it pulled away. He looked back at Helen and Louisa and noticed that they were still standing by the front gate until he was out of sight.

Red was safe now in their barn and the robber's horse he had ridden before was now tied behind the wagon. When they reached close to the border, Hank would let them go and then turn back to Olathe.

Zeke didn't ask for this journey. But somewhere in Missouri were five men who were going to get something they didn't ask for either...

CHAPTER FIVE

SOME TIME BEFORE ZEKE RODE INTO LONE JACK, HE AND HANK
Dawson had camped near DeSoto. For a brief time anyway, Zeke
had actually smiled a couple of times. He had not camped on the
prairie since June, when he joined his father out at Spring Hill.
And the more stories Hank told him, some about his service in
Mexico, some about the freighting business, the more he started to
respect the man.

When Zeke was about to set off for Lone Jack, Hank did pause
briefly when he saw the young Kansan buckle on a holster with
the now-fully loaded Dragoon pistol.

"An army Dragoon," noticed Hank. "Haven't seen one in a
while."

After he strapped it on, Zeke said, "I want to tell you something, Mister Dawson. This isn't mine. I took out my Henry and
filched it from a Union soldier. When two men tried to steal my
outfit back there on the trail to Brooklyn, I shot them both. I took
their gear and whatever they stole from Lawrence and put it in my
saddlebag."

Hank looked at him earnestly. "Are you sorry for it?"

"Yes...But not for all of it. I guess those two men would have put me in the ground if I hadn't gunned them first. I'm ashamed I had to do that."

"Don't be."

"I think of them sometimes. I think that when I killed them, I made myself as bad as they were. Maybe as bad as the ones that whooped it up in Lawrence..."

Hank Dawson then got up and stood across from him in the clearing.

He looked Zeke in the eye and said, "If you're going to have doubts like that, then your sister's done for..."

Zeke stared back at him, taking in all that the older man said without argument.

Hank continued, "A fighting man can't think about the sins of his enemy. And he can't save the world either—at least not all of it at once. Keep your mind on the job. It doesn't get done by itself... We didn't ask for this war, but now we've got it and we can't just wish it away. If you're going to do a job, 'specially for your country, don't do it half-assed..."

Zeke nodded and then stuck out his hand. Hank shook it and Zeke tried hard not to let the older man see him wince.

Then as he turned away, Hank said, "Zeke...use your sights."

"Excuse me?"

"Your sidearm. It has sights for a better aim. That's why Sam Colt put 'em there."

"Thank you, sir."

Hank nodded and said sternly, "I'll be seeing you later."

"Yes, sir."

Zeke rode into Lone Jack practically unnoticed. Whether the townspeople were preoccupied with the comings and goings of bushwhackers or Union patrols in the wake of the Lawrence

Massacre, he didn't know. He had passed a few Union patrols on the way in, and though they looked him over a couple times, no one stopped him. He was, after all, alone. They were tracking many.

Zeke dismounted and tied his horse to a hitching rail near a saloon. He stood to the side of the door, listening to the badly played music from inside. He knew that Lone Jack was full of bushwhackers and figured that a saloon would be the place where they'd congregate and boast of their "triumph" in Lawrence. He might even get a line on Charlie Morse. Roster had said they'd be halfway to Lone Jack—and now here he was. He knew that his gun might be recognized as Union, but he could always say the truth, that he'd taken it off a Yankee soldier.

Zeke was about to enter the saloon when three swaggering men suddenly pushed their way through the door and came outside. They were roaring with laughter and Zeke stepped back quickly before they ran into him. They didn't notice him at first.

They were all young men, barely older than Zeke himself. Yet to him, they all seemed arrogant beyond their years. Certainly, they seemed to be totally ignorant of the fact that other human beings existed besides themselves as they seemed to bludgeon their way around the sidewalk.

As he watched them sway noisily, Zeke caught the odor of the cheap whiskey and almost became ill.

That's when nine-year old Penelope Ryan came down the sidewalk, hugging her schoolbooks. She was thinking hard about something, perhaps school or perhaps something at home; nevertheless, it seemed inevitable what would happen next.

The biggest of the trio of bushwhackers, Dick Lamont, came forward and his huge legs rammed into the little girl as she tried to walk around him. Her books scattered to the ground and she fell forward on the sidewalk, skinning her knee. Almost immediately she burst into tears.

"Hey!" roared Lamont. "Are you stupid, little girl! Watch where you're going!"

Zeke watched all this and would have been angered anyway at what he had just witnessed—only it was different this time. As if a switch had been turned on, a sudden rage came to him, without warning or compromise. His line of vision shook, and he fought to control it. The fingers at his sides were clearly trembling and he instinctively curled them into fists.

He glared at Lamont and said thickly, "Maybe you'd better pick up her books and apologize."

Lamont slowly turned around to face him. At first, he thought he heard wrong. Who, in all of Lone Jack, would have the nerve to say anything threatening to him?

Lamont burned his gaze into Zeke and demanded, "She your kin?"

Zeke didn't answer him. Instead he responded in the same tone. "Are you deaf, mister? I said, pick up her books!"

Lamont paused. His two friends looked at each other apprehensively.

This fellow talking to Dick Lamont that way had to be crazy. Others on the sidewalk and even across the street stopped and ran over. A crowd was starting to form, and some veteran brawl-watchers were shaking their heads in disbelief at Zeke's ignorance of who Dick Lamont was.

Zeke's gaze held on Lamont steadily. The little girl's tears continued and when Zeke heard her anguish, it only increased his anger.

"Sure!" Lamont said loudly, knowing full well he had an audience now. "I'll pick up her books!"

Lamont punctuated the remark by stepping into the street

where Penelope's books had fallen. They were open now, face down on the ground, some pages already torn apart. Quickly Lamont put his boot down and started to crush them into the dirt, swishing them back and forth.

Helplessly, Penelope cried louder.

It was then that Zeke stepped off the walk, yanked Lamont around to face him and punched him squarely in the nose. The blow shocked Lamont, as much for the fact that he was actually struck by someone as well as the impact itself. The boots that had crushed the child's books were now crushing his own fallen hat as he stumbled over it on the way to the center of the street. His big hands went up to his nose and when he looked down at his fingers, he saw blood.

At that moment, Kelly Ryan stopped putting groceries into her buckboard and turned around. As soon as she saw her little sister on the sidewalk with tears in her eyes, she quickly rushed over.

Dick Lamont possessed a certain trait that made him the most feared man in town, and that was his ability to draw a gun and kill a man before he could throw the first punch. Lamont naturally expected his commands to be obeyed without question and others around town usually gave him a wide berth or did as they were told. Zeke's punch had clearly caught him off-guard, and he realized before anyone else that an example had to be made.

Lamont's right hand went down to his Navy Colt, but before he could lift it from its holster, Zeke ducked forward and dove for Lamont's stomach. As Zeke rammed into him, his left hand reached around Lamont's waist and tightly gripped the big man's wrist before the gun could clear leather.

Hank Dawson Jr.'s hat rolled off into the dirt and the two men slammed into the side of a metal watering trough, Zeke's head striking the side. The impact caused him to loosen his grip on Lamont's right hand. His head throbbed in pain and he sat near the trough, giving Lamont time to draw his gun and cock the hammer.

Zeke spotted the move, however, and he quickly forgot the pain long enough to raise himself off the ground and grab Lamont's wrist with both hands.

On the sidewalk, Penelope had stopped crying and anxiously watched the two men, her heart going out to the tall young man who came to her aid.

Briefly they struggled over the gun, until Zeke suddenly shoved Lamont's wrist backwards, close to his face. The movement so surprised Lamont that he pressed the hair trigger and the Navy Colt fired close to his right ear.

Lamont screamed and instantly dropped the gun into the dirt, his hand grabbing his ear painfully. Enraged, Lamont hit Zeke in the eye with his free hand. The young Kansan fell back against the edge of the trough and tried to raise himself up. Before he could, though, Lamont threw himself on Zeke and his huge fingers quickly went to his throat. Already dizzy from hitting his head against the trough, Zeke tried to push him off, but couldn't find the strength.

The bushwhacker's rage had no limit. His fingers went into Zeke's face and was pushing his head back further and further until the Kansan's head went all the way back into the trough. Zeke's hands pushed against Lamont's chest, but it was like pushing down a brick wall. Soon Lamont's hands pushed Zeke's head beneath the water, and he put pressure on them to keep him under.

As the seconds passed, bubbles floated to the surface and Zeke felt the air in his lungs slowly draining away.

Penelope cried to her sister, "He was helping me, Kelly!"

Kelly glared at Lamont's back from across the street. Then she looked at the young man whose head was being held under water and her Irish brogue took on a sympathetic tone.

"Come on, mister, get up!"

Penelope, who hadn't wiped away her tears, echoed, "Please!"

Kelly knelt down to her sister and put her arms around her, ready to turn her eyes away from the scene if, God forbid, the poor man didn't survive.

Zeke glimpsed Lamont from underwater, through the thick fingers pushing him down, and saw his face; straining, full of sweat and without mercy. Then he started to see the blackness of a huge web before his eyes and after that, little sparks of white light. Vaguely he was aware of losing consciousness. In the back of his mind, he remembered hearing stories of men who were hanged and still survived, and though the rope would choke the poor devils, the cutoff of oxygen would leave them brain dead.

Terrified of this fate, Zeke's right leg suddenly hooked around Lamont's left and yanked it over. It didn't make Lamont let go, but the leg-trip caused him to lose his footing and fall to his left, giving Zeke the room he needed to pull both his knees up and push them against the bushwhacker's stomach. Now with Zeke's long legs braced against him, Lamont was being pushed back farther than his arms' length. Still holding onto Zeke, he fell back, taking the Kansan with him.

When Zeke's head broke the surface, he coughed loudly as fresh air hit his nostrils. Zeke's head was throbbing, and his ears were full of water, but he could still see clearly enough to reach out and put his fingers on Lamont's throat.

Lamont tried to push Zeke's head back again, but the attempt was clumsy. With his blood throbbing in his ears, Zeke angrily punched Lamont in the eye and the two men hit the ground with a thud. They slowly continued to roll over each other on the dusty street as the crowd cheered on.

Though Zeke was a newcomer to town, he might have been

surprised, had he been able to hear through an earful of water, to know that most of the cheers were for him.

As the two men rolled further up the street, Penelope said, "He stood up for me, Kelly. Who is he?"

"I don't know, hon," Kelly answered, watching them. "But I wish I did."

Zeke made sure he got to his feet first, yanking Lamont up with both hands. If Lamont had expected a punch after Zeke pulled him to his feet, he was stunned when the Kansan punched him before he could put his feet under him. He tried to throw up his hands to block the punches, but Lamont saw that Zeke wouldn't stop. His anger surfaced, Zeke kept punching Lamont's bruised face and didn't stop until the killer was knocked against a hitching rail and crumpled to the ground. Dust came up in a cloud after Lamont hit the ground and his body lay still in the dirt.

Zeke was breathing hard, gladly taking in huge gulps of air as he wiped his face of dirt and trough water. He glanced down at his holster and relaxed; his sidearm had not fallen out.

The crowd converged slowly around him. Lamont's two friends came closer and they froze when Zeke shot them a look.

One of them said, "You beat up Dick Lamont, mister. He rides with Anderson and Quantrill. He's not the kind who'll forget this."

Zeke replied, "I don't care if he rides with Satan, though I don't see much difference."

He could see the two were insulted, but he didn't care. He was as angry as he was exhausted—which was a lot.

Standing close by, Kelly Ryan was smirking at the remark. In her hands was Zeke's fallen hat. She had made sure she was the first person to retrieve it.

Glaring at the two men, Zeke said thickly, "You tell that son of a bitch that if he so much as gives that girl a dirty look, I'll break his neck."

The two men stared at him and seemed as if they were about to say something, but somehow couldn't find the words. They turned away, and subsequently the crowd drifted off as well.

Zeke started to head back to where Penelope had dropped her books and was shocked to find her standing right there.

The words he had used! And she was standing right there all the time.

"I'm sorry!" he said contritely. "I shouldn't have used those words in front of you."

Kelly's eyes looked at the Kansan admiringly. She watched him now, more closely than she had ever watched anyone.

Zeke knelt down in front of Penelope and asked her gently, "Are you all right?"

He got his answer when Penelope threw her arms around his head and kissed him hard on the cheek. He blushed a little and grinned. "I guess she is," he said.

After he stood up, he saw Kelly, who promptly handed him his hat.

"Thank you, sir," she said, her brogue sounding musical to Zeke's ears. "These border ruffians seem to think that everywhere they trod, the ground is blessed." She looked down at her little sister and stroked her hair. "They don't care if they bully a child or make one an orphan...Dick Lamont has a reputation riding for Quantrill, and I imagine he doesn't like losing a fight." She looked back at Zeke, her eyes searching his. "But I have a feeling you're not afraid of anything."

He asked, "Would it make a difference to you if I was?"

"No, it wouldn't."

"Then I was scared."

"You sure fooled us! Who are you?"

"Ezekiel Tyler...My friends call me Zeke."

"Well...Zeke, I'm Kelly Ryan. We live with our pa about a mile from here." She felt a pull on her riding skirt. "Okay! And this is my little sister, Penelope."

Now that the attention was on her, Penelope giggled and hugged her sister's knee.

"Happy to meet you both." His eyes went back to Kelly. She had dark brown hair and blue eyes that seemed to look right into you. She was tall, and though still in her late teens, she carried herself with a maturity he hadn't seen in many girls her age. Growing up in the West, he realized, especially in the midst of a border war, made one grow up pretty fast.

"Well," Zeke said lamely, "I guess I'll move on—"

"Come home with us!" Kelly blurted out.

"What?"

"Well...To clean up!"

"Listen, Kelly, I was going to do some things after I got here."

"Looking like that?"

She was right. Zeke was a mess and he knew it. Getting cleaned up wasn't a bad idea.

"We have some grub too!" Kelly said, betraying the excitement in her voice. "I'm sure you're hungry from traveling...uh, from wherever you rode in from."

"I rode in from Lawrence."

Zeke knew he probably shouldn't have said it, but he figured he could trust her. There was something about those blue eyes that made you want to tell the truth.

Kelly stared at him for a moment, sympathy in her eyes. Then she said, "Why are you here? I'm sorry! It's none of my business."

Zeke smiled and said, "I guess I could use a bite, huh?"

Kelly smiled back at him.

"My horse is up the street," Zeke said. "I'll be right back."

After he left, Penelope giggled and asked, "Is he married?"

Kelly laughed and said, "I don't think so...Anyway, you're too young for him."

As they started to walk towards the buckboard, Penelope asked, "Can you think of someone who'd marry him who was closer to his age?"

Kelly grinned and said, "I think so..."

It was unusually quiet over at Sni-A-Bar Creek in Jackson County, where restless young men hid from other restless young men in blue uniforms. After the others had laughed at Dick Lamont's bruises, he sat down against a tree stump, nursing his grudges. That's when a knife flew by Lamont and imbedded itself in the wood, not far from his left shoulder.

Lamont shouted, "Hey, Blaine! Watch it with that pig-sticker, will you!"

Blaine came over and yanked the knife out of the stump. He towered over Lamont as the other man glared up at him.

"So, what're you going to do about it?" chided Blaine. "Beat the hell out of me like that tall sodbuster did to you?" Lamont said nothing, but the rage remained in his eyes.

A few feet away from them, the Janey twins laughed at Lamont's despair.

CHAPTER SIX

THE RYAN HOME WAS ACTUALLY TWO MILES EAST OF TOWN ON A small hill flanked by the woods on one side and a trail that led into the main road on the other. Clouds were drifting in from the south and it was overcast by the time they rode up. At times, Zeke looked down and noticed his own shadow on the road fading in and out with the movement of the clouds.

He also made himself look at the ground when he felt a pause in the conversation.

He really liked her. She was a good talker and far more intelligent than her years. In fact, there were times he found himself lacking. In the past, Zeke had had no trouble talking to girls back in Lawrence, though those conversations were infrequent and usually on the lighter side.

Kelly was different.

Zeke hated telling her his problems, especially about Ruth, but she asked him point-blank why he was there, and he couldn't lie to her. There was something comforting about Kelly, something that seemed to make him want to open up to her. Maybe it was those blue eyes that seemed to sense dishonesty. He told her about the

Dawson family and their kindness, especially about their recent loss and Helen Dawson's request for him to return.

After a while, they rode in silence. Even Penelope stopped interrupting. Kelly was sitting on the right side of the buckboard holding the reins as they moved slowly up the road, Zeke riding his horse next to her. Then as they approached the hill, Kelly suddenly reached over, grabbed Zeke's hand and squeezed it.

It surprised him and he gazed down into those eyes. Kelly didn't flinch when Zeke looked at her. In fact, she discovered she liked looking at him.

They were ready to climb the hill when Penelope blurted out, "Hey! Are either of you watching the road?"

The house was a simple one-story wooden structure atop the hill. As they rode up, Zeke noticed a small pasture on one side of the house that had mostly weeds and dead grass. In the midst of it was a wooden board with writing on it sticking out of the ground and a large Celtic cross, also made of wood. Both the board and the cross were tilted forward.

A barn was on the other side, and beyond that a forest which went for a mile and a quarter before it parted for the road to Warrensburg.

Zeke watched the house and quickly noticed a hand, a man's hand, straighten the blinds in the kitchen and then pull away.

After the horses and buckboard were put away, they approached the front door. A big man opened it and eyed Zeke closely, noticing the dirty shirt and pants. He was tall, about as tall as Zeke, with broad shoulders under his work shirt and suspenders. He was bald, with some white hair around the sides and a bushy white mustache above what seemed to be a forced smile. The green eyes were dull under heavy brows and, like the smile, also tried to look friendly.

"Pa," Kelly said quickly, "this is Zeke Tyler." Zeke looked at her, not understanding why she was rushing the introduction. "Dick Lamont pushed Penny to the ground and dirtied her books and Zeke beat him up."

Thaddeus Ryan raised his eyebrows and said, "Well! You don't see that every day!" His brogue was distinctive, and though Ryan sounded jovial, Zeke got the impression his tone was as forced as his smile. Nevertheless, the old man reached out and shook Zeke's hand.

Again, Zeke looked at his fingers. Don't any of these big prairie men have LIGHT handshakes?

"Come on in!"

After Zeke entered, Ryan suggested that he and Penelope wait in the kitchen for some grub and then excused himself as he spoke to his eldest daughter. At a quiet signal from Ryan, he and Kelly stepped outside and closed the door. They walked out toward the low fence, Kelly watching the ground thoughtfully.

She knew what he would say.

After several long moments, he finally said it. "Have you gone crazy, girl?"

Kelly looked at him and said defiantly, "No, Pa, I haven't."

Ryan continued, "We have enough trouble from these Southern scum! Now you invite the man who beat up Dick Lamont for supper." He shook his head contemptuously. "I thought I raised you smarter than that! What do you think is going to happen when word gets around that my daughter is friendly with some Kansas upstart?"

"How did you know he was from Kansas?"

"When you're an immigrant, you notice the accents out here just as much as they notice ours. He doesn't sound a bit like he's from Western Missouri. Besides, only a stranger would have the guts to do what he did; no one from around here would have the nerve! Don't get me wrong, Kell. I'm grateful that he stood up for my little girl, but that's where it ends. He's going to bring trouble down on us!"

"So, he's not staying for supper, is he?"

"I've never kicked out a man who's come to my table. And I owe him something for standing up for Penny. But you mustn't see him anymore."

"That might be easier said than done, Pa..."

Ryan turned back and studied her closely. "Don't you play the starry-eyed lass now. We can't afford it. Look where we are! Maybe you haven't noticed, but right now we're living with vipers! And they won't be too understanding when they find out that you're friendly with their enemy. And they will find out! They have better spies than the federals."

"You're getting yourself worked up, Pa."

"So, I'm—" He glanced towards the house, then calmed down. "We're not native Missourians. We're in enough danger."

"We won't be here long, Pa. The bluecoats will make sure of that."

"Maybe. Maybe we'll live long enough for all of us to get away from here, but it only takes a second for a bullet to strike home! Don't forget that!"

Ryan turned and went back into the house. Kelly knew this was her father's usual way of ending an argument, and quietly she followed him in.

When they entered the living room, they found Zeke and Penelope playfully wrestling on the floor. Penelope had Zeke in a headlock and was laughing as she was trying to pull Zeke's nose off.

"Ow! Ow!"

"I think we're just in time to rescue this young man," said Ryan jovially.

Trying not to smile, Kelly said sternly, "Penny, get off him!"

Penelope reluctantly let go of Zeke and he stood up.

"Sorry about that," said Kelly.

"Don't worry about it," said Zeke. "My little sister used to do that to me a lot." He became quiet for a moment. Then he said to Ryan, "I appreciate your hospitality, sir, but I shouldn't stay long."

Ryan and Kelly looked at each other briefly, then the old man said, "Come on in. I'll have supper fixed soon…"

Zeke had washed up outside and after he returned, they all ate dinner. The subject at the table then turned to Mrs. Ryan. Zeke had seen the crude tombstone outside and didn't ask about her, but Ryan himself brought her up.

Kelly was born and raised in Ireland eighteen years ago, and she and her parents lived in County Cork until poverty and the confiscation of their land forced the family to sail for America. Penelope was born shortly after their arrival, but Mrs. Ryan died in childbirth. Now forced to raise two daughters, Ryan moved to Missouri and found work as a handyman. They had only been in Lone Jack the past year.

"We won't be here for long, you know," said Ryan.

"No?"

Ryan shook his head. "In a few days, we'll all be moving out. The army won't give us a choice."

"What does the army have to do with it?"

Kelly said, "Guess you haven't heard." Ryan passed Zeke a newspaper and he looked at it.

He read, "'General Thomas Ewing Junior, Department of Missouri, has issued Federal Order Number Eleven. All the families of…'" He skipped through the various counties and all the specific perimeters that met the criteria for expulsion. "'…residents are given ten days to pack up and move out'." He looked up at

Ryan. "Why the he—" His eyes wandered to Penelope briefly. "Why the devil would they want to do that?"

"I have three words to explain that," Ryan said. "The Lawrence Massacre."

Zeke's eyes went to the hands in his lap and he said nothing. Kelly looked at him sympathetically.

"In retaliation," continued Ryan, "for the massacre, they're kicking out all 'Southern sympathizers'." He shook his head. "What does that have to do with us? We're from County Cork, way across the sea. What do we have to do with slavery? Much less the massacre? I feel sorry for those folks who got killed, but that is not our problem. Why should we get punished for some Negro-lovers getting killed?"

"Pa!" said Kelly angrily. "Zeke's parents were in that. And they kidnapped his sister."

"I'm sorry, lad," Ryan said quietly. "I figured you were from Kansas, but I didn't know you were that close to the trouble... Don't get me wrong. It's true I haven't exactly been an abolitionist, but when you haven't got much money and two little girls to feed, you become distracted with your own problems. And now we'll lose our home and get absolutely nothing for it in return...Nevertheless, I will pray for the souls of your parents...And I pray for the safety of your sister."

Zeke said earnestly, "She'll need more than your prayers, Mister Ryan."

Penelope was quietly listening to them. Finally, she reached up and put her hand on Zeke's shoulder. "I pray she comes back too, Zeke..."

Touched by her sincerity, Zeke leaned over and embraced her. He said, "Thank you, honey. That's the best prayer I've ever heard."

Kelly's eyes were blinking back tears. "She'll come back," she said quietly.

Ryan looked at her sharply. "You can guarantee that, can you?"

Kelly rose and stopped by his chair. "No," she said, "but maybe you can by taking a side for once..."

Ryan stared at her as she passed by, picking up the plates around the table.

That's when they heard the approaching horses.

Kelly and her father looked at each other.

"Sounds like two riders," said Zeke.

Ryan said, "He's right. Penelope, go to your room. And take Zeke with you."

Zeke looked sharply at him.

"Please, son." The look on Ryan's face was imploring. "I think it would be best if they didn't see you."

Zeke hesitated.

"We'd better go, Zeke," said Penelope, taking his hand. He allowed her to pull him into the room she shared with Kelly, just as two riders dismounted outside.

Kelly stood near the cupboard and watched her father. "It's him again, isn't it?" she said contemptuously.

Ryan tried not to look at her eyes. Instead he scanned the table and said, "Clear those utensils or they'll know we had a guest."

Ryan went to the door and let in two big men. They were in their early twenties and had trail dust on their boots. Only one of them bothered to wipe his feet on the outside mat.

"Hello, Ryan," said the man, a tall red-headed fellow with a mustache.

He nodded in return. "Hello, Cahill...Wallace."

Wallace was a hulking fellow with a granite jaw and hooded eyes. When he entered, he just gave Ryan a blank stare. Every single time he came there, he never greeted Ryan. He always did the same thing when he entered, which was toss his hat on the table and turn and stare for a long time at Kelly. Sometimes she returned his look with a withering stare of her own, but this time she continued to clear the table. She also didn't want to provoke him with Zeke in the house.

After Zeke entered the bedroom and quietly closed the door, he saw a room with two beds and plenty of books.

"Are they your books, hon?"

"Some of them. Most of them are Kelly's. I've almost never seen her without one."

Zeke was impressed. Then the voices from the kitchen caught his attention. He opened the door slightly and listened.

Cahill took off his hat and put it on the coat tree. It was then that he saw Zeke's hat there as well. His eyes went to old Ryan and then back to the hat. His face told nothing, though, as he sat down at the table with Wallace.

"Looks like we missed dinner," he said matter-of-factly.

"Yeah," said Ryan, watching him. "Looks like."

"Sorry about that, but Pete over here had his eye on this new dancer at McGann's."

"She meant nothin' to me!" Wallace said loudly, looking straight at Kelly. "I like brunettes anyway. They stick to their men more than any blonde-haired dancer."

"Yeah," said Ryan, noticing the look, "but some brown-haired lasses have a kick to them that'll send ya reelin'."

Wallace laughed wryly. Staring back at him, he said, "They wouldn't have a kick to 'em for long!"

Trying to sound cheerful, Kelly asked, "Coffee?"

"Please, ma'am," said Cahill. "I don't know about Pete, but I'd be obliged."

Ryan had been forced to sit in a chair at the side of the table, since Wallace had usurped his chair at the head. He looked at them blandly.

"Who was your guest?" Cahill asked suddenly.

The question so shocked Ryan that he paused before he answered. Kelly also stopped in the middle of making coffee to look at them.

"What made you think I had a guest?"

Cahill answered, "You pulled off the plates and the utensils, but I still see the impression of a fourth plate on the tablecloth. Besides, and more to the point, you have two hats on the tree, and they're both different sizes…You wear both of them?"

"A fellow passed through on his travels. He needed to rest his horse and be fed. I'm not going to turn him down…Guess he left his hat."

"Where was this hatless fellow headed?"

"West somewhere."

"You didn't ask?"

"I didn't ask."

"That in itself is strange," said Cahill. "If a man is travelin', folks are usually curious about where he's headed."

"I think he mentioned California."

"Really? You fed a man who's travelin' to a Free State?"

Wallace, without the least bit of inhibition, turned and spat on the floor. "Nigger-lovin' trash!"

"Hey!" said Ryan. "You're in someone else's home!"

Smiling wolfishly, Wallace turned and spat again. Ryan's face grew hard and the hands in his lap tensed.

Cahill asked, "You haven't been feeding any Federals, have you, Ryan?"

"And if they wanted food, how am I supposed to stop them?"

"Hide your food and tell them you're all out."

"I'm supposed to spend my time hidin' food? Then I have to

dig it out again to feed you?" He shook his head. "This America is a strange place. I've yet to see the freedom I've heard so much about back in Ireland."

As Kelly poured the coffee, Wallace stared at her hard.

Kelly said plainly, "You're making me nervous, Mister Wallace. I might shake this coffee pot so hard, I might pour the contents in your lap."

Wallace replied, "And I might slam you in the floor by accident."

"If you do," said Ryan angrily, "you might be hittin' the floor yourself."

"You know," interjected Cahill as the two men glared at each other, "some young drifter came into town earlier today. I heard he wasn't in town five minutes before he got into a fight with Dick Lamont."

"Oh?"

"Yeah, and this is the kicker. The drifter won the fight. Anyone else would be pushing up daisies by now."

"So why are you tellin' me this?"

Cahill's eyes stared straight into Ryan's when he said, "'Cause we tracked him here."

Ryan tried to hide his discomfort and wasn't doing too well. "He said he was goin' to California."

"And your daughter escorted him here. Your buckboard wheels are all over the trail straight from town. Now why is that?"

"He isn't here, Cahill."

"Why don't we tear this house apart?" said Wallace harshly.

"Because we're in a gentleman's home, that's why!" said Cahill, raising his voice to Wallace for the first time.

Wallace looked at him, but then shrugged and turned back to staring at Kelly.

Cahill said indifferently, "Anyway, it doesn't matter.   These folks won't have a house for anyone to search much longer."

"Yeah," said Ryan. "We heard about that."

"Where will you go?"

Ryan shrugged and said, "Don't know.   Unlike the other folks around here, we don't know anyone down South to return to... We'll probably head west."

"To Kansas?"

Ryan stared back at him and answered, "Maybe."

Wallace stared at him angrily and said, "You like livin' with nigger-lovers?"

"I like livin' with people who treat each other decent!" Ryan answered harshly.

"Figures!" said Wallace, as he slurped his coffee.

"A man has a right to live where he pleases, I suppose," said Cahill. Sardonically, he added, "It's a free country..."

"Some say that," noted Ryan.

Wallace suddenly spat a mouthful of coffee on the floor and said, "Girl, this coffee's like birdseed! Gets cold too damn quick! You got a bottle around here so's I can give it a shot?"

Kelly replied, "There's no liquor in this house, Mister Wallace. And my name isn't 'girl'."

"Don't worry, Miss Ryan," said Cahill apologetically.   "All females are 'girl' to him. Please don't take offense."

Wallace's voice rose as he said, "No, I mean it. You people always got a bottle somewhere around."

Cahill turned and glared at him. Ryan's face froze, his eyes hateful.

"You want to rephrase that?" said Ryan. "Like right now!"

Wallace's face reddened in fury.   "No mick is going to tell me—"

"Pete!" Cahill interjected, trying to sound patient.   "Did you ever try to understand the origins of my name, Cahill? Because if you did, maybe you wouldn't be so damn loose with your words!"

Wallace stared back at him, then his eyes veered off. He didn't apologize.

"All right," said Ryan, holding in his anger. "You've had your coffee. You two had better leave."

Before Cahill could speak, Wallace shouted, "When we please!"

"You're leavin' right now!" Ryan put his hands on the table, about to rise, but Wallace got up first and drew his Navy Colt.

"Damn you, you nigger-lovin' Irish pig!"

He fired across the table and a bloody hole appeared in Ryan's forehead. Ryan fell back in his chair and tumbled to the floor.

Kelly's scream echoed around the house, just as Cahill rose and hit Wallace in the face. Wallace staggered back two steps but recovered quickly. Cocking the hammer again, he pointed the gun barrel straight at Cahill's face.

Cahill looked down in horror at Thaddeus Ryan's body, now cradled in Kelly's arms as she cried uncontrollably. Then he looked back at Wallace and saw something he never wanted to see.

"You fool! What did he ever do to you?!"

"You always treated these scum as good as us!" yelled Wallace. He was about to say something else when he noticed a shape appear from the dark hallway. He saw the flashes then and heard the shots which thundered in the small room. The searing pain in his stomach came quickly and he doubled over, still trying to raise the Navy Colt.

From the hallway, Zeke kept cocking and firing the Dragoon until it was empty. Wallace crumpled to the ground, next to Kelly and her father. Contemptuously, she spat on Wallace's body.

"Daddy!" Penelope ran to her father with tears in her eyes.

Zeke reached over and picked up the Navy Colt. Cocking it, he pointed it at Cahill and studied him.

"All right, Cahill...You tell me now and forever...whose side are you on?"

Cahill stared back at the Kansan's eyes, not at the pointed gun.

"I don't side with the killers of families, if that's what you're asking."

"Then maybe you should've picked another line of business."

"You're the man who whipped Dick Lamont."

Through his teeth, Zeke replied, "And you're the friend of the man who killed this girl's father."

Cahill said, "I never wanted this! I knew he was wild, but I didn't think he'd do anything like this!" Cahill looked down sadly at the two girls and when he spoke, the usually cool voice trembled. "I'd do anything to make it up to you girls. I swear!"

Zeke said accusingly, "You say that now, but then you'll ride back to Quantrill!"

Cahill looked up and Zeke saw reddened eyes. "If you think I'd ride anywhere within a hundred miles of Quantrill after this, you might as well pull the trigger on me right now."

Zeke looked at him for a moment and watched the defiant eyes never leaving his. Zeke then cocked the hammer of the Colt back into place and lowered the gun. He stared hard at Cahill before he spoke.

"Will you take these two young ladies away from here? Ride with them to somewhere safer?"

"Where?"

"There's a village over the Kansas line called Brooklyn. It's south of Lawrence, close to the Santa Fe Trail."

"I can find it."

"There's a family on Kent Street, name of Dawson. Father's

name is Henry. You give me your word you'll take these two girls to the Dawson's and protect them every step of the way."

"You've got my word," said Cahill earnestly.

Kelly was now on her feet, tears still running down her face.

"I'm not going, Zeke!" she said, wiping her eyes.

"You have to!" said Zeke sternly. "I'll never live with myself if those pigs do anything to you and Penny."

Through her teeth, Kelly said, "I don't care about your guilt, Zeke. They're not chasing me out! I'm staying here."

"I've already let one girl fall into their hands! I'm not going to let that happen to you and Penny!"

"Then let him just take Penny."

"It's not safe here—"

"I'm not leaving you, Zeke!" Then she added quietly, "Not ever…"

Zeke stared at her, then turned back to Cahill. "Saddle two horses. You lead Penny's and stick real close to her. If anything happens to that girl, you'll answer to me."

"I don't care what you think of me otherwise, but I don't hold to kidnapping girls."

"That's good," Zeke said tautly. "'Cause I'm about to trust you with the safety of one. And after Ruth's kidnapping, I still wonder if I'm crazy to let you ride with her."

Kelly said, "Zeke, he *was* trying to restrain the other one."

"Yeah, I heard," said Zeke coldly. "A lot of good it did…"

Cahill soberly put his hat back on and said to Kelly, "I swear to you, ma'am, I'll give my own life before I let anyone harm Penny."

"Before you set out," Zeke said, "you and I are going to have a little talk about the men you rode with. I'm looking for a few men in particular. Maybe you know them and maybe you don't. Or maybe you just heard their names…but one way or the other you're going to tell me. Then I'll take it from there…"

CHAPTER SEVEN

THE KITCHEN WAS CLEANED UP FROM TOP TO BOTTOM. THADDEUS Ryan was hastily buried next to his wife and prayers were read over his grave. Pete Wallace was unceremoniously buried under loose shrubbery in a draw several yards off the trail.

Zeke had questioned John Cahill at length. He had never participated in the Lawrence Massacre. Like some other guerrillas, he backed out of it rather than harm civilians. He knew Pete Wallace only a few months, but he did ride with him on other raids. He didn't like him, but he was a fellow guerrilla and he knew that as far as the war was concerned, a man couldn't pick the comrades he rode with.

Unlike other guerrillas, Cahill got information from ranchers by being amiable and just engaging them in conversation; by cajoling, not threatening. His methods were scorned by Wallace and other more aggressive band members.

Thaddeus Ryan had wanted no part in the war and Cahill could see that. Yet Ryan did eventually tell him about Union patrols in the area. He had to. Ryan dreaded to think what would happen if Cahill's riding companion did more to Kelly than just look.

Cahill knew that with the issuance of Order Number 11, it would be the end of any "aid and comfort" the guerrillas might receive. With poor Missourians in the chosen counties now being evicted, their belongings divided between Union soldiers and Jayhawkers, and their property burned to the ground, the bushwhackers would have fewer places to be fed and change horses.

Standing outside, Kelly looked at her home sadly. Even if she returned here, there would be nothing left but ashes.

Cahill sat his horse and looked down at the Kansan. For the first time, he saw sympathy.

Zeke said, "Tell the Dawsons she's a sweet kid."

Cahill looked at Penelope, still with tears in her eyes. He said quietly, "I think they'll see that."

"Tell them also that she'll fit right in."

"What do I tell them about you?"

Zeke hesitated. Then he said, "...Tell them I wish them well."

"Penny will get there safe."

"I'm starting to feel more certain of that now."

Zeke shook Cahill's hand. They double-checked the buckboard for bedrolls, provisions, and ammunition for the two- or three-day ride. After she hugged and kissed Kelly, and then Zeke, Penelope was helped onto the horse and Cahill led it out of the yard. They continued down the hill and took the trail west.

After they disappeared down the road, Zeke and Kelly finally faced each other.

"When their gang gets here," Zeke said grimly, "they'll only find an empty house. They'll just think you moved before the soldiers evicted you."

"I guess," she replied, still dazed by it all.

"I'm sorry, Kelly."

"You said that before."

"If there was any way—"

"Listen, Zeke," she said coldly. "I've had my fill of apologies. I'm not stupid enough to blame you for this. When you live where we do, you expect trouble. I know for a fact that if the Union soldiers didn't kick us out, we would've moved anyway. Maybe across the border into Kansas, maybe west, we'll never know now...But it happened. I don't know everything, but I'm quite certain that I will not be the Town Orphan the rest of my life. I'm not the only one around here who's had their parents murdered, as you very well know. As far as I'm concerned, I'm just one of the crowd. Now it's something you and I both share...But I won't fold up on you just because I'm on my own."

"You're not on your own."

Kelly looked back into his face and liked what she saw. Yet there wasn't any time. They had to leave, and the sooner the better.

She turned to the house. "I'll miss this place..."

Zeke said wryly, "I guess this Order Number Eleven doesn't give folks a chance to be sentimental."

"I'm still going to miss it."

"Listen, Kelly," he said urgently. "I've got some money. If there's a good hotel in town for you to stay, take it. Live off it in the meantime. Hopefully, I'll be able to come for you."

"I'll not wait for you, Zeke Tyler. Not unless you want me to go insane in the meantime."

"I'll be worrying about Ruth. I don't need to worry about you too."

"I can handle a gun, if that's what's bothering you."

"Let one of us set up a place to come back to in the meantime. You've been seen in town before...It's easier for me to do what I've come for as long as I know you're safe..."

Kelly had taken some clothes and only the most important belongings in an old canvass bag. After she tied the bag to the back of her horse, she mounted and took the reins. Zeke mounted his horse and they were prepared to go.

That's when Kelly reached out and grabbed his hand, just as she did before.

"I'll tell you one thing, Zeke. If any of those men harm you or Ruth, they'll find out how good a shot I am…"

It was getting late and Kelly had already checked into a hotel in town. The desk clerk, Jake Rule, eyed her suspiciously at first. He had seen her in town and figured her to be a resident. Now she was checking into a hotel. It didn't make sense, but her money was real—good Union currency. He was no Unionist, but he was thankful that the currency in Lone Jack was not Confederate.

He sat back at his desk and eyed the newspaper in front of him, but he was not reading it. Jake Rule knew which way the war was headed and just bided his time. The South, he figured, had Agriculture; the North had Industry. They could always burn crops, they can't burn machines—not when the U.S. economy needed them. He had to deal with bushwhackers; of course, that was mandatory, all part of survival.

Jake Rule was bald, wore small wire-rimmed glasses and a checked vest. He glanced down at the register again. Kelly Ryan? The daughter of the old Irish handyman he'd seen around town? And didn't she have a little sister he had seen her with? If she registered alone, where were they? He certainly didn't get the required information from Kelly herself; she checked herself in and curtly went up to her room without anything else to say besides, "Thank you, sir."

Jake Rule would never be rich running a small hotel in a burgh like Lone Jack, but at least he always knew which side of the street he was on at any given time. It would put him in good stead with the guerrillas if he just mentioned this young visitor to someone in authority.

He slammed the counter bell and called the name of the teenager loafing in the next room. The kid arrived expectantly. He was tall and pimply and looked very bored.

"Wipe that look off your face," said Rule. "I've got something for you to do."

"And that is?"

"Find Dick Lamont. Tell him I'd like to speak to him."

"Ain't here. Heard he was over at the Sni-Bar with Blaine and Chiles and the rest of 'em."

Rule raised his eyebrows and asked, "Who's around?"

"Remember seeing one of those twins going into McGann's. Don't know if it was Tom or Mart..."

"Those two," he said wryly, "would laugh at a train wreck."

The boy started to scratch himself and Rule yelled at him.

"Stop that! Didn't your folks learn you any manners?"

"Yes, sir. And if I didn't learn fast enough, I got hit for it."

"Never mind that. If you see Lamont or Beaucaire or any of 'em, tell 'em I want to see 'em."

The teen smiled mischievously under his old stiff cap.

"Is it about that dark-haired gal who checked in?"

Rule looked at him suspiciously. "How'd you know?"

"I've seen her in town. Tall and Irish. Pretty blue eyes too. Fine lookin' gal..."

"If your parents heard you talk that way!"

Suddenly the boy realized he had spoken out of turn. He swallowed and said imploringly, "I didn't mean nothin' by it! It was just an—an observation, that's all!"

"An observation!" Rule shook his head. "You youngsters are getting more shocking by the minute, I swear!"

"You want me to tell them about her checking in?"

"No, I will. Now beat it and keep a watch out. They may be riding in."

The boy ran out. Rule looked down at the register. A pretty young girl like that here alone. Or was she?

He sat back in the chair. It was not his problem. They wouldn't harm her even after he told them, so there wasn't anything for him to be guilty about. But these were dangerous times, and sometimes a man's—or woman's—associates are what counted. Kelly must be here because of a man, he figured. And those boys out there in the woods might want to know who he was and where he stood.

The rest is up to them...

Zeke rode the game trail quietly, a light wind filtering through the branches above him. He knew it was dangerous. The guerrillas were all over these forests. If the Union Army couldn't find one man, Quantrill, it could take him years to find five. But if he had to, he would take forever to find them.

Forever.

When he looked toward the west, he saw the horizon, a straight crimson line hovering along the clouds. It would be dark in minutes. He knew he had to camp somewhere off the back trail —a Union patrol might mistake him for a guerrilla and parole him —with pistol balls.

Zeke found a hollow among some cottonwoods and tied the horse to a tree. He spread his bedroll out and climbed in, covering himself from a gust of leaves blowing suddenly through the trees.

There was no moon out. Had he raised his hand and held it in front of him he wouldn't have seen it. All was quiet except for the wind rustling the branches.

He didn't miss the irony.

Tomorrow was his nineteenth birthday. And here he was out in the woods looking for a gang of maniacs. How far from Kansas he was. No more birthdays to celebrate with his family.

He thought of his parents then, and how much he needed them now. More than ever, it seemed. Then a gust blew leaves along the ground and made him shiver.

Zeke was alone in the darkness. Just him and his memories.

He turned over in his bedroll and cried...

CHAPTER EIGHT

THE SUN WAS UP FOR OVER AN HOUR. ZEKE WOULD HAVE awakened sooner had he not been sleeping under the full, spreading branches of a sycamore. He stretched and started to adjust his eyes to the sun's glare.

It was his birthday. And what a way to start it.

After putting away his bedroll, Zeke shaved and then washed, using water from his canteen. Afterwards he searched his saddlebag and checked on the various items he took off the dead robbers, as well as the food Kelly had given him from the Ryan kitchen. After building a fire with matches from the Ryan home, he was able to cook bacon and have some bread with it. Then he made coffee, which he had started drinking a year ago (without his mom's knowledge).

Zeke untied the horse and let him picket on the lush grass several yards away. After a few minutes, he walked towards the horse, and as he approached him, he heard something.

He looked up and his eyes tried to search beyond the trees, listening closely. A cool morning breeze rustled some leaves and over it he heard a rushing movement in the distance. At first it was a trickling, then as the wind calmed down, a definite rush of water. He realized a stream had to be there, about twenty yards or so behind the trees.

Zeke took the reins and pulled the horse towards the sound. Then after a few minutes, he parted the branches of a cottonwood and saw the bank of a creek just ahead. He walked his horse through and then stood on the bank as the horse drank his fill. As he waited for him to finish up, Zeke removed the canteen and finished the little water he had left. Then he refilled it in the stream and put it back on his saddle.

It was then that he heard the click of a cylinder and a hammer cocked back. The noise was about ten feet behind him. Quickly his hand went to the Dragoon sitting snugly in its holster.

"Don't try it!"

Zeke turned around and faced a tall man in a dark beard, perhaps two weeks growth. He had a wide, sweaty face under a flat black hat. His eyes were slits of brown with no friendliness in them. The cocked Walker Colt in his hand only emphasized the lack of friendliness.

Behind him were three men; two tall ones and one little one, and further behind them were their horses. *Whoever they are, they sure can make themselves awful quiet when they have to.*

Zeke raised his hands and he could see the man with the Walker Colt grinning through his black beard. He apparently liked seeing other men helpless. Despite their various beards, these men looked as young as Zeke. In fact, it looked like he was the only one who bothered to shave.

"A young man like yourself way out here," said the man with the Colt.

"Don't tell me you came here just to give your horse a drink."

Zeke said nothing. He just kept watching the man and his pistol, not showing fear at either.

"Well," said the black beard, "since you're not in a talkative mood, maybe you can answer one question."

Zeke was smart enough by now to know what that question would be. He had heard about these questions being asked and was appalled by what would happen if someone gave a wrong answer.

"You favor the North or the South?"

A wrong answer could mean a pistol ball in the head. He was prepared to give an answer—but didn't know the right one. He looked at the man and the group behind him closely. What could he tell by their stance, their horses, their weapons, or anything else? If they were bushwhackers, he would have to answer he favored the South; if they were jayhawkers, he'd have to say North.

They would not give him a chance to change his answer.

Zeke stared at the fellow with the Walker and thought of his voice. There was no southern inflection at all; he was from the Midwest. And nowadays a Midwesterner could be anything.

The Walker Colt the man was holding told him nothing. Bushwhackers favored Navy Colts, and if this fellow had one on him it was hidden. The other three were too far away for him to clearly identify their holstered weapons. He looked at them all closely; watching, listening for *anything* that would indicate their origins. Though he was scared, he still faced them, not flinching once.

Pa always said, don't let the animal know you're scared. Face 'em down, even if your stomach is twisted in knots.

The hesitation seemed like an eternity to him and they all noticed the delay—yet it was what he needed. The little fellow, standing with the other two, smiled mockingly, then turned and spat on the ground, uttering an obscenity. Now Zeke knew what to answer.

"I favor the South," Zeke said, trying to sound proud.

The black-bearded fellow studied him a few moments, then cocked the hammer of his Walker Colt back into place.

"That's what I want to hear!"

"Come on, Talley!" said one of the men behind him. "You're going to release him just 'cause he says that?"

Talley answered, "You know a jayhawk that comes riding in here all by himself? Those boys like to travel in a crowd...They can't win a fight otherwise..."

Zeke saw the irony in this statement, which did not include the bushwhackers.

"What are you here for, anyway?" asked Talley.

Zeke put down his hands and said, as convincingly as he could, "I want to join you."

Talley holstered his gun and looked back at the three men. "Well, what do you think, boys?"

The little fellow spoke with a Louisville drawl. "I don't like it! Some tall jasper like him shows up in the woods and wants to join up with Quantrill?" Zeke could hear the contempt from this little man when he called him "tall". "Huh! Maybe your Walker made him answer that way, Herb. He wants to join Quantrill!"

Zeke stared back at the little man and said easily, "You tell me where there's a recruiting station for Quantrill's boys and I'll go there."

The little man's lips tightened, and he grimaced as the other men laughed.

"He's got a point, Will," said Talley, who then turned to Zeke. "What's your name?"

"Zeke Tyler," he said, then without missing a beat, "out of Cass County." He had quickly remembered from the newspaper Ryan had given him that Cass County was one of the areas to be depopulated by Order Number 11.

"You've got a home, Zeke Tyler?"

"Not anymore," said Zeke earnestly. In fact, he said it so convincingly that the men saw real tears well up in his eyes. He stared at them, trying to hold down his rage. "My folks were murdered," he said, through his teeth, "by a pack of animals! And I'd like to see every one of them dead!"

Talley seemed amused. He glanced back and said, "Well, boys, looks like we've got a real hot-tempered man here!"

"It's not funny!"

"Didn't say it was," said Talley, whose face now became as serious as those of the men behind him. "The homes of our kin got the Union torch as well." Then he remembered he had said "Union" and spat on the ground.

"Mount up and ride back to camp with us."

"Where's that?"

"Not far from here. Come on."

The others eyed Zeke as they slowly turned to head back for their horses. Zeke watched them warily. Well, he was in, as far as he knew. He mounted his horse and moved up to join them.

Despite Talley's assertion that their camp was "not far from here", Zeke had ridden with them for well over an hour. The men spoke briefly to each other, but not to him, and the silence was awkward. As they rode, Zeke noticed that two riders, including Talley, were in front; the little one called Will rode behind him.

Though he didn't turn around, Zeke could feel the hateful little eyes glaring at the back of his head, and at times he heard the click of a Colt's hammer being cocked. Apparently Will was taking imaginary target practice at the back of that head and body that sat so *tall* in the saddle.

The camp was so deep in the woods that they had to duck their heads when their horses rode in under the thick branches of cottonwoods. No roads or trails and certainly no streams nearby, at least not where he could see any. It was dense forest and lonely as well—purposely so. *Only a squirrel could happen upon these men.* The camp was so well hidden, Zeke realized that if these men ultimately didn't trust him, they'd have to kill him to protect its location.

This act had better be convincing.

They all dismounted, and the horses were picketed off to a little corral with other mounts. The area was thick with fresh grass and several ropes were tied from one tree to another to keep the horses penned in. Zeke walked into the camp and looked around. Instantly smelling coffee, he saw a few men near a fire, boiling some in a pot.

There were several men about; some sitting near the fire, some resting on logs or large rocks, but all were staring at the new man Talley's group brought in.

One man sat on a curved rock about a dozen feet back polishing the barrel of his rifle. As Zeke walked into the sunlight filtering through the trees, the man froze and glared at him. Then he rose and walked towards Zeke, still holding his rifle. When he got about six feet away from Zeke, he stopped and pointed the rifle at his stomach.

"Well, thanks, Talley," said Dick Lamont. "You done me a favor."

Zeke stopped and watched him closely. *Oh great. Just who I wanted to see.* Lamont's face was still bruised from their recent fight. In fact, the part of his face that still seemed alive were his hate-filled eyes.

Talley stepped forward and all the other men stopped what they were doing, staring at the scene.

"What's up, Lamont?" asked Talley. "You know him?"

"Yeah," answered Lamont grimly, jacking the hammer down on his rifle. "He's got something coming to him."

Talley quickly stepped in front of Zeke and said firmly, "Listen,

Lamont. We just found him a few miles back, watering his horse. Says he wants to join us. Now I don't know what your problem with him is, but you're not shooting anyone here until he's had his say." He turned back to Zeke. "What'd you do to him?"

Zeke, still glaring at Lamont, said, "I just rode into Lone Jack, figuring to find one of Quantrill's boys and get a chance to join up. Then I saw this monkey..." He said the word on purpose and was glad it had the desired effect; Lamont's bruised face twitched in rage. Zeke continued, "I saw him push a little girl to the ground. He not only made her cry, on top of it, he yelled at her. Well, no man is going to push a child around if I have something to say about it...so I whipped him."

Talley stared at him in disbelief. "You whipped *him*?"

Another man sitting on a rock spoke up. "It's true, Herb. There was a lot of talk about it all the way from town. Look at him."

Lamont's fury was rising at the mention of the beating. Talley turned back and looked at his face in the sunlight.

"Yeah," agreed Talley. "Looks like you've been knocked around some, Dick."

"And now I'm going to put this through 'im!" Lamont raised the rifle.

Talley put his hand on it and said, "Save your iron for the blue-coats. If you want him, put that long gun down and get to it." He looked back at Zeke. "Both of you! Take your holsters off and settle it."

As he passed him, Talley said, "All right, Zeke Tyler. Now we all get to see if you've got the stuff that'll make you one of us. I know you beat him up once, but, you see, I'm a skeptical man. I don't believe a word anyone says, no matter how many folks say it...I've got to see things for myself."

Zeke said quietly, "Distrustful soul, huh?"

Talley answered, "I wouldn't trust Jesus on Sunday mornin'."

Zeke looked back at Lamont and saw him removing his holster. He didn't want to go through with it, but there was no way out. If Zeke backed out now, they wouldn't want him as a guerrilla. And if he wasn't one of them, they would have to kill him.

Talley said cheerfully, "Give 'em room, boys!"

The men pulled their little circle back several feet. Lamont took off his hat and tossed it to the ground.

Zeke pulled off his holster and the moment he handed it back to Talley, Lamont dove for Zeke's stomach. The attack happened so quickly that when Talley took the holster, the momentum almost pulled him over as well. Talley quickly caught his balance and cursed angrily—he should have known Lamont would pull something like this.

Zeke had barely turned back to face Lamont when the attack came, and he instinctively put up his arms to block the lunge but didn't have time. Zeke's hat flew off and the two hit the ground with a thud. As they did, two raiders in their path jumped out of the way.

With their arms wrapped tightly around each other, they rolled across the ground furiously, kicking up dust in small but stinging clouds. All heads turned and followed them as they tumbled over each other, knowing full well where they were headed.

They were approaching the campfire and Zeke strained his muscles to stop them before they rolled into it. Unfortunately, when they did stop, Zeke had his back on the ground and Lamont was using every ounce of his weight to pin him down. Lamont was not fat, but he was muscular, and he knew just when and where to apply his strength—and unlike the other fight, this time he was sober.

He punched Zeke across the face with his left hand, a heavy blow that made his head spin. Seeing that the punch had the desired effect, Lamont planted his feet and rose, yanking Zeke up by the front of his shirt. Then he punched Zeke again, while releasing the grip on his shirt.

The young Kansan fell back and hit the ground heavily, the back of his head and neck suddenly feeling an intense heat. He had fallen near the burning wood of the campfire.

Recoiling from the heat, Zeke started to come off the ground when Lamont threw himself on the Kansan. The weight of the man almost crushed Zeke against the ground and his head was now very close to the flames. Still dizzy from the blow, Zeke tried to push Lamont hard in the chest and felt what seemed like one hundred ninety pounds of sheer bone. And then there was the man's rage—it was bottomless.

Lamont pressed his fingers hard into Zeke's face. At this point, his pushed-in nose smelled the bushwhacker's seldom washed hand and he felt like gagging. Behind him, the heat from the fire started to prickle the hairs at the nape of his neck.

A tall young man from Georgia named Jim Gaines was watching the scene. A little concerned, he turned to Herb Talley and asked, "You sure you want it this way, Herb?"

"Why not?" Talley replied. "He bought into it, didn't he? Anyway, you could call this his 'Baptism of Fire'." Talley then looked at Gaines and saw he wasn't smiling. He shrugged absently and turned his attention back to the fight.

Zeke knew that in a few seconds he was a goner. With no room to swing his fist, his right hand reached down, instinctively searching for something he knew would be there. He stiffly kept his head away from the flames as his fingers inched down and then to the right, searching desperately. Soon he could tell by its heat that he'd found what he was looking for. Ignoring the pain, he wrapped his fingers around it and drew it up under Lamont's straining arms.

His fingers were starting to singe. The pain was searing, but Zeke did his best to ignore it as he shoved the stone straight into Lamont's face, aiming instinctively for his mouth and nose.

The rock had been near Zeke's back, and close to the fire. As soon as he'd thrust it into Lamont's face, he knew it did the job. Lamont screamed and his hand came off Zeke's face. The bushwhacker leapt to his feet and his hands were frantically covering his face. As soon as Lamont got up, Zeke tossed the rock away, shaking his fingers desperately. Wasting no time, he pushed himself off the ground with his other hand.

Lamont was still holding his singed mouth when Zeke punched him in the eye with his good hand. The big man fell back against a curved rock as three bushwhackers flew out of the way.

Not finished with him, Zeke reached over and pulled Lamont to his feet by the hair. Then he hit the same eye again. Blood was running down the side of Zeke's mouth and the palm and fingers of his right hand had first degree burns, but he was angry. He had had enough of Dick Lamont's dirty fighting tactics, his brute strength and his attempts to murder him.

The blood was pounding in his head, but Zeke was too far gone to stop. He kept hitting the bushwhacker with everything he had, blackening both Lamont's eyes and turning his face into a bloody mess. Then he grabbed Lamont's head and slammed it several times against the rock behind him. He never noticed when Lamont lost consciousness; he just knew he had to kill him.

Talley turned to Jim Gaines and said, "Stop him before he kills him."

Then he shouted cheerfully at Zeke, "Let up on 'em, wildcat! We've got to have something left for a raid or two!"

Gaines brought another man over and the two of them

grabbed Zeke as Lamont crumpled to the grass. Zeke allowed the two men to pull him away; indeed he had no strength left in him to resist. His head was throbbing. It took a long time for him to relax and control the mounting dizziness. Then, after it passed, he looked down at his singed fingers and the blood on both his knuckles. The raiders nearby looked at him with something close to awe.

Then the two men stepped back and let Zeke stand on his own.

Talley stepped in front of him and said approvingly, "You've got a pair of mean fists there, Zeke Tyler."

"Yeah, I know," Zeke said harshly, then threw up his left hand and punched Talley hard in the jaw. Talley fell to the ground heavily as Jim Gaines and the other man grabbed Zeke again. The other raiders leaned forward as one, ready to grab Zeke as well.

With his hat behind him on the ground, Talley raised up on an elbow and rubbed his jaw. Despite Zeke's weakened hands, the punch still hurt.

Indignantly, he looked up at Zeke and asked, "What's that for?"

Glaring down at him, Zeke said thickly, "That's for doing nothing while I'm bein' burnt to a crisp!"

"I just figured you didn't want any interruptions."

Still breathing hard, Zeke replied, "You interrupted *me* when I almost killed *him*!"

Talley, still on the ground, grinned broadly and said, "Boys, I think we found a real live one!" He then gave a loud rebel yell and the other raiders around them did the same thing. A few of them even patted Zeke on the back.

He was accepted. He could now ride as one of them.

And deep inside him, he had never felt more disgusted in his life...

CHAPTER NINE

KELLY WALKED DOWN THE STAIRS OF THE HOTEL AND WHEN SHE got to the lobby, she was surprised to find the clerk already staring at her. Usually these drab men behind a hotel desk are deep into a newspaper. She knew she was attractive; she had seen that gawky boy with the cap ogling her the other night when she checked in, but she knew that was not the reason the older man was watching her now.

She had paid for her second-floor room in advance. Her belongings were safe (or at least she hoped they were). And to make sure she was safe she had an 1849 Colt pocket revolver in her handbag. Its four-inch barrel sat snugly against a handkerchief and some coins.

Kelly stared back at Rule and finally asked, "Yes?"

"Nothing, Miss Ryan. It's just—you look so lovely this morning."

That was not only forward, it revealed his nervousness when he was caught staring at her. And why should her being lovely "this morning" mean anything to him when Kelly had never stayed at the hotel any other morning.

She went to the desk and gave him the key.

"Will you be out long?"

Kelly's eyes narrowed and she turned to him. He saw the look.

"I don't know, Mister Rule," she said. "Let's say I could be back anytime."

Jake Rule swallowed slightly when he saw those blue eyes. He realized very quickly that those eyes could be charming when she wanted them to be or they could look real mean.

They looked mean now.

"Of course, Miss Ryan! I just thought that...if you're expecting any visitors."

Kelly stared at him briefly, then said, "Yes, Mister Rule, I might be. My young man might be coming by."

"Certainly. What does he look like?"

"Well, he's tall, about six foot-three or so. Sandy blond hair, broad shoulders, blue eyes...Should he come by, please let me know. Thank you."

She turned around and was out the door before Jake Rule could ask her anything else. Quickly she walked away from the hotel, hoping to be cooled by the fresh night air.

Kelly really had nothing to do, but she had to get out of that hotel and its nosy clerks. She knew that nighttime in Lone Jack could bring out the rowdy bushwhacker element, but it would also be the time Zeke would make an appearance and contact her.

Not wanting to appear like she had nothing to do, Kelly stopped at the front of a dress shop and gazed through the window at the dress displays. She had noticed two women standing a few feet away and talking animatedly. So she wouldn't look out of place, she increased her gaze at a lovely sky blue dress on a display, as if she was prepared to buy it.

At first, Kelly didn't pay much attention to the chatter of the two women, but after a moment, she couldn't help herself.

"It's a shame what those Yankees are doing!   Damned shameful!"

"Ellie, don't curse!" said the short brunette in a white bonnet.

"Still, it's true! Heathen pigs is what those Yankees are! Damn heathen pigs!"

Kelly watched them in the reflection. Ellie was a tall blonde woman in a garish dress of dark blue, an equally garish hat topped her head. Her eyes were a piercing blue in a long angular face and her chin jutted out a bit, as if ready for use as a weapon. Her eyes were almost like Kelly's, but they lacked the Irish girl's warmth. Ellie's eyes now shot the brunette a look.

"Don't make apologies for the Yankees, Betty! Every one of them's scum and should be roasted alive...I'm glad our boys slaughtered those nigger-loving trash in Lawrence! Shootin' and burnin' is too good for 'em!"

At the mention of the words, 'nigger-loving trash', Kelly suddenly trembled all over. Her stomach twisted in knots and she struggled to calm herself down. Ellie had the misfortune to use the exact same words Pete Wallace had used before he murdered her father.

Kelly briskly turned around and went up to Ellie. She was inches from her face. The two women stared at her.

Kelly glared at the blonde woman and asked curtly, "Are you saying that those poor souls in Lawrence deserved to die?"

Ellie looked back at her defiantly and said, "Yes, I am!"

Ellie did not see Kelly's right hand come up, despite how close they were standing. Out of the corner of her eye, Ellie just caught a blur heading for her face and had no time to block it. The slap left a huge ugly red blotch on the blonde's right cheek.

Ellie felt her cheek and her glare weakened, but she was still trying to sound defiant when she said, "All I was saying is that those Kansas boys deserved what they got! That's all—"

The second slap was actually faster and had more power than the first, coming from her right hand this time. It stung Ellie's cheek and now there were red blotches on both sides of her face. Now Ellie put her other hand up to her right cheek and stepped back on the walk, her full upright stance and unshakable poise broken forever. Her head was lowered slightly, and her eyes had some tears in them as she stared at the woman who put them there.

Kelly turned and put the handbag with the loaded gun in it on a small ledge near the shop window. Then she turned back and faced Ellie with her hands in front of her.

Kelly's tone was low and challenging. "If you want more of that, just say so..."

Ellie was still holding her cheek as Betty put her arms around her protectively.

"Don't you lay another hand on her!" Betty said, her voice approaching panic.

"Let her fight her own battles," Kelly said roughly.

"Come on, Betty, let's go!" said Ellie, her voice choking.

They quickly turned and Kelly watched them go down the sidewalk.

"Don't start anything with her, Ellie!" said Betty soothingly. "She's one of those shanty Irish hussies!" They continued around the corner.

Slowly she calmed down and turned to look for her handbag, which was no longer on the ledge.

"Looking for this?" asked Jean Beaucaire, holding her handbag.

Kelly turned around and quickly took it from him.

"I hope my money's still inside!"

"There's something else there besides money."

Kelly stared at him, realizing he probably looked inside and saw the gun. Testily, she said, "I have to carry a gun—to protect myself from the slime."

"You can't mean me," said the Frenchman, trying to sound innocent. "I love people. Especially beautiful women."

Kelly studied him a moment, then said sourly, "Good day, sir."

She abruptly turned and went down the street. Beaucaire moved after her quickly and took hold of her arm.

Turning to him, Kelly said, "Mister, you'll remove your hand right now. I don't need the marshal to do my fighting for me."

Reluctantly, he removed his hand. "I witnessed your altercation with those two women, and I have no doubt of your... resolve. I just wanted to tell you about the dress."

"What?"

Beaucaire gestured back toward the dress shop and said with a flourish, "Say the word and it is yours, madam. I'm sure you'd look lovely in it."

Kelly glared at him and said, "Listen, you! If I ever want a dress or anything else, I'll pay for it myself with my own money. I won't be beholden to you or any glad-handing riffraff with the charm of a cockroach and a face to match."

Behind the eyes, Beaucaire was trying to hide his irritation and appear amused.

"I heard the Irish have a sharp tongue. What is your name, Colleen?"

"My name is none of your damn business."

Beaucaire raised his eyebrows. This girl was not responding the way she was supposed to. Perhaps if he mentioned the dress again.

"It's a shame to leave that blue dress in that window."

"Then you buy it and wear it yourself. I'm sure it would look good on you."

As Beaucaire's face grew hard, Kelly turned away from him

and continued down the sidewalk. "Damn mick," he said under his breath.

Oh well. There was still Anita, and her house was just up the street...

Talley's group started to arrive in Lone Jack that night, riding into town in pairs or groups of three. Herb Talley decided to ride in paired up with Zeke. The Kansan's face was bruised, and his right hand was wrapped in a clean rag, covering the palm and fingers.

"Well," said Talley, trying to get a conversation going, "that was some dust-up back there."

Zeke glanced at him but said nothing. With his left hand holding the reins, he turned his attention back to the trail.

"This has got to be some kind of record. Dick Lamont has put near to a dozen men in the hospital and probably a dozen more in the ground. You come along out of nowhere and beat the stuffing out of him, not once but twice! I don't know what they put in the water in Cass County, but whatever it is, I'll have some myself."

Zeke had his eyes on the trail when he said, "You don't have to ride with me, Talley. I can still swing a punch with my left..."

"What?"

"You're keeping me company to make sure some of Lamont's friends don't mistake me for a Yankee and uh...shoot me by accident."

"No!" Talley answered. "I just figured you didn't know your way to town, that's it."

Zeke didn't buy it. He also figured the real reason for Talley's company were all those questions waiting to be asked—and Zeke was right.

"Your folks had a farm in Cass County?"

"Yeah."

"Big farm?"

"Big enough for them to burn."

"Know the Dennisons?"

"There are a lot of folks living in Cass County. Am I supposed to know them?"

"No...Just thought you might. Don't know a man out there who didn't get a horse from their ranch."

"You know one now."

"You ever go fishing around Arrow Creek?"

"I don't fish," answered Zeke laconically.

Talley paused before asking, "So they killed your folks, huh?"

"That's what I said."

"I'm out of Independence myself...I'm the son of a border man. My pa got killed by the Jayhawks in '56 while he was shootin' up Paola, Kansas. They found him later by Arrow Creek—in several pieces."

Zeke said grimly, "Maybe your pa should have stayed on his side of the border."

Talley stared at him and asked, "What did you say?"

Zeke looked back at him and said without hesitation, "Maybe your pa should have stayed on his side of the border."

Talley was holding down his anger. He tried to stare Zeke down, but the Kansan didn't flinch under his gaze.

"You like playin' close to the edge, don't you, Zeke Tyler?"

Zeke said nothing and turned his attention back to the trail. Both men were silent for a while. Personally, Zeke didn't care, but he could see that Talley liked to talk and it unnerved him that Zeke wasn't much for conversation.

"We're just going to town to blow off some steam. Figured after all that brawlin', you could use a few drinks yourself."

"I'm not much of a drinker," Zeke said honestly.

"Huh! Not much of a drinker? How do you have fun when you're in town, play cards?"

"I don't gamble."

Talley stared at him. "You *are* old enough to shave, aren't you?"

"Yeah, I'm old enough to shave."

"Got a gal in town?"

Zeke paused, studying the trail. Then he said, "Yes. I have a girl."

"She pretty?"

"She's beautiful."

"Good. You'll see her in town then."

Zeke glanced at the gang leader, then back to the road. He listened to his horse's hoof beats on the hard-packed ground and felt the light wind filter through the trees above. The night air felt good on his bruised face, and he looked off in the distance, seeing the town itself come into view. Soon, they rode into Lone Jack without either one of them saying a word, then they headed down the main street.

Kelly noticed the riders coming into town in pairs and wondered what was up. Most of them were going into McGann's Saloon. She was just a few feet away when Dick Lamont and the little man, Will Sorrel, dismounted at the hitching rail, tied their horses and headed for the swinging doors.

Before he entered, Lamont saw her and stopped dramatically, staring hard at her face, as if trying to remember her. Kelly looked up at him and gasped—she couldn't help it. Lamont's face had a bright red burn around the mouth and chin. His nose was busted, and he had two black eyes. The rest of his face was covered with bruises, though the eyes still burned with contempt. When she saw those eyes, Kelly knew that the man was still trouble.

Lamont continued to stare at her without recognition until Sorrel spoke up. "Come on, Dick. I got a thirst."

"Yeah," Lamont said absently, and then followed him in. In other times, it was Lamont who had led his admirers everywhere they went.

After they entered McGann's, Kelly quickly put her hand over her mouth to stem the nausea she was feeling. She remembered his face from town, especially lying on the ground after the beating —but he didn't look like this! She paused a while, leaning against a post and let the sick feeling pass. After it was gone, she looked at the saloon doors thoughtfully. Then she heard horses behind her approaching the tie rail.

Kelly's face brightened and something leapt in her as she looked toward the street.

Zeke and Talley got off their horses and tied them at the rail. When Zeke turned and faced the saloon, he saw her, at first not believing it. After all the fistfights, hard riding, and endless duplicity, she was as beautiful to him as any angel he had ever read about or seen in picture books.

Talley saw them staring at each other and asked, "Your girl?"

"Yeah," Zeke answered. He was about to run to her, but she beat him to it, running into him and throwing her arms around his neck. He took her in his arms, and they stared at each other for only a few seconds before they kissed. Then Zeke stopped and looked in her eyes. Then they kissed again, longer and harder this time.

Talley tied his horse and watched them, amused. He said dryly, "Zeke, ol' buddy, either you've been on the trails too long or...you look like you've just found each other."

When they stopped kissing, they pulled back and Zeke stood in the lamplight near the saloon door. That's when Kelly finally got a true look at his face. She gasped and then noticed the awkward homemade bandage on his hand. She almost screamed.

"My God, Zeke!"

Before he could answer, Talley spoke up again, trying to get a rise out of them. "Don't worry, ma'am," he said mischievously, "seems he's always getting himself in trouble."

Kelly noticed him for the first time and her eyes narrowed; her dislike was apparent.

Zeke said, "Kelly, this is Herb Talley. Herb, this is Kelly."

Talley removed his hat and bowed, not taking himself too seriously. "My pleasure, ma'am. Hopefully, you can keep Zeke over here out of trouble."

After seeing Zeke's bruised face and listening to Talley's attempts to treat it all as a joke, Kelly's temper was rising. "You said that before, Mister Talley. Now what did you mean by it?"

Talley saw the anger in the Irish girl's eyes and said easily, "Well, your fella over here likes to mix it up with men I would've laid odds to come out the winner. I heard he whipped Dick Lamont real good here in town and now I got a chance to witness that myself. He was really something, ma'am, though he was almost roasted alive for the privilege of winning—"

"Talley!" Zeke said irritably. He saw the horrified look on Kelly's face, as if something had died inside of her.

He looked at Talley, who was grinning broadly. The more he enjoyed Kelly's hurt, the angrier Zeke got. "Aren't you thirsty?" he asked harshly.

"Yeah," Talley answered breezily, "that's what I came here for, isn't it? Well, ma'am, it was awful nice to meet you...Zeke, the boys will head back to camp late. I'll leave you to your catching up." Still grinning, he winked at Zeke and then entered the saloon.

After he left, Kelly stared at Zeke and asked, "What did he mean when he said 'the boys'?"

"I'll tell you in a minute," he replied, looking around. "Let's move on down the street first."

Kelly put both her hands on his face and couldn't hide her anguish. "Oh, darlin', what did they do to you?"

"In a moment," Zeke said, then put her arm through his and they started down the sidewalk. He knew it might take a while to calm her down.

"You got into another fight with Lamont? Why?"

"When we rode into camp, Lamont was there. He wanted to shoot me, but Talley said we had to settle it with our fists—again. He had to see it for himself." The last statement was said in disgust.

"Why?"

"Guess it was the quickest way for him to see if I belonged with the gang."

"The gang!" She stopped and stared at him.

"Talley and those other men are bushwhackers."

"*All of them?*" Her shout was unexpected, and Zeke looked around to see if anyone noticed. Apparently, no one did—or at least they didn't show it. "I thought it was just Lamont."

"No, Kelly. Every man that's ridden into this town in the past hour, rides for Quantrill."

"Oh, my Lord!"

"I had to, Kelly. I had to get information about Ruth's where-abouts from the inside."

"You're riding with a gang of killers, don't you know that?"

"You think I want to?" he said, turning to her.

"And that's why you had the second fight with Lamont! So you could get yourself cut and bleeding to amuse a pack of animals. Can't you see what they are? You'll ride with them and it won't take long before you get yourself killed."

"Kelly, I'm using them to find her."

"Oh, really?" she said cynically, folding her arms. "Who is doing the using here? I understand what you're after, I want her freed too, but no good can come from these men! Not permanent or temporary. And they're not going to just let you find your sister and leave when you please."

He looked back at her and said deliberately, "I know what they are, and you do too. But you and your father still fed them."

Kelly looked at him abruptly, fury in her eyes.

Her voice choking, she said, "You don't know how many times I had to prepare meals for them. How many times I wanted to take that butcher knife and slit their throats you'll never know. Look at what they've done: Destroyed our families, kidnapped your sister, burned your hometown. And you want to sit in their camp and break bread with them?"

Angrily, he said, "Kelly, stop!"

Kelly still glared at him, but her anger lessened somewhat with his outburst.

Zeke looked at her sadly. Then he took her hand in his and kissed it. He held it close to him and said, "I'm sorry for that...I don't ever want to yell at you."

Kelly's eyes softened and her mouth relaxed into a little smirk. "...All couples yell at each other sometimes, Zeke."

Zeke squeezed her hand and looked into her eyes. "Yeah, I guess they do..."

The gunshot that echoed down the street froze both of them to the spot. They turned and looked back up the street. As other people ran towards the saloon, Zeke started to move away, but Kelly grabbed his arm.

"Zeke, don't go! Those riff-raff are probably shooting each other over some dancer! It's not worth it."

Zeke said coldly, "Somebody could be hurt, Kelly. Now let me go."

Reluctantly she let go of his arm and Zeke headed for the saloon. Kelly watched him go sadly and then followed. With some difficulty Zeke pushed his way through to the crowd gathering at the door.

When he entered, he saw a long dingy room with some light glaring from a cheap chandelier above. Tables were situated along the walls on the right-hand side, the center apparently open for dancing. Everyone seemed to be around the bar, which stretched the length of the room on the left side.

Lying on the floor near a fallen barstool, with blood soaking his shirt, was a young man Zeke had never seen before.

Suddenly Zeke heard Dick Lamont's voice, loud and possibly drunk, yelling for room. Then he saw the crowd near the bar part quickly, some almost tripping over the body on the dusty floor. Zeke could now see Lamont standing at the bar. In his hand was a Navy Colt with smoke rising from the barrel.

An old man was standing near Zeke, nursing his beer. Sadly, he stared at the man lying on the floor and shook his head.

"I'm done shocked over this. Real shocked…"

"Why?" asked Zeke wryly. "You've never seen a dead man?"

"Not him…I'd have sworn Tilton would've had the edge."

Zeke stared at the old man and asked urgently, "Who's that on the ground?"

The old man blinked wide wrinkled blue eyes at him and said, "Greg Tilton. I knew him for the fastest man with a gun in Jefferson County!" He sadly observed the body. "Not no more."

Zeke turned back and stared at the corpse. *If Tilton was here, the others would be too.* His heart leapt when he realized he might be that close to saving Ruth. He *had* to stay here now.

Zeke asked the old man, "Why'd Lamont kill him?"

"Old Greg was making a little too much fun of Lamont's face. I mean, look at it! The man who did that to him must have been eight feet tall and had the chest of a buffalo!"

Zeke looked at the old man and raised his eyebrows. Unfortunately, at that moment, Zeke didn't hear Lamont yelling at him.

"Hey," said the old man, pointing at Lamont. "He's calling you out."

It was true. Lamont stood at that end of the bar, hovering over Greg Tilton's body and yelling at Zeke. Suddenly all eyes at the other side of the room turned and stared at him.

Zeke looked back at them uncomfortably. God, this is embarrassing. What does that lunatic want now?

"There he is!" Lamont yelled, pointing a shaky hand towards Zeke. "The fella they won't let me forget beat the daylights out of me--not once, but twice!" He slurred the final word and as he staggered slightly, a few men, including Herb Talley, rushed forward. But Lamont recovered quickly, raising the gun barrel close to their faces. Hastily, they backed off.

"Come on, Tyler! Get out your iron! You and me are gonna fight again—only this time it'll be to the death!"

Zeke called out, "You mean the other times we *didn't?*"

Some in the crowd actually laughed and Zeke smiled at them good-naturedly. He was hoping to make light of the situation and deflect Lamont's drunken rage. Despite what he was, Zeke didn't want to kill him.

"Oh, that's really funny, Tyler! Really funny...But, you see, I'm at the end of my tether right now. And I think I've been laughed at enough—thanks to you! Now you just stand there—stand there like you are. And when I put my Navy back into my leather, then you and me draw. Me with my Navy, you with your Yankee pea-shooter. Understand me, Tyler?"

Zeke replied grimly, "Yeah, I understand..."

By this time, Kelly had pushed her way in, but there was no room for her to squeeze her way over to Zeke's side.

Herb Talley stepped forward and held up his hands. "Now, Dick," he said consolingly, "let's just settle down. You've got a whole bar full of liquor behind you. Let's forget all this and just fill our bellies. What do you say, Dick? Let's get to it!"

"Yeah," said Lamont, a sudden gleam in his dull eyes. Talley didn't know if it was a reflection off the overhead lights or he was lit from within. Either way, he had a bad feeling about it.

"That's right, 'let's get to it'. That's the same thing you said when you insisted me and him fight. Well, now look at me! I should thank you too!"

Talley's face became still, and he stepped back. His eyes watched the Navy Colt in the drunken man's hand. The hammer was already pulled back and his finger tightened on the trigger.

Everyone around them stared at the scene as if frozen in time. No one made a move to interfere. Lamont said nothing. His eyes were dead holes in his head and at that point, it was hard to tell what he was thinking. The gun barrel gleamed as it pointed at Talley's stomach.

Then Lamont pulled the trigger.

A second after this, a shot was heard. Talley instinctively recoiled and looked at his stomach. Then he looked up towards the front of the saloon.

Zeke stood there grimly holding the Dragoon pistol at arms' length, its barrel smoking.

Lamont turned toward Zeke, his stomach bloody and a look of shock and pain on his sweaty face. He tried to lift his Colt, but it was too heavy for his hand. After it fell to the floor, his body followed it.

Little Will Sorrel stood next to Talley and looked down at Lamont's body. He shook his head.

"He must've snapped or something..." He looked up at Talley. "He shot Tilton, but this time the gun misfired. You're a lucky man, Herb."

Talley stared at Lamont's body and answered, "You've got to keep your Navy dry...I figure some moisture got into it. It happens. Percussion cap just misfired..."

He looked towards Zeke gratefully, then scanned the noisy crowd.

Some men came forward, picked up the two bodies and carried them out. Kelly winced as she saw them go past.

Talley said to the crowd, "Folks, I want you to gather 'round and know that fella with the Yankee sidearm in his hand. His name's Zeke Tyler! And he not only saved my bacon, he's the toughest son I've ever seen anywhere with two fists and the fastest man with a gun I can mention!"

Zeke stared at his gun, then absently holstered it. He was dazed by it all, but the crowd around him didn't seem to notice. Some men slapped him on the back and moved him toward the bar. Rebel yells suddenly filled the air, rising to the rafters and beyond.

To Kelly, the noise was deafening. Woefully, she watched Zeke being herded over to the bar by his newfound friends. As tears ran down her cheeks, Kelly pushed her way back through the crowd rushing past her and fled out into the street.

It was lonely now, with most everyone in the saloon or headed towards it. She ran up the street, feeling suddenly lost and empty.

In her eyes, it was the second time in just a few days that she lost someone close to her. He belonged to someone else now. And she didn't know if she was ever going to get him back...

CHAPTER TEN

HIS HEAD FELT LIKE IT WAS IN A VISE AND THE PRESSURE WAS STILL there when he woke up.

"All right! Sleepy-head is up!" Jim Gaines turned around and shouted, "Yeah, get another plate!"

Zeke put his hands on his face and opened his eyes slowly. He looked up from the ground and the sun seemed to shine its glare just at him and him alone. Recoiling, he turned away until he could adjust his eyes. When he did, he looked up from the ground and saw a tall young man with brown hair and a lean, tanned face looking down on him with some amusement. He seemed to be chewing on something. When Zeke's eyes cleared, he saw that the young man was holding a tin plate in one hand and stuffing some buttered bread into his mouth with the other.

Zeke squinted into the sun again and sat up slowly. The pounding in his head was incredible, but he forced himself not to cover his eyes. The rag tied around his hand was off, and though his fingers were still achy, he could still move them. Then he suddenly looked at his feet and noticed his boots were off. A glance to his right told him they were just a couple feet away, next to his hat.

Zeke looked up at Gaines again.

"Yeah," said lean young man with a deep southern drawl. "I pulled 'em off."

"How nice," said Zeke, feeling his skull. "Who're you?"

"Jim Gaines."

"That's nice…Who am I?"

Gaines said good-naturedly, "You're Zeke Tyler. The toughest man in Quantrill's merry band, with his fists *and* his gun! Anyway, according to Herb Talley."

"Yeah, I think I remember him."

Gaines looked at him seriously and said, "He didn't forget you, that's for sure. He was talking you up good at McGann's. Not that I didn't believe him. I was there when you tanned Lamont's hide the other day and I was there in McGann's when you paroled him."

Zeke's head throbbed again as he tried to move. What he had just heard didn't alleviate his pain either.

"You know," said Gaines, "for a man who doesn't drink, you downed that whiskey pretty fast."

"Guess I didn't want to taste it."

"Then why'd you drink it?"

Zeke was shaking out his boots as he said, "I don't know… Everyone was there at the bar, patting me on the back and all… They were all pushing that stuff on me."

As Gaines chewed a mouthful of bread, he said, "Just 'cause all of them was at the bar beltin' it down doesn't mean you have to."

"You drink some?"

"Sure. I like a bottle sometimes—and a woman along with it if possible. But I know when to straighten my elbow too. The gals aren't much fun if you can't see 'em straight."

Zeke looked down and grinned. Then he felt his head again.

"Get yourself a plate. Got coffee too."

"Is it hot?"

"Scalding."

It was a chore, but Zeke made himself get up. He got a plate and was able to collect some cooked meat and bread and found out that Gaines wasn't lying about the coffee being hot. He went back and sat down near his hat. Gaines was already seated next to him with a fresh cup.

As Zeke ate his fill, he looked at Gaines and asked, "How long have you been riding with 'em?"

"Since what they called the Battle of Lone Jack a few months ago...Had an older brother who served in the Fifth Georgian Infantry. Way I heard it, he's now lyin' somewhere along the Chicahominy River in Shenandoah with a ball in his skull. So, I came of age and left Georgia. I didn't feel like sittin' still on a battlefield and wait for a Union slug to get me, so I joined up with Mosby for a while. But then it looked like the Federals were hangin' all of Mosby's bunch they could find, no questions asked. I heard that fightin' for Quantrill was tough work, but it put a crimp in the Federals' bonnet, so I came up here to do my part. Besides, when I was with Mosby, I did one or two things that, let's say, would not meet with the approval of polite society, so Bill Quantrill here I come!"

Zeke looked at him seriously. "You ever been to Lawrence?"

Gaines stared back at him as if he were crazy. "Lawrence? Hell, no!" He looked around to see if anyone was close by, and then said quietly, "I'll admit I like stealin' a whole lot, but I never killed no clerks or storekeepers to do it.   Nor somebody's husband or father—least none that didn't wear a blue uniform. I'm in it for the coin, pure and simple—and harassing old Johnny Yank...Now what happened to Lawrence..." He shook his head regretfully. "I bailed out of that stew before we got to Mount

Oread. And I was right. Heard it was some bad business down there..."

"Yeah," Zeke said grimly.

"You got kin?"

"Dead."

"Oh...I'm sorry. My folks are still wonderin' what happened to me. I don't know about them either. Quantrill's boys don't really have a mailin' address."

"Can't you get to a post office and mail a letter?"

"With Grant's boys layin' across the country like a randy cowpoke on top of a loose woman, that might be a problem..."

Zeke blushed at the bawdy imagery, and Gaines noticed.

"You turnin' red, Zeke?"

It was then he realized that he had said nothing to Kelly.

"How long have I been here?"

"Well, you passed out some time last night. Then when we were ready to pull out, we tied you to your horse and I led him as we headed back to camp. It's about eleven in the mornin' now."

Zeke stared aimlessly in front of him. The food and coffee had energized him, but when he realized he had left Kelly back in town without telling her where he was, the headache returned with a vengeance.

"We're supposed to meet up with Quantrill in a few days, I heard."

"What for?"

Gaines looked at him curiously. "What do you think for?"

Zeke stared at him. It didn't take much imagination for him to realize exactly what they were going to do after meeting with Quantrill. Absently he picked up his coffee cup and started to drink, then realized it was empty.

Gaines watched him closely, noticing the empty coffee cup.

"Where are we going?"

"I don't know. I figure Kansas."

"Why's that?"

"Well, with old Landlord Ewing's Eviction Order in force in western Missouri and the Union Army ridin' the counties, Quantrill might figure to have another raid on their side of the border. Kind of thumbin' our noses at them, you might say."

"I see."

"Ever shoot a man from a horse?"

"I shot two getting off one."

"Yeah? Northern boys?"

"I didn't have a chance to ask."

"Hmm..."

"Let me ask you, Jim..." Zeke looked at his boots for a few seconds. "You ever hear of someone named Charlie Morse?"

"Yeah! He's a roughneck from way back! Good man with a gun or a knife. I'm surprised Quantrill didn't promote him or something. But the last time I saw him was, oh...let's say, two months before Lawrence. I heard that he 'acquitted himself quite well'. That's what they said. That's not how I would put it, but I guess they know what they're talkin' about..."

"And how would you put it, Jim? What Charlie Morse did?"

Gaines looked at him seriously. Then he looked at his boots and seemed to be chewing the last of his breakfast still stuck in his teeth. Finally, he spat the morsel out on the ground and turned back to him.

"What am I supposed to say? He's one of us, isn't he?"

Zeke looked disappointed but tried to hide it.

Curiously, Gaines asked, "You sure you have a stomach for this, Zeke?"

"Sure, I do!"

"Well," said Gaines, less seriously, "who am I to question the man who brought down bad Dick Lamont?"

Zeke knew he was pressing the issue, but he didn't care. "Would Morse be coming around?"

Gaines stared at him for a few moments, then said, "We've got a couple hundred men spread from here all the way over to Sni-Bar Creek. I don't know where he is at the moment...but I will say that he comes into Lone Jack often. Him and those laughin' twins I used to see him with...You want to talk to him?"

"Maybe I'm wrong," said Zeke, choosing his words carefully, "but I heard that there's some boys on the border who have their own slave business going...I'm not saying anyone here, but some boys take to grabbing up women, maybe young girls, and selling them somewhere for profit."

"Yeah?" said Gaines, sounding interested. "Sold to who?"

"Maybe down south. Especially since so many Negroes ran away because of the war."

"Yeah," said Gaines wryly. "Ran away to put on blue uniforms and then come back to us, this time with *guns*..." He pursed his lips, then looked off toward the horizon. "Old Charlie used to recapture runaway slaves and sell 'em back to their owners, just like ol' Bill Quantrill used to do...Or Charlie would hear about some plantation owner or other such person who had their Negroes run away or join the Union or whatever...and uh, replace 'em. That's what I heard."

Zeke's face was taut as he asked, "Replace them with who?"

Gaines kept his eyes on the horizon as he answered reluctantly, "Children...Not young boys so much, even though you could get them to do the tougher work, but...like you said, young girls. But I have a feeling they weren't kidnapped just to do the household chores...if you know what I mean."

The tension in Zeke was so obvious, it caused Gaines to ask, "What's wrong?"

"What?"

Gaines shrugged and said indifferently, "I don't know, it just seems like you're gettin' upset."

"I had a night of hard drinking I never had before. How do you think I'd—"

"What do you want with Morse anyway?"

"To see him."

After a while, Gaines realized that Zeke wasn't going to say anything further and just sat drinking his coffee. They didn't speak for several minutes, both lost in their own thoughts.

Finally, Gaines asked, "You got a stake in this girl-grabbin' business you don't want to talk about?"

"Nope," Zeke said quickly. "I just wondered what kind of a man would deal in such a thing..." Then he looked Gaines in the eye. "...Or condone it."

"It's his business. It isn't a matter of condonin' or not condonin'. I've got my affairs, Charlie's got his."

"You mean you'd let him take your little sister?"

"He'd have trouble with her."

"That's not the point."

Gaines stared at him, confused. "Zeke, do you know someone who's been through—"

Abruptly a big man with a foghorn voice yelled, "Mount up! Everybody! We're heading west!" Zeke looked up at the man as he turned away to yell at others. West; he knew that meant Kansas. He had wanted so desperately to return there—but not this way...

CHAPTER ELEVEN

THE ROAD OPENED UP TO THEM AS THEY APPROACHED RED BRIDGE at the border. There were about forty of them altogether. In light of the devastation that occurred at Lawrence, what they had in mind was not an overly ambitious plan. There was to be a raid on the small Kansas town of Desoto, south of Olathe, with plunder and the requisitioning of much needed supplies the main goal. With the bulk of the raiders still at Sni-Bar Creek and Quantrill himself off in Blue Spring visiting Kate King, there were rumbles from within the group that there were not enough men for this raid. But the nearest Union fort was miles away, said Talley; the town's garrison small. And anyway, there was all that plunder.

The bushwhackers that rode to Kansas that day wore blue Union blouses and caps, especially those men at the head of the column. As in Lawrence and other places, this was to fool the defenders, or at least make them hesitate before opening fire. The preparation at camp was, as usual, frenzied and chaotic, with men scrambling to find the right size uniform and then scrambling to change into them.

Already wearing a Union blouse and yellow neckerchief, Jim

Gaines stared at the Union cap he was about to put on. Wincing, he remarked, "If my mother saw me in this, she'd just as soon get out my daddy's long gun and blow my head off!"

After Zeke put on his blouse and neckerchief, he looked down and felt the material reverently. This is what he had always wanted to be--but not quite this way. The blouse fit comfortably, but when he felt further along the stomach lining and looked down, he saw a dark patch of red and a huge hole. Suddenly he felt sick. Whoever that soldier was, he was a hero, and Zeke felt he didn't deserve to wear the man's uniform.

Later as they were mounting, Zeke had practically begged Talley to let him stay behind.

"I can't go, Talley. I'm not trained." Zeke knew perfectly well that it took no specialized training to rob and murder.

"Got to have you come along with us, Zeke," said Talley, climbing onto his horse and looking quite official in his Union outfit, that of a cavalry captain. "We've got to see you handle yourself in battle."

Battle? What kind of a battle is it to go against mostly unarmed and untrained civilians? He wanted to stay in Lone Jack and search for Ruth. He wanted to see Kelly again and try to explain.

Reluctantly he mounted his horse, trying to keep his hands steady as he grasped the pommel.

Talley studied the Kansan and said, "Now I know you're not scared, Zeke...It's something else, don't know what."

Will Sorrel rode up to them and said, "Herb, why don't you let him stay here and babysit the horses? Can't you see he's not man enough to fight? One drop of blood and he'll skeddadle."

Zeke wanted to hit him desperately but restrained himself in front of Talley. Perhaps the little scum might help Talley change his mind about bringing him along.

Talley looked back at Sorrel and said, "Alexander the Great had to see his first drop of spilled blood sometime. It's what's called the evolution of great men..."

Sorrel stared at him, baffled. Then he moved his horse away, shaking his head.

Talley turned to Zeke and said, "He's a good man to have in a fight. He always manages to kill at least one person on these raids and he's pretty consistent but mention any word more than two syllables and he's as lost as a Yankee in Savannah." He looked at Zeke. "Don't you want to get back at the Yanks?"

"Sure, I do. I just don't want to mess you guys up, that's all."

"Well, that's right considerate of you, but as far as my command is concerned, the only ones that'll mess up are the Yanks. And once they see us, fear will take hold and they *will* mess up. Mark my words. Now come on..."

Zeke quickly realized that that was the end of any arguments. To push his reluctance any further would be dangerous. No one would find his body in the woods for months, if ever.

They rode off.

This was now getting beyond his control. He wanted information from the bushwhackers, not participation. And now he was riding toward Desoto, Kansas, wearing the bloodied shirt of some poor Union private—an infantryman yet. As he put on the worn private's cap, he realized that the Dragoon pistol he always wore at his hip now ironically fit in with the rest of his outfit.

Zeke could pull up his horse and light out; just part from the column and ride off into the woods before they got to town. It was simple. He would somehow ride back to Lone Jack, track down Charlie Morse, and beat the living daylights out of him until he revealed exactly where Ruth was. And then he knew what would happen as soon as he left the column: He would be shot in the back from a dozen Navy Colts and his body unceremoniously dumped in the ravine under Red Bridge. And the one who'd open fire first would be that little weasel, Sorrel.

Nope. Zeke was stuck and he knew it.

They were now several miles inside Kansas. Zeke knew it was nothing short of miraculous that they didn't run into anyone yet, friend or foe. The sun shone brightly over the land and patches of sweat appeared on their Union blouses. A few miles from Desoto, they spotted a fork in the trail and, like the cavalry officer he was playing, Talley raised his right hand and halted the column. Everyone looked around expectantly.

Zeke briefly took off his cap and ran his fingers back through his hair as he scanned the area. There was a dense forest on either side of the road, and everything seemed as calm and peaceful as could be. He put his cap back on and turned around. He saw Jim Gaines sitting his horse, obviously uncomfortable in his under-sized Union private's uniform. Talley had ordered him to take rear guard, as if he wanted to keep him from being too chummy with their newest bushwhacker.

During the ride, Zeke had fallen way behind Talley and was now somewhere in the middle of the column. Not that he disliked Talley, but rather he wanted to ride some distance behind Will Sorrel. He figured that at the first opportunity the little man would put a slug in his back and then whine that it was an accident during the heat of battle. Even now he saw Will Sorrel sitting his horse several yards ahead, his right hand nervously fingering the butt of his Navy Colt tied down at his hip.

He glanced around and still couldn't understand why they were stopping. Then he noticed that the column was shielded from the merging road by the dense foliage. He also noticed that none of the riders had spoken a word, knowing already that when Talley halted them, it was for a reason.

That reason appeared shortly.

At the fork ahead, five Union men appeared from the merging road and continued toward town. Had Talley not halted the column, the northerners would have seen them first. They would've seen those in the forefront of the column wearing Union blue, but they also would've seen the riders behind them who were *not* wearing uniforms and realized immediately that they were bushwhackers.

The riders were silent, almost held in awe at the five innocent lambs up ahead of them. Zeke watched the soldiers in disbelief. *Come on, fellas. All you have to do is turn around and see us.*

But the five men were ignorant of the danger. Zeke quickly saw that they were all tired—dead tired. They had probably been in the saddle for a full day and night still hunting the perpetrators of the Lawrence raid. Their horses were sad specimens, desperately needing to stop and rest.

He shook his head sadly, still not believing it all. He had read of animals in Africa who attack and devour helpless smaller creatures and couldn't miss the parallel. There certainly was no fair play in the jungle, and he was about to witness a good example of savagery right before his eyes. Sweat appeared on his forehead and he looked around anxiously. He wanted to shout a warning, anything!

And he knew he would be just as dead as they were about to be.

Already most of the riders had their guns out and pointed them toward the soldiers as they awaited a signal from their leader. A few yards ahead of him, Will Sorrel also had his Navy Colt out, its hammer cocked.

Zeke then got an idea. Slowly he walked his horse forward, heading for Sorrel's mount. His eyes, like everyone else's, were on Herb Talley.

Talley, meanwhile, watched the Union soldiers with amusement and took his time. This was easy! And they could always use five more uniforms...

Zeke knew he had to act now, before Talley gave the signal. Suddenly he jammed his spur into the horse's side and braced himself. As expected, the horse screamed and pushed forward, ramming Sorrel's palomino. Jolted by the impact from the rear, Sorrel dropped the hammer on his Colt, and it fired.

Zeke certainly didn't expect the chain reaction that followed.

When Sorrel's gun went off, the bullet went directly into the back of Hal Bartlett, a small but corpulent man who sat his horse just a few feet in front of Sorrel. Bartlett screamed and fell off his mount dead.

Sorrel cried out "Hal!"

Talley and the others all turned to look at Will Sorrel in shocked disbelief. The Union patrol also turned around quickly and now saw the column back up the road. Realizing they were just seconds away from certain death, to a man they turned their horses and rode for town.

"Damn you!" screamed Will Sorrel. He raised his pistol, but Zeke's arms were longer and a lot faster than the little man's. His fist shot forward and struck Sorrel squarely in the nose, knocking him from his horse. Sorrel hit the ground hard as the others backed their horses away to avoid trampling him.

"Come on!" yelled Talley. "Forget him! Get those troopers before they warn the town!"

As raiders spurred their horses around him, Talley glared back at Zeke in anger and disbelief, slightly shaking his head. Partially to avoid his eyes and partially to keep up the act, Zeke also spurred his horse and rode right past Talley along with the rest. Even as he rode past, he could feel the hot stare of the man in the stolen captain's uniform.

After they were all gone, Talley rode back to help Sorrel back on his horse.

Enraged, the little man said, "Herb, I don't give a hang if he saved your neck, I'm gonna kill that tall son of a bitch!"

"Don't do nothin', Will. Not until I talk to him."

"Talk is cheap, Herb! And you've been doing too much of it!"

Sorrel turned his palomino south.

"Where you headed? Desoto's west."

"There's a cut through the trees. It'll get us to a back road into town. It's narrow and wouldn't have worked for the column, but it'll be good for one or two men. And if you want to beat those bluecoats into town, then you'll ride with me!"

"Let's go!" said Talley urgently.

Talley sped off, following Sorrel's lead through the woods.

Further up, Zeke spurred his mount on. He saw the raiders galloping far ahead to overtake the soldiers and that's when he knew what he had to do.

He had ridden from his aunt and uncle's house in Olathe many times, and often he had cut through Desoto. Using his knowledge of the area, he veered off to the left and cut into the woods, ducking low hanging branches and circling dense underbrush for several miles.

Finally, what he was looking for appeared a half mile in the distance. A small game trail, not known to many, appeared before him and Zeke rode into it without slowing down for the turn. The horse strained in the stifling heat, but it kept up the pace without difficulty. It had been, after all, a bushwhacker's horse.

Sweat was pouring off Zeke, but he was never more determined to reach a destination. He had to get to town before the others did. Maybe there was a Union garrison worth its salt somewhere in Desoto, but he couldn't take a chance. By now, he was bathed in sweat and getting cramps in his sides, but he had made his decision. He knew he was jeopardizing his life, but he could not sit by and let this bunch of rough-necks murder anyone. He would fight these men if he had to.

He couldn't let the atrocities happen.

Never again!

CHAPTER TWELVE

THE QUIET OF THE WOODS WAS BROKEN BY THE GALLOPING HOOFS, one set after another, growing louder until it seemed to fill the air. His horse charged through the trees with almost as much determination as its rider. The sweat on his forehead was a salty curtain covering his eyes, and several times Zeke wiped it off only to have it appear again and continue his agony. He desperately wanted to remove his Union cap, but the low-leaning branches of the lush forest kept scratching him every now and then and he needed the Yankee headgear for protection.

At times through the journey, Zeke could have sworn he heard other horses behind him, but he wasn't sure. If he was being followed, they would have to keep up his pace, not an easy feat.

Were they this fast when they rode through Lawrence? Were they this fast when they torched the village of Brooklyn?

He didn't know or care. It was time for his mind to sit back and let the horse do the work—at least for now. Then he had to warn the town, that is, if those soldiers didn't arrive there already. He would soon know. The back end of the street called Brookville Lane appeared a quarter mile ahead.

His horse shot into the back street and continued for a half mile, the town's main street just ahead. It was the middle of the day; stores would be open, and families would be all over the street. Mothers with their children, fellows with their girlfriends, fiancés, wives...

Then he thought of Kelly.

Zeke quickly shook the thought out of his head and rode fast into the town's main street, the place the bushwhackers would hit first. He was ready to give his best impression of Paul Revere when he saw the pandemonium ahead of him.

He pulled the horse up short, and the momentum almost threw him off. Zeke set himself right and looked up the street, not believing the sight.

Bushwhackers were riding into town, giving the rebel yell and shooting at the townspeople—only the difference this time was that the citizenry was shooting back. Immediately around him, people had run off the street and back into the safety of their homes. Zeke suspected, to look for their guns.

Zeke was still close enough to the action to see the town's main square. Blood flowed freely at the foot of a statue of some long-forgotten politician. Three of the Union soldiers were laying there, their faces in the dirt, indicating that they had been shot in the back. Indeed, Zeke saw three rider-less cavalry mounts wandering aimlessly around the square.

Yet they had accomplished their goal: They had warned the town.

Young men and old, even wives and mothers, had taken up shotguns and pistols, anything they could find to stop the raiders. The street ahead was a mass of gunfire and smoke. Some raiders lit torches and ran to the sidelines to set fire to various buildings. Yet no sooner had they put the torch to some-one's residence, a loud shot would be heard, and the arsonists would die where they stood, their torches falling uselessly to the ground.

They did manage to kill some of the defenders, but not as many as they would have. Zeke kept his distance, watching the battle carefully, and it looked like the townsfolk were doing all right. Some bushwhackers were being picked off by citizens firing from behind windows, and then, hearing gunfire from above, he looked up and saw several men with rifles and shotguns firing from rooftops on both sides of the street.

He couldn't help but smile.

But then he grew reflective. It was Lawrence. What happened there had spooked a lot of people. Nobody wanted to be caught off-guard again.

Still, where were the other two privates? It was sometimes hard to see through the smoke-filled battle and rushing figures on horseback, but he kept looking for the two soldiers. He pulled the stallion more to the side as some raiders headed in his direction, townspeople firing after them.

Zeke didn't have long to wait to find the two men. They were both now on foot, running towards him. The two were among a group of seven or eight men running down the street with mounted bushwhackers in pursuit. The horses were riding down the screaming men as they turned to fire back. One of the riders, a burly man in a Union shirt and wide-brimmed hat, wasted no time trampling one of the soldiers. As the hoofs went over the screaming man, the rider's hefty bulk erupted in laughter.

All pallor went out of Zeke's face and his hands gripped the reins tighter.

The main column of bushwhackers continued their ride, firing at all targets when they could, but something was wrong now. The fighting was losing its intensity, and the skirmishes were now just individual gun battles around various parts of the street. The element of surprise was lost, and with it, the ability for the raiders to overwhelm their opponents.

Zeke pulled his horse back further behind the side of a building as the raiders charged past him, heading to the other end of the street. It was then that he spotted the fifth soldier running right past him. Zeke was startled by his sudden appearance and instinctively pulled the horse out of his way. The bluecoat was firing back at his pursuer until his Dragoon pistol was empty.

Then, in that second it took to pinpoint his surroundings, the soldier spotted Zeke. Almost in a panic, he turned to his right and ducked into an alley. It then occurred to Zeke that the poor man had mistaken him for a raider.

Unfortunately, the burly guerrilla also spotted the private and turned his horse into the alley, giving the rebel yell as he pursued him. Warehouses on both sides towered over the soldier as he frantically ran down the long alley searching for a doorway.

Zeke spurred his horse over to the mouth of the alley and rode in after them. Up ahead, he saw the big man lift his Navy Colt and fire at the fleeing soldier as he charged at him. Then, to Zeke's horror, he saw another building, the back of a general store, blocking the soldier's way at the end of the alley. Only a weathered door faced the alleyway, with cans filled with garbage standing in front of it. Zeke figured the door must have been sealed long ago, after its use as a receiving entrance for goods.

When he got to the end of the alley the soldier literally ran into a wall. Panic-stricken, he started to throw the cans aside.

Tossing away his empty Navy Colt, the big man pulled out another one and fired as he closed in on the frantic man. Then Zeke saw the private cringe suddenly, as if someone had kicked him in the back.

Zeke's heart went out to him, yet he was still too far back to help.

Suddenly the soldier turned around, grasping one of the trash cans. With an effort he shoved the full can directly into the path of the bushwhacker's horse. Whinnying, the horse stopped suddenly and reared on its hind legs as the can almost rolled into it, spilling rubbish onto the ground. The big man held on, tightening his grip on the pommel. Then, cocking the hammer of the gun, he fired again at the soldier, but the horse's rearing spoiled his aim.

It gave the soldier a chance to use all his strength and throw his weight against the recalcitrant old door. The sound of a weathered bolt breaking from inside was heard and, encouraged, the soldier hit the door again.

It swung open then, and the wounded private leaped within, his body piling into several boxes in his path. His body was wracked in pain as he made the effort to crawl away. Then he froze in fear as he heard a familiar click of a Colt's hammer pulled back. He heard the shot and the ball struck his hip, causing him to roll back on the floor, already covered with spilled sugar. It seemed the burly raider had already dismounted and was now at the stockroom's entrance.

Looking past the burly man standing with his back to him in the doorway, Zeke could see a bit of sunlight and some toppled boxes. Moving inside, the big man cocked his pistol again and Zeke heard another shot. Hurrying now, the Kansan drew his army pistol and dismounted.

Zeke stepped inside and the first thing he saw was the raider's back. The big man's wide shoulders were shaking and then he heard the laugh, deep and loud and obnoxious.

Enraged, Zeke shouted, "Turn around!"

The burly man suddenly stopped laughing. He paused just a second before he raised his Navy Colt and whirled around, firing as he turned. As the raider's bullet hit the wooden door jamb above him, Zeke fired the Dragoon. The raider's face froze in pain as he grasped his throat, feeling the blood coursing from his severed esophagus. He hit the dirty floor heavily, the impact shaking a few jars off the shelves.

Stepping closer, Zeke stared at the body and said quietly, "Try laughing now..."

Then he heard the moan. Zeke looked quickly to his right and saw that the private was still alive.

He ran outside to his horse. Zeke removed his canteen from the saddle and looked down the alley. No one else had heard them. He figured the owner of the general store must have run to a safer place when he heard the shooting coming from his stockroom. He went back inside.

Zeke put his gun down on the floor and lifted the young man's head, feeding water through his dried lips. The wounded soldier looked up gratefully and drank. He coughed loudly and tried to swallow again, but he couldn't.

"Thanks," he said weakly, and looked again at Zeke. "You one of us?"

Zeke said earnestly, "I never left you..." He pushed the canteen on him again. "Now drink up. We'll get you to a doc..."

"Save your water, soldier...I've been killed, and I know it..."

"And he ain't the only one!" The voice was just six feet behind him and had a Louisville accent.

Zeke rose quickly and faced Will Sorrel, or rather looked down on him. A Navy Colt was pointed at Zeke's chest. The look on Sorrel's face was as mean as Zeke had seen on any man—except perhaps Dick Lamont.

"Drop the canteen." Zeke dropped it careful it didn't hit the soldier.

The little man stepped closer to him, hatred in his eyes.

"You made me shoot Hal Bartlett. Beau Jackson is lyin' there dead and now I find you feedin' the enemy! Hell, maybe puttin' on that damn bluecoat gave you some funny ideas! That coat fits perfectly, don't it? A tall uniform for a tall man."

Zeke wasn't sure where this conversation was going until Sorrel suddenly backhanded him in the mouth. He turned with the slap, but still felt its sting. Putting his hand on his mouth, he was about to say something until Sorrel spoke.

"Shut up! I've had my fill of you tall sons of bitches getting away with everything. You jaspers get it all! All the women. All the admiration of your buddies. I don't. Not a little cuss like me." He emphatically pushed the gun barrel under Zeke's chin as the Kansan stood there with his hands raised. The hammer was cocked back, and it would drop and fire if he made even a slight move.

Zeke just stared at him. Then he said, "You gonna shoot already or just bore me to death?"

Sorrel was so surprised by the remark, he stepped back, the gun sliding off Zeke's throat. He looked at Zeke and was about to say something else when the click of a cylinder was heard at his feet.

Sorrel spun around and pointed his gun at the floor just as the wounded private fired the Dragoon. The little man doubled over as he heard the hammer pulled back again. Another bullet hit his stomach, and then he crumpled, his fall to the floor not as loud as Beau Jackson's and certainly not as far.

Zeke looked down at the private weakly holding his Dragoon pistol.

"Here, soldier," he said, handing the gun back to Zeke. "Thanks for the use of your sidearm...That felt good..."

"I bet."

"I'm afraid you're empty though."

"I'll reload later."

Zeke holstered his gun and bent over to pick up the canteen. When he turned back to the soldier, the young man's head was back on the floor and his eyes were closed. Zeke reached out and felt his chest. The soldier was gone. After he rose and turned around, he saw Herb Talley standing in the back doorway.

Lord, this storeroom is getting more crowded than Chicago during Christmas season.

Talley was no longer wearing the Union blouse and cap and had changed into his own shirt and Stetson. Stepping into the room, he looked around and quickly saw the bodies. "Must've been quite a party," he said wryly. Then he spotted the body of Will Sorrel and asked, "How'd he get it? You and him have it out?"

Zeke told the truth. "The dead Yankee shot him."

Talley stared at the huge body on the floor. "Beau Jackson." Then he looked Zeke in the eye and said, "You're telling me that Yankee got Will and Beau Jackson too?"

Zeke made no reply. Talley was holding his Navy Colt loosely in his hand. Zeke wasn't sure whether he was pointing the gun at him or not, but he had to be careful.

Then Talley's eyes went to the canteen on the floor, next to the soldier's body. "You're a merciful man, Zeke Tyler." This was not said as a compliment.

Again, Zeke said nothing. He felt like he had to raise his hands, but with Herb Talley one wasn't sure where one stood. He'd have a hard enough time trying to explain things.

Talley said. "Couldn't find you in that fiasco up the street, so I was wondering what happened to you. Then I hear some shots from this storeroom. Figured some of my boys are here, but I didn't expect to find you...The boys are starting to ride out. It looks like those Kansans just won't quit...Take off your Yankee duds, they're a target to these folks. You bring your shirt and hat like I told you boys?"

Zeke nodded.

"Good. We'll ride out of town real quiet…We're going right back to camp. Since they whipped us, they won't see any need to follow us…"

Zeke was careful not put his hand near the empty Dragoon pistol. The gun in Talley's hand waved at Zeke dangerously and he quickly realized that Talley's suggestion was really an order.

When he heard other bushwhackers outside calling Talley's name, that clinched it.

Like it or not, he was going back to camp, where he had some explaining to do…

CHAPTER THIRTEEN

As they rode into camp, they saw that most of the men were already there; some of them with minor wounds. The ones with serious wounds did not make it back to camp.

After they rode in, Zeke and Herb Talley dismounted. Then, just as Zeke was about to turn the horse into the corral, Talley stepped in front of him and landed a perfect punch to the jaw. Caught off-guard, Zeke fell back on the ground. With his hat behind him in the dirt, he sat up on his elbows and stared at Talley. His jaw hurt, and as he felt it, he noticed he didn't lose any teeth.

Talley looked down at him and Zeke saw his rage. The others around them stopped what they were doing and stared at them.

"If you hadn't saved my life," said Talley, trying to control his fury, "I would've killed you long before this."

Zeke got up quickly, his fists at his sides. The fact that Talley had waited until he was surrounded by his own men before he punched him angered Zeke even more. "Don't let that stop you, Herb," he hissed. "What saved your bacon was a misfired Navy Colt, so don't let any false sense of gratitude stop you. If you want to take me on, let's go. 'Let's get to it,' as you said to me and Dick Lamont not too long ago..."

Talley stared at him resentfully, trying to shame Zeke, but it was impossible. Whatever Zeke had done back in Desoto, he was proud of it and Talley saw that right away. He wanted to beat the living daylights out of Zeke, but then Talley's glare weakened and the tension in him started to go away.

Talley slowly shook his head and said plainly, "No, Zeke...I'm not fool enough to go against you hand-to-hand...But I still feel like tearing you apart...Why, boy? Why the hell did you do it?"

Zeke stared back at him, almost with sympathy. In a way, he could understand the position Talley was now in.

Then Zeke looked around and saw the others glaring at him. Perhaps Talley could restrain himself, but he knew that sooner or later the others would definitely kill him, with the odds being sooner. Only Jim Gaines, gratefully pulling off his Union clothing, watched the scene without anger.

Still, a few men had their pistols out and were pointing them straight at Zeke's belly. The Kansan only returned their angry looks.

"Well, come on," he said to them. "You live your whole lives by gunning down unarmed men. Why should that stop you now?"

Zeke could see that his words were having an effect. For the few that had their pistols out, it took all they had in them to restrain themselves. Talley just stared at Zeke, his own rage giving way to a kind of wonder. If anyone was filled from head to foot with nothing but pure gall, it was this man, Talley thought.

He tried to hide his admiration as he said, "Still playin' close to the edge, eh, Tyler?"

Zeke said nothing. He knew that they were waiting for some kind of apology or explanation or plea for mercy and they slowly realized they weren't about to get any, not from him anyway.

When he realized that Talley and the others had nothing more to say, Zeke turned and picked up his hat.   He was about to mount his horse until Gaines stepped up to them.

"Hold on, Zeke," he said, looking at Talley.

The Kansan stood by his horse and said, "Forget it, Jim..."

"No.   Not until I've said my piece...You can't kick him out, Herb."

"I can't?   Well, let me tell you something, Jim.   At this point, kicking him out is about the nicest thing I can do!   You see the guns around him?   If he doesn't light out now—"

Gaines said, "Zeke didn't kill Hal and you know it!   Will Sorrel did.   I know it was an accident, but—"   He looked around.   "Where is Will?"

Talley looked at Zeke resentfully and said, "A Yankee killed him!"

"No great loss if you ask me...Still, what happened was an accident.   Zeke was just anxious to get into the fight and his horse bumped Will's."

Talley's eyes looked past the southerner.   "What're you waitin' for, Tyler?   Mount up and ride out of here!"

Without a word, Zeke mounted his horse and prepared to ride off.

"Hold on, Zeke!" urged Gaines.   "I want you to hear this too...I held on for a while, Herb.   And I've been loyal too.   But ever since Lawrence I've been thinking."

Talley's eyes showed amusement.   "Have you, Jim?"

"Yes, I have.   And I don't want to see any more of that, if I can help it.   That's what we were supposed to do in Desoto.   Sure, we needed supplies, but it wasn't going to end there.   We were going to dry-gulch nothing more harmful to the Confederacy than farmers and storekeepers, maybe young boys, like in Lawrence.   I joined this outfit to fight bluecoats, not old men and children!"

Zeke saw the rage in Gaines' face for the first time and felt something close to admiration.

Talley stared back at Gaines, almost matching his indignation. "Do you see what the Yankees are doin' in the Shenandoah and the rest of Virginia, what they're doin' all over the south?   Huh? They're burnin' our farms and our crops and you're tellin' *me* you feel guilty about killin' folks!"

Gaines glared at him and said patiently, "First of all, Herb, they aren't *your* farms or *your* crops, 'cause you're from goddamn Missouri!"

Talley couldn't answer, he just glared at Gaines.

"Maybe Zeke suddenly got religion.   Or maybe he didn't want to see towns full of crying women and children like what ya'll did to Lawrence.   Either way, he's got something and I'm pulling out with him.   And you know why, Herb? Because I know now that if I stay, the day will come when people will visit my grave and curse *me* out as a mass murderer just as they will *you*!"

Talley's rage subsided and he watched helplessly as Jim Gaines got his outfit, went to his horse and mounted up.

Zeke said wryly, "Our backs'll be turned, so you'll have no trouble hitting us…"

They all watched as, without a word of farewell, Zeke and Jim Gaines rode out.

One man with his gun out walked up to Talley. He stared incredulously at the pair as they rode away.

"You gonna let 'em go, Herb?"

Talley didn't answer him. He just looked at the man, then at all the others. In his heart, he knew he had just lost two of the finest men he'd ever have…

They ducked branches and skirted dense shrubbery and before long they hit the game trail that took them on the road to Lone

Jack. They were both silent until they had put several miles between themselves and the camp. They rode their horses at a walk, as if both men were relaxed for the first time in a long while.

And then, without looking at him, Gaines asked, "You blew our position on purpose, didn't you, Zeke?"

Zeke looked at him and said nothing.

"Outside of Desoto," Gaines continued. "You wanted those bluecoats to know we were there, didn't you?"

"Yes," Zeke said calmly. "I did want them to know."

"And they'd run and warn the town about us?"

"That's right."

And then they were silent again. Both men held to his own thoughts for over a quarter mile until Gaines spoke again.

"There was something between you and Talley back there. I saw the way you two were giving each other looks—like you two knew something we didn't. What was that about?"

"You ever hear of a big man who rode with us named Beau Jackson?"

"Sure. Used to play cards with him. Stud poker."

"I killed him."

Gaines paused, taking this in. Then he asked, "Why?"

"He was riding down soldiers and townsfolk alike. He killed one running away from him who had nothing but an empty gun…"

"Um-hm," replied the Georgian, as only the sounds of the horse's hoofs on gravel could be heard. Then after something like a minute, he said, "Well…he always cheated at cards. Where I come from, they would have killed such a man anyway…What about Will Sorrel?"

"He got himself killed."

"I heard. You have something to do with it?"

"I would say so."

Gaines looked at him finally and asked, "And why are you telling me all this?"

"'Cause you asked me." Zeke looked at him seriously, but then gradually he smiled.

To his surprise, Gaines smiled back. Then they both faced the trail and relaxed.

"You're one of a kind, Zeke Tyler," Gaines said good-naturedly. "What got you to Border Country? I mean, what really got you here?"

"Jim," Zeke said quietly, "I've got troubles. It's getting late and there's a clearing just outside of Lone Jack that I've been using. We'll camp there and I'll tell you all about it..."

Jim Gaines had taken some extra food before he left the bushwhacker camp, so now he was able to sit quietly with a plate of beans before him as he stared into the fire. It was night. Zeke had already eaten and was now looking out into the forest to see if he could spot anyone hiding among the trees and twisted shrubbery. Instead, he saw only blackness. He pulled out his pistol and loaded it, then put it back into its holster. His hand rested on the butt.

Without looking at him, Gaines said, "Sit down, Zeke Tyler. They didn't follow us."

"You sure of that?"

"Positive. They don't have any time to waste with us."

Zeke turned around and looked at him. "Why is that?"

"'Cause they don't, that's all."

"They're planning something else?"

Gaines shrugged. "Maybe. They're supposed to link up with either Quantrill or Anderson, I'm not sure which. As far as I'm concerned, that's their business."

Zeke glanced back at the woods, then walked back to the fire and sat down next to Gaines.

They said nothing for a while, both men vaguely watching the fire.

"You know," Gaines said, "I never would have believed that today I'd be sitting down and having supper with a Yankee…"

Zeke looked at him. "Disappointed?"

"I don't know." He glanced at Zeke and then looked back at the fire. "You're one of the nice ones, I guess."

Zeke looked down and grinned.

Gaines continued, "Don't get me wrong. I'm no Yankee-lover…But I admire a man who can fight, and one could do something right for folks—on either side of the line…Anyway, you're not a lowdown jayhawk and that's one thing in your favor."

Gaines put down his plate and washed the food down with a mouthful of coffee. He looked into the fire again.

"Poor kid," he said. "How old is she?"

"Thirteen."

Gaines' face became hard and his pale green eyes reflected in the fire. "'…Suffer the little children…'"

"Yeah."

"I sympathize with you, Zeke Tyler."

Zeke looked at him. "I don't want your sympathy!"

"Well, you're gettin' it!"

Zeke suddenly got up and threw his coffee grounds into the fire and tossed down the cup. The fire hissed sharply.

He walked over to the edge of camp and gazed into the forest, as if he could actually see what was in the darkness. His broad shoulders tensed up and unconsciously his hands curled into fists. Gaines watched his every move.

He said tautly, "I don't need anyone's sympathy! Right now, I'm so angry inside, I just want to ride out and beat the hell out of every border man I can get my hands on."

Gaines shouted at him across the fire. "Maybe you better wake yourself up, Zeke Tyler! Look around you and see where you are! Other families are hurtin' too. I'm sorry for Ruth, but other families haven't got the hope that their young ones are still alive. They did their burying and read their prayers and angry as you are, your feelings are nothing compared to what they went through. Hell, some families got children who will never reach thirteen. Where I was growing up, I got to know those families real well..." Then, calming down, he said, "It's getting late, Zeke. Get a few hours' sleep. The way you are now, you're too wound up to go out looking for her and know what you're doin'. Hell, I bet you can't even see straight..."

Zeke finally turned around and faced him. Quietly, he said, "You talk too much, Reb...If you're up after ten, wake me. Then I'm going to ride into town. I figure I'll be able to see straight by then..."

Kelly Ryan was on her horse and skirting the southeast border of town, watching the trail as she headed deeper into the woods. The moon shined through the clouds and gave her some light to see, but she was still a little uncomfortable. She rode slowly, aimlessly. A light wind came, rustling the tree branches above her.

And then she forgot the darkness of the trail and her thoughts were far away. She thought of Zeke and hoped that, wherever he was, he was still in one piece. Kelly had never felt this way about anyone and her realization of it only bothered her more. She had always scorned her contemporaries for what she felt was a senseless waste of affection for any boy who came along, in or out of uniform. She knew she was smarter than they were; her grades proved that.

Kelly sighed and looked at the bright moon, all alone. She felt ridiculous; a pulp romance writer couldn't come up with a more saccharine moment.

Earlier in the day, she had written a letter to the Dawsons. She appreciated the fact that the war was not as intense in the border states as it was in Virginia; the mails could still get through. She introduced herself as a friend of Zeke's. Then she wrote several pages about what a wonderful child Penelope was, and if half of what Zeke had told her about the Dawsons was true, she would be more than happy if they would take care of her. As an afterthought, she finally got around to talking about herself. She mentioned that, after her father's murder, she insisted on staying in Lone Jack and helping Zeke in any way she could.

Would they detect her real feelings in that sentence? Perhaps, but at that point she wasn't too ashamed of those feelings.

Kelly rode into a hollow just off the trail. She started to feel good out there; it gave her time to think. She was away from the bushwhackers' town, with its noise and swaggering, and also away from Jake Rule and his staring eyes. She had mailed the letter to the Dawsons straight from the post office, rather than turning it over to Rule.

A sudden rustling in the branches above made her look up. The squirrels were scurrying away, and birds were taking flight. She knew what that meant. Without thinking twice, Kelly reached into the saddlebag and drew out the pocket revolver, then set it in her lap within the fold of her riding skirt. Soon the noise from the branches subsided and she heard the sound of horses' hoofs on the trail.

"Well, well!" said a man's voice.

Kelly turned and saw them, four men in Union blue sitting their horses and watching her. The one who seemed to be in the lead was a young fellow with a blond mustache covering his lip. His cap was on crookedly and he had a huge grin on his face. Kelly figured he was the one who spoke.

"Well, well, yourself," she said indifferently.

"And what would bring you all alone way out here?"

Kelly studied him with narrowed eyes. "I'm not exactly in the desert, private. The town's less than half a mile from here, and I'm just taking a ride."

"All alone."

"The wildlife doesn't bother me."

"Oh-ho!" he said, smirking. He glanced back at his amused comrades. "A tough Irish lass, eh? I like 'em spit and fire myself!"

"How nice for you."

"Yeah! Now tell us, gal, what really happened to you? I mean, why're you here? Boyfriend troubles?"

Kelly just sat her horse and stared back at them. Three of them were smiling, but the fourth one in the rear was looking down periodically. Was he ashamed? Kelly wasn't sure.

The one in the front looked Kelly up and down and his eyes grew larger. "You look kind of lonely..."

Kelly glared at him and said, "I'm not *that* lonely."

The front soldier looked back at his friends and laughed. Then he looked at Kelly and with the slight prod of his boot, his horse pushed forward. Suddenly, he reached out with his right hand and grasped Kelly's forearm.

"You're comin' with us, gal," he said.

Kelly said tautly, "Private, I'm asking you to let go of my arm."

"Oh!" he said, gripping her arm tighter. "You're *askin'* me to let go of your arm!" The way he said it was in vicious imitation of her brogue. Then he turned around and laughed. As expected, his companions laughed too. Facing her again, the smile disappeared, and a grim hatred showed itself. The grip on her arm tightened and Kelly saw by the look on his face that he knew he was hurting her.

He leaned even closer and it was then she got the full force of the liquor on his breath. She felt like throwing up.

"Come one, gal...You shanty whores are made for this..."

The gun came out and struck the soldier's temple so fast, it shocked the other three as they witnessed it. Releasing her arm, the soldier felt the crushing pain on his skull and with the impact, toppled from his horse. He hit the trail hard and a cloud of dust flew up after him.

The two soldiers behind him gaped at her and both reached back to their holsters. Kelly quickly brought the gun into position and cocked the hammer back. Seeing the gun, they all raised their hands uncertainly.

"What're you gonna do now, gal?" said one of the soldiers, his voice trembling.

Finally, the soldier in the rear spoke up. "She can do whatever the hell she wants to. She's got us and that's that. I knew this was stupid!"

Kelly said indignantly, "Then maybe you should've spoken up before that pig put his hand on me!"

The soldier spoke to the other two. "Put Edwards back on his horse. Tie him to it, if you have to."

"No," said Kelly. "Let him rest a bit. Perhaps a spell in the dirt will make him lose some of those wicked thoughts he's been having. And maybe after I ride away, you'll think on it and come to believe the same thing—after you lose your sidearms."

"What?"

"Remove your guns and toss them into the woods."

The soldiers looked at each other.

Finally, one of them said, "Do as she says."

They all unbuckled their holsters and tossed them into the forest, then obediently raised their hands again.

Kelly moved her horse back, still pointing the revolver at them. In the moonlight they could clearly see the rage on her face.

"Here you are, the noble Union Army! Going after women like a randy bunch of cowhands, when young girls are being kidnapped and taken away on your watch."

One of them said, "What're you talkin' about?"

She grew angrier as she spoke, and her words made them shift in their saddles uncomfortably. "Ask yourselves what some border men are doing with young women, with girls not old enough for fifth grade. Ask yourselves what happened to girls like Ruth Tyler of Lawrence, Kansas!" To her captive audience, the next words were venomous. "I'm sure you remember Lawrence, the town that burned while the Union Army fiddled."

"Now hold on—"

"You sorry examples of fightin' men! Why don't you ask yourselves what happens to those you're sworn to protect while you're out here dallyin' with me? But it doesn't matter. Because you and that pig on the ground and Quantrill's bunch are all made of the same stuff. I'd shoot all of you right now, but bullets are a nickel apiece and I'll not be wasting my money on the likes of you!"

Kelly then whirled her horse around and rode back towards Lone Jack. After putting her gun away, she tried to calm herself down, but couldn't. The tongue-lashing she gave them felt good, and they deserved it, but she didn't like the knots in her stomach that went with it. All in all, she felt that she spoke for Zeke, Ruth, Mr. & Mrs. Tyler and all the other poor souls whose lives were ruined. She thought of her father then, and gradually the tears came. All through her ride back, she thought of him most of all.

By the time Kelly entered the hotel, the tears were all gone. And then, as soon as she came through the door, she spotted the teenage boy with the cap. His feet were on the desk and when he saw her, he almost fell out of his chair.

When Kelly approached the desk, he looked up and tried to leer at her, but was met with the fiercest look he had ever seen on any woman—even his ma. His body seemed to shrink back in the chair, and he swallowed plainly. Kelly held out her hand and he gave her the key without hesitation. Then she went to the stairs and marched up to her room. The slam of her door made him jump. Normally he fell asleep when he was on night shift. He would have trouble doing that now...

CHAPTER FOURTEEN

BEFORE ZEKE PARTED COMPANY WITH JIM GAINES, THEY HAD BOTH wished each other luck. And he remembered the Georgian's words as he was about to ride off.

Gaines had said, "It's best I not help you right now, Zeke. For a man who's got to keep his mind on his chosen profession of destabilizing the Yankee regime, I'm afraid I'm in danger."

Zeke looked at him curiously. "What danger is that?"

The southerner looked down at him sternly and said, "Danger of liken' you folks..." He waved at him and then turned his horse and fled down the trail.

When Zeke rode into Lone Jack it was after ten and a full moon shone on the town's main street. It was quiet at first, but as his horse ambled down the street, the noise level picked up. He stopped a few doors down from McGann's and tied his horse to the tie rail. The one in front of the saloon was crowded enough with bushwhackers' mounts.

After Zeke entered McGann's, some men turned and looked at him. They recognized the young hellion who had killed Dick

Lamont and, with a little prodding, drank himself into uncon-
sciousness afterwards.

Zeke looked around and moved deeper into the room. The
loud talk and harsh laughter were all around him as smoke rose in
thick clouds and stayed near the ceiling. As he passed tables with
men playing cards and smoking cheap cigars, he coughed audibly.
Zeke hated being there. The smoke made him sick and the drunks
disgusted him. Still, Charlie Morse wasn't going to be found at a
church social.

Zeke inched his way up to the bar, the men on either side
making way reluctantly, until they saw who he was. Both men
were rough-looking, and they stared idly at him, making no
comments.

When Zeke lifted his hand to get the bartender's attention, he
was surprised to find the man heading right up to him, ignoring
another man looking to order a drink.

The bartender was tall, an apron around his dark pants and
checked vest. Zeke detected a welcoming smile under the
handlebar mustache.

"What can I do for ya, Zeke?"

At first, Zeke was surprised, but quickly dropped the look. It
was dangerous for a man to be surprised at the respect he gets
from a tough reputation. And Zeke was well aware that the men
on either side of him were watching him closely.

He would've spoken quietly to the bartender, but he knew that
it was impossible in that place. Instead, he leaned forward and
said, "Well, first, I'd like a beer." He had never drunk a beer before,
but it had to be easier to take than the stuff he had the other night.

"Coming up, Zeke!" The bartender left to get it and the man
on Zeke's right side then spoke to him.

"Nice shootin' the other day, Tyler."

Leaning forward on the bar, Zeke replied with an indifferent, "Yeah."

"You don't sound too happy," the fellow said.

Zeke looked at him and asked, "Does it matter to you if I sound happy?"

The man backed off a little and said, "No, no...Just makin' conversation."

Zeke ignored him and continued staring absently at the mirror across from him. The bartender returned and presented a full mug before him.

"There ya go, Zeke," he said and was about to move away until Zeke reached over and grabbed his hand.

"Wait a minute!" he said, letting go of his hand. "Just want to ask you something...You ever hear of a man named Charlie Morse?"

Briefly the barman's eyes narrowed as he looked at Zeke. Without thinking, his eyes then went to the man on Zeke's right. Zeke noticed the look and then quickly took a swallow of beer to imply that he wasn't waiting with baited-breath for the answer.

"Well..." started the bartender.

The man on Zeke's right cut him off. "He's in town."

As he drank some more beer, Zeke eyed his reflection and saw the two men near him giving each other knowing looks.

"You know him, Zeke?" asked the man on his right.

Zeke couldn't pretend he had ever been friendly with Morse; he might even be facing him right now. The thought that this might actually be the man who had stolen his little sister from her home made him feel tight little knots in his stomach. Without thinking about it, the hands he was resting on the bar became fists, and the man noticed.

He raised his eyes to Zeke again.

"Why would you want to see him?"

Zeke pushed the angry thought out of his mind and forced himself to relax. *Control yourself. You're tipping your hand before you've even met the man.*

Quickly Zeke took his hands off the bar and rubbed them together easily. "I'd just like to see him," he said casually.

A look from the man made the bartender go down to the other end of the bar suddenly. As he sipped his beer, Zeke noticed that too.

"We can take you to him," said the man.

"So, he's in Lone Jack," said Zeke, trying not to sound excited.

"Yeah. Yeah, he is. My name's Jack Blaine." He held out his hand.

Zeke pretended not to see it as he leaned over the bar and sipped his beer. He knew he wasn't being friendly, but he would be damned if he was going to shake hands with anyone who was even remotely connected with his sister's kidnapping.

Blaine motioned to the man on Zeke's other side and said, "That's Fred Chiles."

"Hi," said Zeke, without looking at him.

Chiles gave Blaine a questioning look and the other man quickly put a coin on the bar and both men rose.

"Take you to 'em," said Blaine.

"He's far from here?"

"Nah. Just come with us."

When Zeke reached into his pocket, Blaine said, "I paid it. Let's go."

Zeke finished the last of his beer and got up. He followed the two men outside, plainly glad to be away from there. The odor of cigar smoke left him, and the cool night air was refreshing.

"This way, Zeke," said Chiles, as they moved down the sidewalk. At first Zeke followed them, but then they slowed down so that he could walk with them. Both Blaine and Chiles were big men, as tall as Zeke, but thicker in the body. They wore range shirts and neckerchiefs, their boots dirty from too many spilled drinks. Their Stetsons were black and worn well. To Zeke, they seemed to be men who clearly fit in, and for picking up information this appearance was as important as the Colts they wore on their hips. Had these men appeared drunk, Zeke would never have gone with them. He wanted information, not drunken fables.

There were few men on the street and Zeke quickly noticed that his companions were now becoming his escorts; they were on either side of him as they moved down the walk.

Zeke tensed up as he realized a robbery might be in the works.

As he slowly reached back to the butt of his Dragoon, Chiles yanked Zeke's arm from the gun. Blaine suddenly grabbed Zeke's shoulder and swung him around to face him. Blaine's fist came up quickly and struck the Kansan hard across the mouth as Chiles pulled him back into the alley behind him. The blow stunned him, but it wasn't a total surprise. He could only blame himself for being careless—two big men taking him to an unknown destination—and he fell for it.

Though Chiles had locked Zeke's arm up behind him, his left arm was still free. Blaine didn't have to move in for a second punch, but he did and an experienced fighter like Zeke quickly saw his opening. He swung his left fist straight into Blaine's nose and the impact caused the bigger man to slam into a wooden post, his hat falling in the dirt. Sharp tears came to Blaine's eyes and his mouth tasted blood.

Reaching back with his left hand, Zeke struck Chiles in the head several times until the enraged man released Zeke's arm and swung him around. As soon as he did, he realized his mistake, forgetting about Zeke's quick left arm. With all he had, Zeke threw the punch and felt bone break as he struck Chiles' nose. The big man screamed and fell back hard against the brick wall behind him, a trash can spilling over noisily.

The noise from the falling can echoed around the alley and Blaine looked back down the street to see if they were heard. Moving back into the alley quickly, Blaine drew his gun and raised it to use as a club.

Zeke saw him coming just in time, ducking his head in reflex and then piling hard into Blaine's midsection. The two fell against the wall, Blaine taking the full impact. As Blaine tried to catch his breath, Zeke pinned the outlaw's gun hand against the wall, punching him repeatedly with his other hand. The bigger man groaned painfully, his strength ebbing.   As Blaine slid to the ground, Zeke yanked the gun out of his loosened grip and whirled around to Chiles.

The barrel almost touched the outlaw's stomach as he moved in on Zeke. In another moment, Zeke would have shot him, but for the shout from the street end of the alley.

"Put it up, son!"

Chiles froze where he stood, his frightened eyes on the gun barrel. The voice drew Zeke's attention, but he resisted turning and instead kept his eyes on Chiles. The gun's hammer was pulled back.

Still looking at the gun at his belly, Chiles said, "Don't worry, Ben! We was takin' 'em!"

"Yeah," the man called Ben replied sardonically. "I saw how well you were 'taking him'...My Lord, had you two tough men continued to fight like you have, you'd both be lying on the ground dreaming of women you'd never get."

Chiles stiffened noticeably and his bruised mouth became a taut grimace.

"You could put it up, Tyler," said Ben. "He won't do anything."

Zeke kept the gun on Chiles.

"Stubborn son, aren't you, Tyler? ...Fred, do yourself a favor and move away from him before he puts one in your belly."

Reluctantly Chiles backed away from Zeke and then went towards Blaine, who was lying on the ground and grasping his stomach painfully.

"Yeah, Jack," Ben observed, "you always did have a weak breadbasket."

Cocking the hammer of the gun back into place, Zeke then turned and faced Ben at the end of the alley. He was tall, with a slightly bent carriage that gave the impression of his leaning against a wall that wasn't there. His blue eyes were small and watchful, though his manner seemed relaxed, even lazy. An impudent smirk topped the appearance and Zeke didn't know whether the smirk was meant for him or the men he just beat up.

When he spoke to Zeke, the tone was respectful. "We've got something for your lip, that is, if you'll come with us."

"Why should I come with you?" Zeke asked. "So you can dry-gulch me again?"

Ben looked down at his feet briefly, then faced Zeke again, his eyes full of humor. He was clearly trying to make it all sound as unimportant as mud being splashed on a pair of old boots.

"This was no dry-gulching," said Ben lightly. "Just a couple of overzealous boys just trying to get a little extra drinking money, that's all.'

Zeke's tone was anything but conciliatory. "They ever hear about getting jobs?"

Ignoring Zeke's anger, Ben shrugged carelessly. "Some boys work a counter, and some work an alley. Who are we to judge who's more productive to society?"

Zeke picked up his hat as the other two men wandered past him to stand behind Ben. Their hateful eyes spoke volumes.

"I don't go anywhere I don't want to," said Zeke glaring back at them. "Especially with pigs."

The two outlaws tensed up at the remark, but Ben remained casual.

"My goodness, Zeke Tyler, the things you say! I was only suggesting that if you want to see Charlie Morse and maybe seal that cut, we can accommodate you. However, if you want to go on knocking the hell out of each other, be my guest."

"That's up to them," said Zeke grimly.

Before Ben could look at them for their reactions, both men shook their heads.

"The votes are in!" said Ben good-naturedly. "Come on, Zeke Tyler. A couple blocks north of here is where you'll find ol' Charlie. And no side trips to no alley either! If you really want to find him, you don't have to walk ahead of us. You can follow us at any pace you please. So if there's any monkey business, you're right behind us and you can get the drop on us at your leisure! So, what do you say, Mister. Tyler?"

Ben's tone was clearly facetious, but Zeke got the impression his intention was genuine. Zeke knew he had opened the ball and now he had to go through with it.

"My name's Ben Connelly," he said, holding out his hand as Zeke approached. When the Kansan made no move to respond, he eyed Zeke's right hand. "Yeah," he said wryly, "I noticed back at the saloon, you don't like shakin' hands too much. When I was a boy, my old man brought me over to Fort Smith. A Yankee colonel bent down and shook my hand and patted me on the head. Had I known then what I know now, I would've spat on his boots and rubbed my palm until the skin came off." He looked at the two men near him. "Let's get on."

Connelly moved down the walk and the other two followed him. Zeke hesitated, then walked right behind them as they led the way.

Connelly spoke quietly to Blaine. "Look at you two! He worked you over so bad you both look like you've come out of a stampede. And he didn't even get a chance to draw his sidearm. God help you both if he had."

"This doesn't finish it!" hissed Blaine.

"Sorry, Jack, I didn't get what you said. Maybe you'd better clear that broken tooth out of your mouth..."

In the few minutes it took them to arrive there, Zeke wasn't attacked by hidden assailants on the progressively dark street, yet his hand was resting on the butt of the Dragoon pistol just in case.

A one-story frame house stood off a lonely road by about fifty feet. It looked ill-used, if the short wooden fence fronting the yard was an example; it looked ready to fall down. When Zeke looked at the house and the word *ramshackle* floated through his mind. The house was once a comfortable dwelling for a local politician and his family. Eventually they headed back east with the first sounds of gunfire from across the border, sometime in the 1850s. It had aged considerably since that time and the once fresh grass had faded to a dirty brown and unsightly weeds grew everywhere.

As they approached, Zeke saw a lamp burning behind crooked shutters. He regarded the house apprehensively, wondering if there was more in the house besides the shutters that was crooked.

"Our headquarters!" said Connelly grandly, though there was still a twinkle in his eye.

Zeke hesitated and Connelly noticed right away.

"Listen, Tyler," he said soberly. "If we wanted your wallet, why bother bringing you all the way out here to get it?"

"Well," said Zeke quietly, "it's your place. Lead the way, you know where everything is."

Connelly looked at him briefly, then turned and they all followed him up to the house. After climbing the first few

decrepit steps, Connelly pushed in the door. The creak was loud—
Zeke suspected that was on purpose.

The hallway was in shadows and Zeke saw a light several feet
away from him and to the right. An archway stood before them.
Zeke followed his escorts through it and soon found himself in a
brightly lit room that smelled of musty air and spilled liquor. A
card game was going on and the three men at the table were a
distinguished bunch.

One man, hatless, had dark hair and a tanned face which could
only come from hard riding under a Southern sun. The face was
stern, and Zeke figured it was always that way, not just when he
was studying his cards. He was a young man, about Zeke's age, but
he had a seriousness to him that added to his years. On either side
of him were two corpulent men who were exact twins, both
dressed the same; matching battered hats, sweaty old shirts and
suspenders over worn trousers.

So, these were the Janey twins—

"Charlie Morse," said Connelly, getting to the point.

Morse looked up from his hand. He didn't like the interrup-
tion and it showed in his face. This was a man used to having
things his way. He regarded the others with familiarity but stared
outright at Zeke.

Although telling himself he would not show anger, Zeke
couldn't help but glare at Morse. Had there not been men with
loaded guns all around him, Zeke would have surely leapt across
the room and wrapped his fingers around the bushwhacker's
throat with little hesitation. Morse had not even opened his
mouth, yet Zeke knew he hated him more than he had ever hated
anyone.

"You know me, mister?" Morse asked in his Tennessee drawl.

When Zeke didn't answer immediately, Morse addressed the
others in the room.

"Does he talk?"

"When he wants to, I guess," said Connelly off-handedly.

Morse went on as if Zeke wasn't in the room. "He's lookin' at me as if I shot his ma!"

Zeke consciously swallowed in an attempt to calm himself. He forced his hands to stay at his sides.

Connelly said, "Well, ya see, Charlie—"

"I wanted to see you," Zeke finally said.

Both twins laughed then, a derisive laughter done plainly to unnerve Zeke.

"Hey," chuckled Mart Janey, "he *does* talk!"

"Yeah," answered his brother, Tom, "but it looks like he's still teethin'. He bit his own lip!" They both bellowed in laughter again and Zeke tensed up at the sound of it.

Connelly said lightly, "Ahh, now don't laugh at this one. He was mixin' it up good with these two stout symbols of Rebel manhood and was movin' in for the kill when I showed up."

"Ben!" Blaine said irritably, his face twisting in suppressed rage. Chiles just went over to a chair in the foyer and sat down, sulking.

Connelly said lightly, "Tell me it's a lie, Jack, and I'll forget I ever said it."

Blaine's jaw tightened and his eyes shifted away from him.

Morse asked, "You beat up these two?"

Zeke didn't answer; he only stared back at him.

Connelly said quickly, "He's shy."

Morse scowled at the Kansan and said, "Yeah, I guess so."

"Speak your piece, Zeke Tyler," said Connelly, who then went over and dropped into a chair, his long legs pushing against the wall.

"Tyler?" said Morse, now getting curious. "Where you from? Or do you care about answering that question?"

The tone was clearly sarcastic, and it infuriated Zeke but he knew he had to control his temper this time. He had to.

"Cass County," he answered. "I rode with the bushwhackers for a while. Herb Talley's group."

"I know Talley," said Morse. "He's a good man with a gun. A good leader. Though personally I think I can come up with someone better." At this remark, both Janey brothers giggled infectiously.

"One day," said Mart Janey, "Charlie's going to have his own revolution. He's going to be top man for all time! Maybe he can take Bill Quantrill's place too."

A deadly look from Morse stopped Janey from saying anything else. Then he turned his attention back to Zeke.

"How come you're not with Talley anymore?"

"I was kicked out—" answered Zeke, "—for fighting. They say I've got a temper."

Connelly said breezily, "Somehow I can't believe that."

Zeke looked back at Connelly and tried hard to stifle a grin. Despite the company he kept, Connelly seemed smarter than those around him and Zeke tried his best not to be charmed by his irreverence.

"We playin', Charlie?" asked Tom Janey.

Morse threw his cards down on the table. "I'm out. Not in the mood anymore." He then got up and walked over to Zeke. He was a tall man, somewhere around Zeke's height, though he had slightly more weight on him. As he faced the Kansan, Morse studied him.

Morse instinctively felt the tension from Zeke and couldn't figure out why; he had never seen him before. His curiosity only grew as to why this man should risk physical harm to seek him out.

Then, as if Zeke had read his mind, he answered his question.

"Heard you got a business going."

Morse looked at him with narrowed eyes. "Yeah? What else did you hear?"

Zeke answered, "Quantrill's boys don't usually grab people from their homes and take them away never to be seen again. But under the cover of a bushwhacker raid, your boys could kidnap young ladies so you can sell them to Southern aristocrats."

Charlie Morse stared hard at the Kansan. It wasn't the recitation of these facts that surprised him, it was Zeke's apparent insolence that made him uncomfortable, and it showed. Still, it was hard not to admire someone with that kind of sand.

Morse smirked at him, his black eyes staring into Zeke's. Then he said quietly, "I could use a man to replace Tilton..."

Zeke relaxed; instead of confrontation, he decided to sell himself, "Listen, Mister Morse, I'm good with a gun. And your foreman here..." He gestured to Connelly. "...was a witness to how I can handle myself in a fight. I'm young enough to stay in the saddle for a day and a half and, let's face it, it's hard to find a good man nowadays who's not on the battlefield."

"And..." asked Morse, "what would you do?"

Zeke paused before he answered, "Anything you tell me."

Charlie Morse reached over for a whiskey bottle near the table and poured himself a drink. After downing the glass, he continued to stare at Zeke; what was on his mind was anyone's guess.

The Janey boys laughed again for no particular reason. Blaine and Chiles exchanged looks and neither of them were happy ones.

Only Connelly appeared not to be following the conversation between them. He looked down at the palms of his rough, somewhat rope-burned hands and regarded them carefully. He wondered if too much dirt had gotten into his skin, and whether he would ever get them clean again...

CHAPTER FIFTEEN

An hour after his meeting with Morse and "the boys," Zeke was camped about a mile outside Lone Jack, in a hollow about fifty yards off a game trail. The fire crackled before him as he sat on the ground with his arms around his knees. His eyes averted from the fire. He didn't want to stare into it and spoil his aim should trouble arise.

Fireflies flitted about him so closely, Zeke could hardly tell the difference between them and sparks from the fire. He shooed them away absently, his mind far away.

Zeke was deeply disturbed about something, and it wasn't insects or the lonely forest around him or the crackling of the fire before him.

Here he was, still alive and free. And his parents were dead, dead for all time. And not only dead but turned to ashes. They were human beings one minute, then dust and ashes the next. And his sister? Taken away from home, never to return?

The rage coursed through him just thinking about it. He wanted these men dead as well—dead for all time.

Zeke looked up and saw his horse tied to a cottonwood, his

nose in the thick grass. A few feet away, his crumpled bedroll was on the ground with his hat next to it. He had tried to lie down but couldn't relax. He had even forgotten to remove his boots.

Then for some reason, something made him turn around. He looked up towards the cottonwoods and saw nothing but fireflies flitting about in the darkness. All he heard was the fire crackling away and the sounds of his own breathing. He faced front again, his thoughts turning to the next day's events.

After the meeting with Morse, it was decided that Zeke would ride to a farm owned by a man named Ferris Walker which was somewhere on the road between Lone Jack and Warrrensburg. It was not a big trail and therefore chosen because of its remoteness, especially from Union patrols. It was a small place, and as such, had only as many horses on hand for replacing bushwhacker mounts. There was no other stock on the property.

Yet there was a covered wagon in the barn, kept out of sight. Zeke was told only as much as they wanted him to know. There was mention of a basement that had been dug as a safe-haven in case of Indian attacks, now used for another purpose. Zeke wasn't told what that was for either—but he could guess.

Ferris Walker was the ornery and obnoxious example of human flotsam who owned the farm. He had no wife, not since she left him anyway. His only friends were a bottle and a deck of cards and he could never keep away from either of them for very long.

To the authorities, he called himself a simple farmer. To Charlie Morse and his assistants, he was a trafficker of kidnapped women who were kept in a basement and fed very little.

But Ferris Walker was no loyal Confederate or Southern sympathizer. He was, or had been, a staunch Unionist. He was a local informer for a Major Clark of the Ninth Missouri Cavalry. He profited financially from this arrangement until Major Clark was killed by Quantrill's men some time ago. Clark's replacement balked at Walker's salary demands and said in no uncertain terms that money would be slow in coming, if at all.

Ferris Walker was not one to sit idly by and wait for opportunity to come to him. Poking about Lone Jack, he got wind of Charlie Morse's "business" and quickly changed sides, offering his services to the bushwhackers. To Morse, the lonely farm seemed a perfect transfer point for slaves to be held until Union patrols thinned out enough for them to be run down South past the Arkansas border.

The next morning, Zeke was to ride to the Walker farm, meeting Blaine and Chiles on the trail to Warrensburg. It seems that Walker was complaining—again. He wanted more money, or he would report Charlie's activities to the nearest Union outpost. To Charlie Morse, there was only one answer to all this greed: Replace Ferris Walker—and now that he had fortuitously appeared on the scene, Zeke Tyler would be the one to commit the murder —as a sign of his sincerity anyway.

When Zeke was told that he was the one would do the killing, his face was outwardly calm, though inside him, he was appalled. He decided he would play along as much as he could until he could search that farm and hopefully find those kidnapped women.

It was then that Zeke heard what he thought was a snap of a twig off in the distance. He quickly sat forward and drew his Colt, aiming it at the trees before him. He listened but heard only the fire.

He scanned the area. The noise was definite, but not enough to guarantee that a man had made it. It could easily have been made by a squirrel or a rabbit.

Then he slowly sat back, holstering the gun. Realizing it made no sense to stay awake all night just on a suspicion, he went back to his bedroll.

All right. So let them watch me sleep. If Blaine or Chiles were out there, I'd be dead already.

Still, within the fold of his bedroll, he quietly pulled out the pistol again, just in case. Ironically the thought of someone keeping tabs on him made him defiant enough to show that their presence wouldn't bother him.

All the tiredness of the day came upon him suddenly as his eyes closed. Before he could think about it any further, he was asleep.

The sun shone on a crisp morning on the trail to Warrensburg. It seemed uncommonly cool and the wind blew through the trees and swayed branches. Zeke felt a chill as he sat his horse and looked around. He considered putting the Colt in his waistband for a quick, easier draw in case of trouble, especially since Blaine and Chiles were escorting him.

Zeke sighed and pulled up his shirt collar. *Why is it so cold? This is late August.*

He tried to relax and then the thought of Ruth possibly being at this farm comforted him and gave him courage. He would tear that place apart and these men as well if they laid a hand on her.

Zeke waited some twenty minutes before the two riders appeared out of the woods like two ghosts. They rode up to him slowly, their horses several feet apart and their faces grim under their beards.

Zeke eyed them warily. Their being that far apart looked like a prelude for an attack, with Zeke's attention drawn to one man as the other opened fire. When they did approach him, they said nothing, but their faces held an obvious contempt.

Blaine, who was chewing tobacco, suddenly spat a mouthful past Zeke. His horse's head came up briefly, but Zeke kept his temper down and just watched them.

Blaine spoke first, sneering at Zeke. "So, our little gunman came after all."

"We thought for sure you'd light out," said Chiles, behind an ugly smile.

Zeke said grimly, "Sorry to disappoint you."

"I have a feeling," Blaine said while chewing, "that we won't be disappointed at all. Nope, not at all."

Zeke looked him in the eye and said, "We are talking about the problem of Ferris Walker, aren't we?"

At that comment, both outlaws looked at each other knowingly, but said nothing. Then they both stared at him, trying to suppress their grins.

Zeke was infuriated but restrained himself. Instead, he simply said, "Remember something. You two aren't doing your fighting in an alley anymore."

The smirks disappeared and they both glared at him. Zeke knew he was playing with fire, but he felt he had to knock them down a few pegs.

"All right," Zeke said decisively, "Charlie would want us to get this over with, right? So, let's go."

He took a chance by riding past them up the road. There was silence as he rode on, his back to them and his hand not far from his holster. If need be, he was ready to hit the ground at a moment's notice.

But then they trotted up to him and went slightly past him, leading the way. He relaxed for the time being, but the tension in the air was thick on every foot of the trail as they rode in the direction of Warrensburg...

A couple hours later, they turned off the main road and stepped into a smaller trail. A mile further, the trees opened up on the left to a clearing thick with tall weeds and patches of dead grass. They were now on the Walker property and Zeke could tell immediately that it was not well kept. What grass there was, had already been eaten by the farm's stock long before. The fence they approached was in need of repair. While riding in, he could have sworn he had seen a huge pack rat scurrying through the weeds.

Zeke could see the buildings ahead, the house where the owner slept, a small bunkhouse where the ranch hands usually slept and further off to the right, the barn and outbuildings besides it. As they approached even closer, Zeke spotted the two old iron doors with a padlock on them, protruding from the ground at an angle next to the barn. His heart leapt at the sight. *The basement where the women might be kept...*

He was brought back to reality when Blaine growled, "Leave the horses here."

They all dismounted and tied the horses to the old fence. Zeke looked to Blaine expectantly and saw him put his hand on his holstered gun. Chiles stood behind Zeke, watching him.

"You go up the path first," said Blaine.

"Why should I?" asked Zeke. "I don't know the man."

"You will," Chiles hissed.

"Come on," urged Blaine. "You want to be one of us, prove it."

Zeke returned his look and then glanced at the main house up the path.

"Don't worry," said Chiles, grinning. "We'll be right behind you."

"I wasn't worried about that," said Zeke, walking around them and going through the gate.

A stone path led up to the front steps of the house, a good sixty feet away. The house was as old as the fence, yet Zeke could tell that the structure may have *looked* weathered but was actually well-built. As he scanned the front porch, he spotted portholes that were drilled into the walls, with removable metal disks covering them. *This place is old. Those portholes are for sticking a rifle barrel through in case of Indian attack.*

He figured that was the reason for the basement as well. There were the iron doors now, but years ago the basement entrance could easily have been hidden by bushes that were no longer there. An escape tunnel during an Indian raid? Zeke guessed that if that was where they held the women, the tunnel must have been sealed up long ago.

Zeke walked slowly up the path, his arms loosely at his sides. He was all too aware of his two "companions" coming up the path close behind him, hearing their boots crunch down on the weathered, cracked stones imbedded in the ground.

When Zeke was about thirty feet from the front steps, a voice called out, sharp and clear through the wind.

"That's far enough!" the voice said, sounding ancient and cantankerous.

Zeke stopped.

"Don't listen to 'em!" Blaine hissed. "Keep going!"

Zeke didn't move. Unlike the other two, Zeke had kept his eyes on the porthole besides the front door. Its cover was off, and the long, thin barrel of a rifle protruded from it, the sight aimed at Zeke.

"I said keep going," Blaine repeated, "or so help me I'll give it to ya in the back!"

Zeke didn't respond to the threat. He didn't feel a gun barrel pressed in his back, so he knew Blaine hadn't drawn his gun yet. Instead he called out to the man in the house.

"Ferris Walker!"

"Who're you?" The old voice called out from the open first floor window and sounded baffled. "I never seen you before."

"You know Blaine and Chiles?"

"Yeah, I know 'em! I got 'em in my sights!"

Blaine hesitated and Chiles glanced around nervously. They looked at each other, then faced the house.

"What's wrong, Ferris?" asked Blaine, finally finding his voice.

The old man responded, "Nothing's wrong, Jack! Not now it ain't—as long as I got you and your trained monkey in my sights."

Chiles scowled at the remark and glared at the house.

"What's eatin' you, old man?!" shouted Chiles, hoping the *old man* remark would rile him.

"One more word out of you, Chiles," shouted the voice from the house, "and I got a ball with your name on it aimed at your fat neck!"

"What's gallin' you, Ferris?" asked Blaine. "We just came here for a transfer."

"Yeah," said Chiles, following the other man's lead. "We've got a buyer down past the border wants two of 'em."

"I told your boss I wanted more money!" said Walker angrily. "And if you think I trust Charlie Morse, you're crazy!"

"So, what do you want us to do?" asked Blaine. "Stand here like fools?"

"Jack," the old man answered, "you can be a fool without just standin' there! No, I just want you boys to drop your holsters."

"What?"

"You heard me! I want you boys disarmed. Now!"

Zeke saw the rifle push further through the porthole and recognized it as a Spencer rifle. With the hammer pulled back, he knew what a hair trigger that could have and figured the man holding it matched the trigger perfectly.

Blaine and Chiles exchanged looks again.

Blaine shouted, "Now, come on, Ferris—"

Before he finished the sentence, Zeke knew what he had to do. He dropped to the ground quickly, his body hitting the broken stones with a thud.

Caught off-guard by the move and now completely exposed to Walker's rifle, both Blaine and Chiles reached for their guns in a panic.

The rifle blasted from the house, and Zeke looked up in time to see other rifles fired from back in the trees, from two separate locations. Blaine and Chiles were hit from three directions, shotguns and rifle slugs riddling them as they both hovered momentarily, their hands still on holstered guns. They both wavered, blood covering their backs and even more coming out of their chests and stomachs. Zeke figured they had been killed half a dozen times by now. They tottered and fell heavily to either side of Zeke's prone figure.

With the air thick with gun smoke, the noise of the rifles slowly died and was replaced by Ferris Walker shouting at him.

"All right, you! Get up!"

Zeke hesitated.

"I still got a bead on you, boy! Get up or I'll snuff ya right there on the ground!"

Slowly Zeke rose and looked around him. He saw two young men come out of the trees, cross past the fence and walk towards him. Both had shotguns pointed at him, smoke curling out of the long barrels.

Both of them were hardly older than twenty and their lanky frames ambled out of the woods with a confidence that belied their years. Their faces were cold and impassive, and it looked to Zeke that if he so much as scratched himself, a spray of buckshot would cut him in half.

"Off with it!" said one of them.

"Slow!" said the other one.

With hands raised slightly, Zeke watched them and knew the seriousness of their demand. With one hand, he unfastened his holster and let it drop to his feet. As one of them held the shotgun pointed at Zeke's stomach, the other bent over slightly and peered at the holster lying on the ground.

He whistled and said, "Yankee sidearm! What're you doing with this, boy?"

"Wearin' it," Zeke answered, not liking the "boy" label.

Suddenly the other one whirled the shotgun around and struck Zeke on the left shoulder. Zeke felt the stinging pain go down his arm and the impact threw him off his feet. He hit the ground on his stomach, the dirt flying up in his face. He lifted his head slightly and coughed.

The other one laughed. "What do you know? He can't take a little tap."

Zeke reached out and felt along the ground, as if trying to push himself to his feet.

The one who struck Zeke, said, "What you're going to learn is not to come back with no smart answers. You hear?"

The other one roughly kicked Zeke's boot and said harshly, "Thor asked you a question!"

Zeke rolled over and looked up at them. He said coldly, "Tell Thor to die!"

He brought up the Dragoon Colt, cocked it and fired it point blank into Thor's stomach. The discharge at close range caused Thor's stomach to recoil violently as blood appeared on his white shirt and quickly spread. A look of shock appeared on his face as he dropped the shotgun practically at Zeke's feet.

As Thor fell, the other youth quickly spun the long-barreled shotgun towards Zeke but being so close to him the turn was awkward. Zeke cocked the Dragoon again and put a ball in the youth's chest before he could react. Not waiting to see the youth fall and conscious of Ferris Walker's bead on him, Zeke sprang up and headed for some bushes several yards off to the right. A rifle ball hit the dirt right where Zeke had been.

Several balls were fired into the bushes as Zeke hugged the ground.   He couldn't remain there forever, and he knew it. He opened the Colt's cylinder and reloaded as there seemed to be a pause in the gunfire.

"Come on out, boy!" said the ornery voice. "Can't stay there all day.

"As soon as you get up and make a move toward that fence for your horse, I'll cut ya down. And we've got guns at the side windas. You so much as look at your horse, we'll open up on ya! Like you did on Joseph and Thor! You hear me, boy?"

Zeke heard him mention *we* and thought about it. Were there others in the house or was that just an old man's bluster?

The bushes were thick and effectively hid Zeke from Walker's rifle, yet they were also thick enough to obstruct Zeke's aim. There was no way he could possibly see the front window, much less Walker himself without peeking out from behind a bush—which was suicidal.

As he tried to think of a way out of his dilemma, he suddenly heard a hammer being cocked a few yards behind him. Zeke turned to the sound, instinctively keeping the Dragoon at his side.

He saw a young woman standing by the fence holding a rifle. She was tall and her red hair shone brightly in the sun. Zeke was struck by how pretty she was, though her range clothes slightly dampened the effect. She wore a blue-gray blouse and a riding skirt over a pair of worn boots. Her eyes were a limpid blue, but their gaze held on Zeke steadily. The look was not friendly.

She called out to the house. "I got him, Pa!"

Zeke stared at her. This was Walker's daughter? It was interesting to note that when Morse told Zeke what a double-dealer Ferris Walker was, he neglected to mention he had a family.

She gestured with the rifle barrel and said, "Put it on the ground, son."

She was hardly older than Zeke, but the grim expression on her face was all business. Realizing that she was close enough not to miss, Zeke reluctantly dropped the pistol at his feet.

He heard a door creak open, then footsteps on the front porch behind the shrubbery; two pairs of footsteps, in fact. They continued on the gravel path.

Two men appeared in front of him, holding rifles. One was close to sixty. Stringy white hair curled around the sides of an otherwise hairless head. The face itself was lean and weathered with bags circling the eyes. Though the blue pupils had a trace of the redhead's coolness, they were now watery and weak. His white brows knotted close together as they watched the Kansan.

The man next to him was much younger, closer to the redhead in age. His hair was light brown with a reddish tint and his lean face had the same thin pointed nose as the gun-toting redhead before him.

Obviously, her brother.

Ferris Walker looked at Zeke as he was still crouched behind the shrubbery. He studied him carefully: the look was not at all friendly, but still curious.

The young man next to him said, "Look at him, Pa! Still hiding like a scared rabbit."

The old man said, "He was man enough to get Joseph and Thor."

"Get up!" the young man said to Zeke. "We want to shoot you on your feet. Be a real sight to watch you fall."

"Not till I ask him some things," said Walker. He turned to Zeke. "Get up, boy..."

Slowly Zeke stood erect. He watched all three of them and was forming a verbal response to Walker's questions when he noticed the redhead's gaze. Her eyes were fixed on him so intently, he knew it would have taken an awful lot to distract her. Was she attracted to him? He quickly dismissed that thought. He was an intruder on her father's property and had killed two of his men.

Walker asked, "What's your name?"

"Does it matter if you're going to shoot me?"

The younger man raised his rifle. "I'll settle his hash," he said.

"Hold it, Cal," said the old man, putting his hand on the rifle barrel. "Your name! Now we ain't foolin'!"

"Zeke Tyler."

Suddenly there was a pause in the redhead's stare, and it looked like she felt something in the pit of her stomach. Zeke noticed she was breathing faster and almost looked like she was going to faint. All this at the mention of his name.

Zeke didn't know why she was reacting the way she did; he had never seen her before.

"You were with them," said Walker, indicating the bodies of Blaine and Chiles with his rifle.

Zeke answered, "I just joined up with Morse. But those men weren't my friends."

Cal said, "He's just lyin' to save his skin."

"No," said Walker, still watching Zeke. "He was walkin' ahead of them like they was usin' him for a shield. I saw their hands, they was on their gun butts. His were at his sides. Also, I never saw him with those two before...Still, he killed two of my men. They were good boys too."

"Oh, please, Pa!" The redhead finally broke her silence. "They were good for nothing trash you found in a saloon in Warrensburg. They would've dry-gulched you for the price of a bottle."

Cal said, "Let's open 'em up, Pa."

"Forget it, Cal," said the old man.

"But why not?" Cal sounded disappointed.

"'Cause he's going to carry a message back to Morse. Those two on the ground, tie 'em to their saddles." He spoke to Zeke. "I don't care what you say about how they got killed. Tell Morse that's a warnin' if he tries any more shenanigans. And you also tell 'em that he'd better give me a damn good reason as to why I don't send my boy ridin' out to the nearest fort and tell the Yanks all about Charlie Morse and his slave runnin'. And that good reason better be a pack of money. Money to keep this thing goin' and also to hire a couple of new men..." Then for the first time, his thin lips almost grinned. Eyeing Zeke, he said, "That was awful good shootin' though." He turned to his son and said, "Go on. Tie 'em to their horses. He's goin' back."

"Pa!"

"You heard me, boy! Bring his horse too."

Cal hesitated, then turned and went back up the fence for their horses.

Walker pointed the rifle at Zeke. "You're leavin' here..."

Zeke stared back at him and said sternly, "Not without my sidearm."

"Boy, you're lucky I'm lettin' you live, now don't push it!"

Zeke stared back at him, unflinching. "You heard me."

"Oh, let him have his gun, Pa!" said Martha irritably. Zeke watched her as she turned away. Did he detect a feeling of disgust with the whole situation? He would have been sure had she not turned her face away.

Walker glanced at her, then back to Zeke. The rifle barrel never once turned from Zeke's stomach.

"All right," he said to Zeke. "Put it on. But if you point that thing at us and I'll empty this Spencer right in your guts. Is that understood?"

Zeke looked back at him and nodded slowly. Then he picked up the Dragoon by the barrel and held it harmlessly at his side as he went over to retrieve his holster. As he pulled on the holster and dropped the Colt into it, he looked down at the two dead men on the ground. Awkwardly Cal was dragging the two bodies of Blaine and Chiles to their horses, glaring at Zeke all the while. Cal took the ropes from their saddles and effortlessly tied the two men to their horses as Zeke watched, the old man's rifle on him all the time.

As Cal finally completed the knot to the rope that held Chiles, he glared at Zeke. "Too bad it wasn't you," he hissed.

Zeke stared back and the old rage came through. "If I find out you were doin' more to those girls than just watching them," said Zeke quietly, "you're going to wish you were as dead as these two…"

Cal's eyes blinked rapidly, and his fingers tightened on the pommel. If the horse had not been between them, Cal would have gone for Zeke right then and there. He held himself back though; there would be another time.

When Martha brought over Zeke's horse, he glanced at her as he was about to mount. As he suspected, she was still watching him closely, but not for the same reasons her father and brother were. Her eyes seemed to be searching his face, taking in his eyes, mouth, every facial expression.

Zeke mounted his horse and looked at the grisly picture before him. The dead men were both in their saddles, their limp arms tied tightly around the horses' necks.

Zeke said wryly, "Good job. Your boy do this before?"

"And for you," said Cal bitterly, "I'd gladly do it again."

Martha looked at her brother and her cool eyes grew wide briefly. Zeke saw the look. After her brother's threat, it seemed like she was scared for him. Finally, Martha reached up and handed him the reins to the two horses, but as he took them, her fingers went around his hand and squeezed it. Zeke looked from his hand and up to her eyes. They were large and blue, but he now realized what else he saw in them.

Sympathy.

Zeke quickly looked at the trail ahead and hoped Walker didn't see their eyes meet. Presently he didn't know what to make of her, but he couldn't worry about that now. They were watching him.

"All right, Tyler," said Ferris Walker. "You ride out and talk to your boss. Tell him what I want—in twenty-four hours from now."

Zeke looked at him and asked quietly, "If he doesn't give you your money, what'll you do with the women? Let 'em go?"

"Hell, boy, I'm not stupid!" Walker said. "First I'll tell the Yanks about Morse...Then I'll shoot the women—every damn one of 'em."

Zeke tensed up. He would have jumped the old man right then and there if Walker's rifle was not pointed at him. And even if he did, Cal would gladly back-shoot him. Either way his death wouldn't benefit Ruth.

He did pause to look at Martha though. She was staring at her father as if she couldn't believe her ears. Cal was just grinning at him.

"And if anyone shows up to claim the merchandise," Walker continued, "we'll kill 'em anyway. No ifs, ands or buts. Is that understood?"

Zeke's eyes burned at the old man. He could hardly speak. Looking down at him, he kept his hands on the pommel, his fingers tightening on the reins.

"Yeah," said Ferris Walker, as he watched Zeke and smiled. "I can see you understand very well."

"Pa," said Martha.

"Later, girl. I want my money by the same time tomorrow—or else me and my boy go down in that basement with our long guns and open up on 'em." Then Walker pushed the barrel roughly into Zeke's side and said, "Now, get off my property!"

Zeke felt the pain in his side but said nothing. He looked at Walker, then shook the reins and moved the horse forward, his eyes catching both Cal and Martha as he rode past. He saw that she was trying to keep her composure after listening to her father's demands, and the strain showed on her face.

He rode slowly out of the farm pulling the two nags with the two dead bushwhackers tied to them. The dead men tottered slightly in their saddles, but Cal had tied them securely. Zeke was right; Cal had done this before.

Zeke rode back down the trail he had taken to get there, his mind far away. He thought of Ferris Walker and his son. He thought of his daughter especially. Where was she in all this? He wasn't sure, but most of all he thought of those women. He had to get them out of there, but if he showed up with a Union patrol, Walker would kill them, this much he was sure of. He saw the old man's eyes—a killer's eyes. He saw them in Charlie Morse as well. Shooting down a woman would be no more of a task to them than breathing.

He sighed grimly.

The war was full of such men...

Watching Zeke ride off, Martha held the rifle at her side and wondered if she had done the right thing by capturing him. At that point, she figured it wouldn't matter now.

She knew he would be back...

CHAPTER SIXTEEN

When Zeke had gotten about a mile from Ferris Walker's farm, he stopped. He had ridden slowly, taking his time and thinking things out. Behind him were two horses with dead men on them. They were shifting to the side occasionally and looked to be in danger of falling off, but ultimately, they stayed on.

He looked around carefully. The forest was thick with cottonwoods
and shrubbery. If Cal Walker had followed and had any idea of sneaking up on him, Zeke would be alerted by the sounds of something coming through the underbrush. He dismounted and pulled his horse several yards off the trail, finally pouring some canteen water into his Stetson and letting the grateful horse drink. He wished there was a stream nearby, but he was in no mood to look for one. After tying his horse to a tree, he went over to the other two mounts, blood already covering the saddles.

He watched them from a distance, trying to calm his stomach. He wasn't going to deliver them to Charlie Morse. He wasn't about to bury them either, especially without a shovel. Instead

Zeke figured to give it a few hours, then turn them loose—dead cargo and all. Let the woods have them.

Zeke pulled out his bedroll, found some bare ground and spread it out. He took off his hat and laid back, staring at the dark clouds above. They formed quickly, blocking out the sun and causing Zeke to suspect a storm was imminent.

He waited, but there was no thunder; only darkness.

He sighed. Trying a rescue during a storm might have made things easy for him, with Walker and his son distracted by the weather enough to let their guard down.

There was a broken fence around the place and the ground was not well cared for. Indeed, the Walker Farm was hardly a fortress. Yet with a large group of women held hostage, he knew that the farm might as well be surrounded by a moat of crocodiles.

He was a tall man, getting broad in the shoulders already. He realized that sometimes big men getting into small places can be clumsy. One noise might trigger a massacre, and he would be damned if he was going to be responsible for one, even indirectly. He had seen too many massacres already and he was barely twenty.

But then again, so had those on the battlefield...

Night would seem the best time to try anything. Whether he liked it or not, he had to wait...

Kelly Ryan sat on a bench across the street from McGann's for close to two hours. It was now midday. She was reading a cheap romance novel and glancing up periodically to look across the street. She had bought the book for five cents and had absolutely no interest in its contents, using it instead as a pretext to look occupied.

The horses galloping in from the east end of the street finally alerted her. She looked at the men riding in and quickly pocketed her book. Then she got up and crossed the street carefully, making sure she was at the saloon's entrance by the time these men got there.

Kelly stepped to the walk and planted herself between the doors and the already crowded hitching rails as six men dismounted and strode eagerly for the saloon.

When Herb Talley swaggered up to the doors, Kelly stepped in front of him and looked up at his face. For a moment Talley didn't seem to recognize her. Then slowly his face brightened as his friends passed him and went inside.

Talley swept his hat off and said, "Miss Ryan! How are you today?"

The tone was clearly sardonic. Herb Talley hadn't greeted anyone like that in years.

Kelly noticed the tone and responded in kind. "And how are *you* today, Mister Talley?" She still detested him, but felt she had to put that aside for now.

"Fine, thank you, Miss Ryan!"

"May we step away from here and talk?"

"Oh," he said, with a gleam in his eye, "we can talk right here! I have no secrets from my friends!"

She sighed and said patiently, "As a favor to a lady then. Please, Mister Talley."

"Oh, all right then, ma'am...For a lady."

They crossed the street and stood in front of the general store as Kelly looked around uncomfortably.

"They all know me, ma'am," said Talley. "They know not to listen in on *my* conversations."

Not trusting his words, Kelly made sure they were alone anyway. Then she turned to him and urgently asked, "Where is he?"

Talley looked at her with amusement. "You're his girl, don't *you* know?"

"If I did, would I be asking you?"

"Believe me, ma'am, if you were my girl, I wouldn't leave you hangin'. No, sir! You'd know *everywhere* I went." Talley was having fun with her, enjoying her anxiety.

"Well, that's all very nice, Mister Talley, but that doesn't answer my question."

Talley looked at her earnestly and said, "We kicked him out of the gang a few days ago."

Kelly's blue eyes bore into his deeply. She said quietly, "I'm glad..."

"He's as wild as an unbroken stallion and twice as stubborn. I don't know what your plans are, ma'am, but if you're fixin' to put a bridle on him, you might have some trouble."

Kelly reddened, and then said curtly, "That's our business, Mister Talley."

"Suit yourself, ma'am, but if you want Zeke Tyler, you can have him! The boys want no part of him, and if they did, I suspect it's to use him as a target."

Kelly's curiosity was aroused further. Trying to suppress her anxiety, she asked, "While he rode with you, did he kill anyone?"

Talley said gravely, "Yes, ma'am, he did—and they were all my men!"

Kelly relaxed then, but she saw Talley's resentment. "I'm sorry about that," she said awkwardly.

"Are you?"

Kelly then looked into Talley's eyes and saw the hurt in them. Still, she had no sympathy for the deaths of murderers.

"How do you mean that, Mister Talley?"

Talley glared at her and she saw his anger building. He said, "Maybe someone used their influence to hold him back instead of doing what a man's supposed to."

Kelly's eyes narrowed and her face grew tense as she watched him. Defiantly, she said, "If you mean that I influenced Zeke Tyler not to kill innocent people, I hate to disappoint you, but he had that decency long before I met him. And if you think you're going to shame me into feeling sorry for the deaths of some young murderers—"

"Those boys were people too, Miss Ryan!" Talley's face was twisted in anger. "They came from good homes and good families, except now the Yanks have burned those homes and murdered those families! And if I might say, you're dismissin' the deaths of those boys as unimportant is the height of arrogance—prominent in your people, I might add!"

It was too much. Kelly stepped forward and slapped him hard in the face. She was trying desperately to control her trembling.

"That was for my ancestors!" she said furiously. "A hard-working people who were kicked off their land a generation ago and cast into the sea to starve! To have their children taken from them by a dozen maladies. They were kicked off their land by men like you, Mister Talley! The 'righteous' men who wanted to make theirs a better world by getting rid of a certain people they felt weren't up to their standards. I was going to ask where Zeke might be, but I'll find him on my own. I'd rather choke than ask for your help! Go on across the street and have your drink with the other righteous folks who talk themselves into thinking they're better than the people they're fighting..."

She abruptly turned away and started down the walk until Talley called out to her. "Miss Ryan!"

Kelly turned around.

"Last I saw him, he rode off with a Georgian boy named Jim Gaines...Then I heard that two fellas named Blaine and Chiles took him toward Warrensburg,,,Don't know the reason...I heard they left this mornin'..."

Kelly stared at him and her face was completely still as she thought about it. Then she said, "Thank you," and quickly turned away, walking back toward the hotel.

As he watched her go, Talley put his hand up to his reddened cheek. He had been slapped by women before, and he always shrugged it off.

But not this time...

It was dark enough for the moon to rise, but even moonlight had trouble getting through the dense grove where Zeke had situated himself. He sat by the fire, having already eaten and had coffee. He had a few hours' sleep and he yawned as he kept his eyes away from the fire. Slapping the bugs off the back of his neck occasionally, he waited impatiently. *Would the Walkers sleep sometime? When did they sleep?*

Zeke had reloaded the Dragoon and checked the Henry rifle. A couple hours before, he had slapped the rumps of both horses and sent them with their dead riders careening down the trail due west, back towards Lone Jack. Would they instinctively ride back to the place they came from? He didn't know, but he certainly wasn't going to hold onto them with two dead men tied to their backs. If a Union patrol did happen to show up, he'd have a lot of explaining to do.

Zeke was thinking about this when he suddenly heard the sound of a branch being pushed aside. Then he heard more rustling sounds, clearly getting closer. He drew the Dragoon pistol and got up, backing himself further into the trees. He didn't bother dousing the fire. Whoever it was, they were too close now for him to pretend the place wasn't occupied. All he could do now was find a hiding place and see who entered the clearing.

Zeke put his back to a thick cottonwood and peaked through its low-hanging branches. Being in the brush now, the insects were eating him alive, but he contained himself and made no move to slap them away. The hammer of the Dragoon was pulled back and the gun barrel was flat against his chest, his thumb holding the hammer in place tightly. He couldn't risk a gleam off the gun barrel alerting his visitor.

There were now footfalls in the thick grass. Then he heard the sound of his bedroll being prodded by a foot. Cautiously he looked out from behind the tree and saw who it was.

Finally, he stepped into the open, pointing the Dragoon at the figure.

The noise startled Martha Walker and she turned her rifle to the sound.

"Hold it!" said Zeke, before she completed the turn. Paraphrasing her when she pointed her rifle at him earlier, he said, "Put it on the ground, girl."

"I knew you didn't ride away," she hissed. "I waited till Pa and Cal were getting tired, then I rode out here."

"Picked up my trail in the dark? That's pretty good."

She shook her head. "I followed you ten minutes after you left the farm. Figured you'd plant yourself out here somewhere, just waiting for a chance to come back...After I found you here, I rode back to the farm. Then I waited for Pa and Cal to drink themselves to sleep before I came out here."

Martha was still dressed in her faded blouse and riding skirt. Her boots were still unpolished and her red hair, now piled on her head, was under a gray Stetson with a little band around it.

"Are you going to drop that long gun?" Zeke asked sternly.

She noticed his tone and resignedly dropped it to the ground. Then she removed her hat and Zeke saw her red hair shine in the firelight. She purposely tossed the hat onto his bedroll.

Zeke saw this and said, "You're not staying for dinner."

"Kind of hot here with that fire," she said. Her chest was heaving faster and she wiped her forehead with her hand. Then she unbuttoned the top button of her blouse so naturally, Zeke almost missed the gesture.

"Are you going to shoot me?" she asked.

Zeke paused, then uncocked the hammer of his gun and holstered it. "All right. You're here. Now why is it so important for you to find me?"

Martha's face became serious and her clear blue eyes bore into his deeply.

"I know you..." she said quietly, her voice suddenly full of emotion. "You're her brother."

Zeke quickly went up to her and grabbed her by the shoulders. He asked urgently, "She's there, isn't she? Is she all right?"

Martha looked into his eyes and saw the rage behind them. She knew better than to hesitate but found she couldn't help it. That something in his eyes froze her voice.

The pause did not help Zeke's mood. He shook her violently. "I asked you, is she all right? You heard me!"

Her red hair dropped loosely to her shoulders and she winced, trying to free herself.

"You're hurting me!"

"I don't care!" he said through gritted teeth.

Then, not liking the way he sounded or the way he acted, he stood back and abruptly let go of her shoulders.

His voice sounded calmer then, "Is she all right?"

"...I don't know."

Zeke didn't like the answer. "What do you mean, you don't know?" he almost shouted. The voice then took on a sarcastic air. "You've been holding her prisoner for the past week!"

"I've been visiting kin in Sedalia for the past few days!"

"But you've seen her?"

"Yes, I have. Before I left. She's a little blonde-haired girl, about ten I guess." She looked into his eyes and said weakly, "Got the prettiest blue eyes I ever saw." Then she seemed to snap back to reality as she said resentfully, "And she's got your stubborn chin too!"

"You haven't seen her since you left for Sedalia?"

"No, I haven't," she said quickly. "But I haven't seen any of them. Pa and Cal don't allow me near those iron doors. I don't know what kind of shape those people are in."

Zeke said furiously, "You stand there and admit to having kidnapped women on your property and you live with that? What kind of a woman are you?"

She glared at him resentfully and said, "You have no idea what kind of a woman I am, Zeke Tyler."

Zeke's gaze burned into hers. "I've got a good idea what you are!"

He went back to his bedroll and folded it up, unceremoniously throwing her hat on the ground. After tying his bedroll onto the saddle, he picked up his hat and put it on. Martha watched him as he did all this, his movements all measured out carefully, so full of purpose it stunned her. After untying his horse, he removed the Henry rifle from the scabbard, checked the ammo again and put it back.

Finally, she found her voice and asked, "Where are you going?"

"You said they were asleep," Zeke answered. "Sounds like now's a good time to bring this to an end."

"Neither of them sleep very soundly."

Zeke said wryly, "Wonder why...Doesn't matter. They're going to sleep permanently when I get through with them."

Martha stared at him and said, "You'd kill my father and my brother, just like that?"

Zeke looked back at her and his eyes seemed so small in the firelight she could hardly see them. "Yes, Miss Walker," he said quietly. "I'd kill them...just like that."

"Do you think I'd let you do that?"

"If you try to stop me, I'd kill you too." His voice was hardly above a murmur.

Martha was shocked at his candor. She looked at him strangely, as if seeing something in him for the first time.

"Listen to yourself!" she shouted. "You sound exactly like my father did this afternoon when he threatened to kill those women!"

"Don't compare me with your father!" Zeke spat out the statement. "Your father's a filthy leech! He profits off the bloodshed in this war! Hell, you can't even give me a noble speech as to why he's doing this. Selling young girls for money and you go off seeing your kin in Sedalia. Did they feed you well while my sister's starving? Don't you dare ask me to spare your father! You don't deserve to even ask God any favors."

Martha's tone was wry as she stepped close to him. "Oh, I see," she said. "So now you're God. You give life and you take it away, is that it?"

Zeke said nothing. He just walked over to his horse, and with a quick movement, pulled himself into the saddle. It was then that he heard the sound of the rifle being moved and he turned to see the barrel pointed at him from across the campfire.

Just like at the farm earlier, and Zeke couldn't miss the irony.

"Seems you just love pointing rifles at me..."

"You ride out of here to kill my father," she said grimly, "and I swear I'll put one right through the back of your head."

Zeke looked at her blandly. Then to her surprise, he drew his pistol and pointed it straight at her. His eyes were cold and the voice coming out of him didn't sound like his at all.

"I never killed a woman before, but I meant what I said if you tried to stop me..."

Behind her rifle, Martha's eyes were suddenly frightened. In all her days, she had never seen a man's personality change as rapidly as Zeke's. Looking at his eyes, even at that distance, she saw the hate.

Hesitantly she lowered her rifle, but not until the barrel was pointed completely to the ground did Zeke holster his gun. Then he shook the reins and rode on, passing her horse tied to a tree a few yards off the trail. Gradually he picked up speed and headed east towards the Walker Farm.

He tried to calm down as he rode.

Zeke didn't like the things he said back there. Or the things he'd done. He had pointed a loaded gun straight at a woman's heart and threatened to kill her.

Zeke spurred his horse faster down the road, as if speed and movement would make him forget what was happening to him.

Something in him had died.

And he wondered if he'd ever get it back...

CHAPTER SEVENTEEN

When Jean Beaucaire left the room of a young woman who lived at the east end of Lone Jack, he was holding his Stetson in his hand and feeling pretty good about himself and the world. He breathed in the mid-afternoon air, which was uncommonly cool, then looked at the sky. Dark clouds drifted in, blocking the sun, though no rain had appeared, as yet. Coupled with the unusually cool afternoon, Beaucaire thought it was rather strange.

He took his eyes off the gathering clouds for just a moment and then caught something out of the corner of his eye. Beaucaire turned to his right and looked at the grove of trees a hundred feet away. He saw something move among the cottonwoods. At first, he thought it might have been tree branches being blown by the unusually strong wind, but the size and shape discounted that.

Beaucaire smoothed back his hair and put on his Stetson as he curiously watched the movement in the distance. Something was back there in the trees and it wasn't a squirrel. He looked around, saw no one else nearby and then trotted over to the grove.

When he got there, he realized he wasn't seeing things. One horse was grazing in a hollow a few yards off the trail. The body tied to the saddle was starting to slump noticeably. Beaucaire went over to the body and lifted the head up by the hair. Immediately recognizing Jack Blaine, he dropped the lifeless head and looked off to the other horse some thirty feet away. He didn't have to see the face to know who the other corpse was; Blaine and Chiles always traveled together. Somehow, it was in the cards that they would end up dying together—for what else could they be now but dead? Dead and sent back to where they started like two packages that were refused delivery.

Beaucaire had known about their trip to the Walker Farm the other morning and that they were accompanied by some young roughneck who had whipped both of them in an alley. He didn't get the fellow's name, Taylor or something like that. Still, he knew of the trouble Charlie was having with the old man and figured they were all out there to make a clean sweep.

He looked grimly at Blaine's body and figured that broom swept both ways.

Beaucaire pulled in both horses and decided to show them and their dead riders to Charlie and the others (He could *tell* him, but he knew Charlie Morse never took anyone's word for anything). And after he showed them to Charlie, he knew that his boss would make the decision to head for the Walker Farm and clean things up once and for all...

Later in the day, Kelly Ryan was on a horse riding towards Warrensburg. She had packed her bedroll and some food, had plenty of water and bought some extra ammo for her revolver before she left town. She left the rest of her belongings back at the hotel room, already paid for with practically all the money Zeke had given her. But she figured to return—and to return in one piece with the man she had stuck with all this time riding beside her. She thought that perhaps it was asking a lot of the

Fates to have her find him in all of Warrensburg, but she was through sitting around that awful town and waiting. She was sick of Jake Rule and his prying and that young idiot who leered at her and especially that arrogant Frenchman, Beaucaire. She had seen him ride out earlier in the day with a group of other young men. She assumed it was his "gang". He seemed the type to ride with one.

The cool wind blew through the trees and swayed the branches of cottonwoods on both sides of the lonely trail. It was quiet except for the gentle rustling of leaves and the sounds of the horse's hoofs on the ground.

Suddenly the mare's head lifted, and she whinnied loudly. Kelly looked at her curiously and it was then she heard the sound of more hoofs on the ground immediately behind her.

The three of them had come out of a side trail, where they had waited for her to pass before coming up behind her. Kelly turned in her saddle to look at them.

The sun glinted off the visors of their Union caps as they got closer to Kelly's horse. The one on the right looked familiar—especially with the bandage pulled tightly across his head. The other two she recognized from their encounter with her the other night.

Edwards, the one with the bandage, smiled crookedly. His next move, though, was unexpected. He drew his Colt and pointed it at her.

This time her own pistol was still in her bag.

"This is a surprise," said Edwards, without humor. "You sure do like riding the trails, don't you girl?"

Kelly stared at him and said nothing. Unconsciously she swallowed at the sight of the drawn pistol. Still, her mind was working, thinking of what would happen if she had a chance to throw something from her saddle right at him and then ride away fast.

She discounted that when she looked at his hooded eyes and realized he'd probably shoot her as soon as she lifted her hand.

He smiled at her, but he spoke to his companions. "Told ya if
we patrolled the road long enough, she'd be back this way." Then
to her, he said, "I owe you for this!" He tapped the cloth on his
head with his other hand.

Instead of feeding her fear, she decided to confront him.

"You'd shoot me, would you?"

Edwards answered her by riding up to her and putting the gun
barrel to her head. Then with his other hand, he grabbed her
wrist and gradually started twisting it. Predictably, she felt the
same pain as when he grabbed her wrist the other night. The end
of the gun pressed into her forehead, already sweating under her
Stetson.

Through her agony, she glimpsed the other two. Their
twisted smiles said it all; there would be no interference from
them, much less pangs of guilt.

As soon as Edwards started to pull her, though, her other hand
came up in a fist and socked the private in the eye. His cap flew off
and he cried out shortly, but his grip around her wrist still held.
Then, with an angry yell, he pulled the arm as he backed his horse
away.

Kelly struggled to stay on her horse, but the pain was too much.
Her eyes widening in fear, she lost her balance and fell to the ground,
her hat rolling away in the dust. With dirt in her nostrils, she
coughed sharply and then looked up into the angry face of Private
Edwards, his hand rubbing his wounded eye below the bandage.

The gun was pointed at her as Edwards started to grin. The
other two soldiers moved their horses around her, and their faces
said it all.

"Pull her back in the trees," said Edwards blandly.

One of them said, "Captain said he might patrol this road himself later in the day."

"That's later in the day," replied Edwards. "But I owe this shanty bitch for sluggin' me..."

Kelly raised herself off the ground, but Edwards' boot came out of the stirrup and shoved her back down. She fell back in the dust, bruising her arm as she hit the ground.

Edwards spat near her and said, "The luck of the Irish ain't gonna help you, you stinkin'—"

A Spencer carbine was fired back off in the woods and a nest of birds immediately flew off into the sky. Their fluttering wings could be heard above the heads of the group in the middle of the lonely road. Above the bandaged head of Edwards, still pointing his Colt down at his victim; above Kelly, who looked off into the woods with curiosity, and above the other two soldiers, one of whom made a grab for the hole in his back and then fell from his saddle, his body missing Kelly by a foot.

The second soldier turned and reached back for his pistol. The move was the last he would ever make as a Spencer slug pierced his forehead and he slid easily from the saddle. Kelly quickly rolled aside as his body, thicker than the other man's, fell heavily to the ground.

Edwards seemed frozen in his position, his gun still pointed down, though not at Kelly now. Sweat appeared thickly on his bandaged forehead and his other hand shook nervously on the pommel.

Like a ghost, Jim Gaines rode out of a cluster of trees and into the middle of the now crowded trail. He came out of his hiding place leisurely, unhurriedly. The wry smile on his face seemed to say that he was now in his element.

The smoking barrel of the carbine was pointed at the sky,

purposely it seemed. There was a mischievous gleam in the south-erner's eye.

"Get up, ma'am," he said in his thick Georgian drawl.

Ignoring Edwards' still-pointed gun, Kelly pushed herself to her feet. "You don't have to tell me twice, lad," she said.

Then, with one quick movement of his other hand, Gaines drew his Navy Colt and tossed it over to Kelly. The pistol landed at her feet.

Kelly saw the gun, then looked up at Gaines curiously.

"Pick it up," he said, his eyes still watching Edwards. "Pick it up, ma'am, and get satisfaction."

Kelly bent down and reluctantly picked up the Navy Colt. She cocked the hammer, a tougher pull than her lighter pocket revolver, and pointed the gun up at the scared private. Edwards watched Kelly with contempt, but his real concern was the south-erner at his back and his eyes darted back to him whenever he had the chance.

"Go on, ma'am," said Gaines earnestly. "Blow his thievin' Yankee hide all over this trail!"

Breathing fast, Kelly watched the private closely and saw the fear in his eyes. The gun was aimed at his rapidly heaving chest. At that range she couldn't miss, but still she hesitated.

Finally, she said to Gaines, "Sir, I thank you for stepping in when I needed help. But if you'll pardon my reluctance, it's not for any lack of gratitude that I say, don't rush me!"

Gaines looked at her and shrugged. "Suit yourself, ma'am," he drawled. "No one ever said Jim Gaines never gave a lady a sportin' chance."

Kelly's face brightened as she stared at the Georgian. Gradu-ally tears came to her eyes. "Jesus is on my side after all!" she said. "You're the same Jim Gaines out of Georgia, are you?"

This time it was Gaines' turn to looked surprised.

"Well, well!" he said, with a big smile on his face. "I always fancied myself a great and famous man! Known all over the west for his many acts of kindness and valor—and his reputation for being every inch a woman's greatest fantasy! I just didn't know the Gaines name had spread this far up."

"I'm glad I found you, Mister Gaines."

"The feeling's quite mutual, ma'am."

At that moment, Edwards spun around and fired his Colt. As Gaines dropped the barrel of his carbine towards the private, one shot exploded and echoed around the forest.

Edwards stooped low on his saddle with a bullet in his chest. His face showed pain, but his gun still remained gripped in his hand as his gaze wandered down to Kelly. She was looking at him, a seething anger in her blue eyes. Smoke drifted up out of the barrel of the Navy Colt she held.

Gaines' smile had disappeared, and he watched Kelly uncertainly. He saw that Kelly had less trouble cocking the hammer back a second time. His carbine was still pointed at Edwards, but he held his fire. This was the Irish girl's show.

As Edwards weakly pointed the gun down at Kelly for one last try, their eyes met. And when the mortally wounded soldier saw the steady blue eyes and the rage behind them, he swallowed in fear.

Holding the Colt with both hands, Kelly fired again. The bullet pierced Edwards' throat just below the chin. The dead soldier recoiled with the impact and fell backwards out of his saddle, hitting the ground heavily. The rider-less horse quickly trotted away from the scene.

Gaines slid the carbine back into his scabbard as he watched Kelly gravely. Then he rode up to her.

Looking down at Edwards, he said, "Guess this old Yankee rat turned his gun on the wrong party."

Kelly had the gun at her side as she looked down at the body. "I never killed anyone before, Mister Gaines."

Gaines watched her and said, "It's war, ma'am. The boys fightin' out there didn't come into this with any experience in killin' either. You just ended up killin' a sick man who would've given a lot of women a great deal of pain." He then pulled out the makings and rolled himself a cigarette. "Anyway, you saved my bacon. And for that, ma'am, I'm obliged to you."

As if waking from a dream, Kelly looked at him suddenly.

"Good Lord, did he get you, Mister Gaines?"

"I heard a ricochet off a tree back there. The ball probably killed some squirrel doin' nothin' more harmful to the Union than gatherin' food for the winter—which seems to be startin' early..." Gaines looked around and saw the branches of cottonwoods swaying. Then he looked down thoughtfully as he exhaled some smoke. "I wonder..."

"Wonder about what, Mister Gaines?"

Not wanting to alarm her with something he wasn't sure of, he asked her a question instead. "Well, for instance, how is it you know me?"

Kelly looked up at him earnestly and said, "You rode with Zeke Tyler. I've got to know what happened to him!"

"Damn it!" he exploded.

Kelly was taken aback and watched him curiously.

"Just when I find a beautiful girl," Gaines said, in mock irritation, "a true angel, with the prettiest blue eyes anyone could ever see—" Kelly faced the ground and blushed. "Just when I find the girl of my dreams--and a sweet-talkin' Irish lass too, of whose people I have the greatest respect for their perseverance through all their sufferin' and hardship--" He tipped his hat to her. "Just when all this happens in my heart, that tall Kansan comes along and takes you from me." He shook his head and took a drag on his cigarette. "What's a handsome young Reb like me to do?"

"First of all," Kelly said, "I'd like to know how you showed up when you did."

"I was watchin' you, ma'am."

"What?"

"I was watchin' you—straight from town. You see, I happen to know ol' Jake Rule would sell his own mother to the bushwhackers. And probably for a low price too! So when he mentioned to some friends of mine that a beautiful Irish lass was stayin' in his hotel, a girl who was *very* friendly with a certain Kansan we both know, and when the word spread around that you might help him, I figured to keep an eye on you, just in case."

"My thanks, Mister Gaines."

"It was a pleasure, ma'am. But you threw me back there when you mentioned my name and where I hail from. I thought I was watchin' you, not the other way around."

"It's a long story," said Kelly, handing him the Colt.

"Hold onto it, ma'am. You use it well."

"No, it's all right," she said, patting her saddle bag. "As you would say out here, I'm heeled."

Gaines paused before putting the cigarette to his lips and said, "Yes, ma'am. I believe I'm in for a few surprises myself..."

That night, as the winds brought a strange chill to the countryside, Zeke had arrived within sight of the Walker farm. He slowly dismounted and tied his horse to a large tree a few yards from the broken fence. Then he slid the Henry rifle from its scabbard and again checked the ammo. Slowly he walked towards the farm, his throat dry as the tension coursed through him.

Zeke's eyes searched the area as he carefully made his way around the twisted trees and patches of cedar. He saw the worn fence up ahead and his fingers tightened around the trigger guard. An owl hooted as he approached the neglected area, its dead grass and well-trod soil making small cracking noises as he walked. Despite the fact that he was coming to a clearing, he noticed that something still darkened his path. The moon was shining as brightly as ever, yet a black shadow covered him. He knew that the branches above him were thick, but he didn't think they cast that much of a shadow.

Curiously Zeke looked up and the sight hit him like a punch in the chest. He gasped and then staggered back a few steps, the rifle falling from his hands.

Up above him, Ferris Walker dangled aimlessly. A growing wind then blew him to the right and made him sway under a heavy branch. Whoever had done this knew just the right branch to do this from. Walker's eyes were rolled back in his head and his weathered face appeared dark blue, even in the moonlight. The rope around his neck was thick and rough.

Zeke looked deeper and deeper into that horrible face; he couldn't help himself. And that's when he turned around and dove behind a tree, vomiting uncontrollably.

Finally, after a few minutes, his head started to clear. His hat had fallen off and his mouth had an ugly taste in it. He reached up and wiped his mouth with a sleeve, then sat back on the ground, still not believing it.

Gradually, Zeke made himself look upward and found that he still winced at the sight.

He picked up his hat and put it back on. Then he got up off the ground as he gathered his thoughts. *Well, one thing's for sure: The old man didn't kill himself.*

Zeke quickly picked up the rifle and then looked towards the house.

It was dark. But that didn't mean it was empty.

With Walker dead, were the women still all right? Were they even there? His heart raced as he thought of the dreadful possibilities.

With the Henry rifle in front of him, he approached the fence with caution, especially now that he no longer had the cover of the trees. Then, a few yards further, he spotted a part of the fence still in the shadow of a cottonwood. Moving quickly, he went over to the section and silently climbed over it.

The timing seemed to be right, with the moon now hidden behind some drifting clouds. With his head low, he ran swiftly in the darkness, his memory mapping out the grounds as he remembered them that afternoon. He ran quickly and soon got behind those same bushes he had hidden behind earlier.

Out of the corner of his eye, he saw something gleam from the direction of the barn. He turned the rifle towards it and immediately felt his heart sink. Between the house and the barn, he saw the iron doors of the basement prison sticking out of the ground. They had been thrown wide open.

His heart raced now. *They couldn't still be there, could they?* One way or the other, he had to find out.

Zeke looked again at the house. It was still dark and still quiet. Not a light, nor a sound or movement. *Where was Cal? Was he hanged also?*

Then he looked toward the barn and froze at the sight. Those doors had also been thrown open; not one bit of stock was left. The covered wagon was gone too.

Zeke rose and went quickly across the clearing, his eyes taking in everything that was possible to see in the semi-darkness. He watched the house closely as he passed. Yet the moon was still behind the clouds and when Zeke looked toward the windows, he couldn't make them out.

Then he remembered the portholes in the front wall.

As if answering him, the clouds parted then, and something made Zeke look again at the house. There, it took him but a second to spot something that caught a spill of moonlight.

A gleam off the end of a rifle barrel as it poked its way through one of the portholes. He saw it just before it exploded, a sharp flash aimed in his direction.

Zeke's dive saved his life. A rifle ball flew through the air at the very spot his chest would have been. Now he was just inches from the open basement doors, his rifle falling away as he hit the dirt.

Then dense clouds drifted in again and covered the moon completely, plunging the clearing into total darkness. Zeke frantically searched the ground as another ball buried itself near his boot. He scrambled forward like a crab, inching ahead as yet another ball flew over his hat.

That was when the earth seemed to open up before him and he fell, his outstretched arms reaching out for something to catch hold of and finding hard wooden steps. The momentum carried him forward and then he tumbled, over and over again. His body bounced against the wooden steps and his hands bruised as he tried to lessen the impact of the fall. Finally, after what seemed like forever, his body hit the bottom, his hat flying off somewhere.

The basement floor was hard-packed dirt. A harsh light glared at him from ten feet away. Focusing his eyes to the light, he saw a lantern that had been set on the floor, its flame withering slightly as the wind blew down through the open doors. Someone had apparently forgotten about it, perhaps someone in a hurry.

Zeke sat up, his body wracked in pain, especially his left hip. The fall, he realized, probably would have killed an older man. Then, remembering his present situation, the adrenaline within him took hold and he did his best to shake off the pain. He remembered his sister and quickly looked around.

The lantern was at low flame, but not low enough to obscure his surroundings. Then he spotted something that brought back the old rage and tightened his stomach again.

Attached to the walls were pairs of manacles, the ends driven firmly into the sod. They now dangled empty before him. Yet even in that harsh light, he spotted the dried blood on the shackles.

He smelled the putrid stench of rotting corpses coming from the dark corners of the cellar, with the squeals of what sounded like very large rats not far away. They were cowed for the present; Zeke's sudden appearance making them scurry back into the room's black corners.

Zeke pounded his fist on the dirt. Then tears came to his eyes, his body shaking violently as he cried. He had blundered into a chamber of horrors. Zeke had expected to find some evidence of their confinement—but not this...

He tried to focus on what he was doing, on what his next move should be, but when he thought of the dead women lying in the shadows, their bodies mutilated beyond recognition, he found it impossible. The tears stung him as he sat there and tried to understand why it had happened, but the answer eluded him...

His hat had fallen on the ground and a large rat started to approach it, hesitating, still cowering in the shadows. Zeke's hand closed around a rusty padlock lying on the ground and, in a rage, flung it at the creature with all his might. He saw it land in the shadows and heard it make impact. A painful squeal followed, and something flew back into the corner.

The footsteps from above approached so rapidly they shook him out of his daze. At the head of the basement steps, he saw the silhouette and a rifle pointed down at him.

"I'm so glad you came back." *Cal wasn't hanged after all— damn it!* "I said I'd give it to you one day and that day has come."

Zeke knew he didn't have time to draw, but it was almost worth a try, at least for the sake of those women...

The tears went away as he looked to the top of the steps; he was thinking fast now. He considered his position: Sitting on the ground, his right boot touching the stairway post. If he could dive behind it, he might buy the time to draw his sidearm and even the odds. Though the shot would be from a bad angle, it was worth a try.

And then he realized that Cal was the only one still around who could provide information. If he had any hope of surviving this encounter, he had to find out what happened there.

Zeke looked up at the young man at the top of the steps. He only saw a silhouette with a rifle cradled in its arms. *Get him to talk. Whatever you do, keep his mind off pulling that trigger.*

"I see they didn't get you," Zeke said quickly.

The voice hissed with malice. "Your friends hardly left a rock unturned..."

Cal still thought he was a bushwhacker. Then Morse's gang was responsible for the hanging and taking the women away. But where?

"Oh, they took the women already?" Zeke asked, trying to sound as if he expected it to happen.

"You know it!" Cal replied bitterly. "I hid in the barn, up in the loft. Figured they'd come back to burn the place. What happened? They send you back to destroy the evidence?"

"You know," said Zeke, "when Charlie gets those women further south, he's going to get a good price for them. There's still time to let you in for a cut of the profits."

The young man's tone was resentful. "Gee, thanks! It's a long way to Arkansas. Anything can happen, and I hope it does! I hope the Yanks come along and fill those buzzards full of holes, every stinkin' one of them! Especially those bitches!"

With those last words, the façade Zeke had carefully built up dropped immediately and his casual stare quickly turned mean.

Seeing the look, even in the shadows, Cal crowed, "That's right, Tyler! You said that if I had treated those girls in—let's say a less than gentlemanly way—that I'd wish I never was born or some such nonsense. Well, I just want to tell you I got so much out of those women that if they live through all this, I'd daresay there'd be nothin' left for any decent man to fool with."

As Zeke sat on the ground his knuckles grew white and it took all he had in him to control his shaky vision.

Then he calmed down all at once and when he spoke to Cal, the voice coming out of him was cold as ice.

"What happened to your father, Cal? Did he run off like a yellow dog when they showed up—like you did?"

"My pa's probably trackin' 'em."

"All the way to Arkansas? Come on, boy, where is he?"

Zeke couldn't clearly make out his face, but it was obvious the young man was confused.

He didn't know. Now to get him riled. It might even affect his aim.

"I found your father."

"What do you mean you found him?" Cal's voice was rising as Zeke relished the young man's confusion.

"He's dead, that's what I mean," Zeke said deliberately.

"What?"

"Yeah. Dead as your brain."

"You're lyin'!"

"Look outside the fence! He's back up in the trees, about twelve feet off the ground!"

Then Zeke heard angry tears in the young man's voice as he repeated, not too convincingly, "You're lyin'!"

"Go see for yourself!" Zeke's hand drifted down to his holster.

Then he saw the silhouette raise the rifle and aim. Tearfully, Cal shouted, "You're a damn yellow liar!"

Now.

Zeke threw himself behind the post and drew his pistol, instantly cocking the hammer. In that quick moment, he heard a rifle discharge, then a second shot.

Zeke paused. At first, he couldn't figure out why, but the reports sounded far away.

Suddenly the steps shook violently, and the sound grew as he realized a figure was tumbling down. He looked through the gap in the bottom step and saw Cal Walker hit the ground noisily, his rifle fallen away, and his limp arms stretched out on both sides. Zeke slowly rose and stared at Cal's body. Two rifle balls had gone clean through him and come out of his chest. His lifeless eyes stared at the ceiling. Just then, two rats appeared from the shadows and experimentally sniffed the fingers of his left hand.

Zeke didn't bother to shoo them away.

As he got to the stairs, he heard someone call out to him.

"Hello! Who's down there?" The voice belonged to Martha Walker.

"Zeke, you down there? Speak up!" There was no mistaking the Georgian drawl; Jim Gaines was up there as well. When he heard the third accented voice, he knew he was dreaming.

"Darlin', are you all right?" *Kelly too?*

Zeke quickly reached over and picked up his hat. Slowly he climbed the stairs. The climb was painful, and his hip still ached from the fall, but he managed to reach the top without faltering.

When he saw Jim Gaines, he grabbed the southerner's hand and shook it. "Thanks, Reb..."

Gaines looked at him and shook his head. "Wasn't me, Kansas."

Zeke looked to Kelly expectantly.

A look of sadness crossed Kelly's face as she shook her head. She was about to say something but decided against it.

A harsh realization hit him, and he faced Martha, just noticing her smoking rifle.

"It was dark," Zeke said grimly. "Maybe you didn't see him…"

"No," said Martha, her voice almost a whisper. "…I saw him."

Zeke said quietly, "You shot your brother." Then he felt like kicking himself for saying it.

Martha's voice was quivering, but she fought to control it. "No…He was no longer my brother…Not with what he's done… I'm not absolving my part in this." She looked Zeke in the eyes then, and to her surprise, found the words tumbling out. "I knew about the women. They told me they were being used as barter to free southern prisoners. I accepted that. They told me they were being treated well and I believed that too. And all this time I kept my mouth shut and went about my business. And then I noticed things. I'd be in the kitchen fixin' supper and I'd hear noises from the basement. I kept telling myself they couldn't be screams I heard—not from women who were treated well. My father and brother are not like that…Then my father tells you he's going to kill them, and I saw the look in his eyes, and I knew then and there that he meant every word. Then he calls them merchandise…like some white trash slaver! This war killed my family. Both my father and brother…dead inside." Her lower lip started to tremble, and tears came suddenly. "…And I let it happen…" She clasped her hands then, and when she looked at them they were shaking. "Jesus, forgive me!"

Kelly watched her briefly, then put her hand on her arm and turned her towards her. She stared at Martha's tear-streaked face and said quietly, "'Neither do I condemn you'…"

She fell into Kelly's arms as the Irish girl attempted to soothe her.

Zeke stared at them briefly and then turned to Gaines. "You won't believe what's down there."

"I can imagine."

"No, Jim. What was left down there…"

"And they did this to women, huh?" He raised his carbine and said, "Let's pay 'em back."

"It's not your fight, Jim."

"It's the fight of any decent man!" said Gaines, surprising Zeke with his anger. "Besides," he said quietly, leaning forward and eyeing Martha, "we saw what they did to her father. I'm also goin' along to straighten out things for her."

Then a horrified look came to Zeke's face.

Gaines asked, "What's wrong?"

Zeke was now sorry he hadn't cut down Walker's body. "She saw him?"

Gaines nodded. "She saw him. We left our animals back there where you tied yours. Then we heard shots. We kept telling Martha to slow down and be careful, but she'd have none of it. She ran up here first, and in this moonlight, she saw what she was shootin' at. She thought her brother was going to shoot one of the women…"

"We've talked enough. Morse and his friends are taking the women to Arkansas."

"Let's ride!"

Kelly gently let go of Martha and said, "Yes, let's get to the horses."

"Wait a minute!" Zeke said impatiently. "You're not coming with us."

Gaines said, "Damn right. You gals are staying here."

"No!" said Martha, drying her tears.

Kelly's voice was firm. "We're coming with you!"

"We haven't got time to argue!"

"Now you listen, Zeke Tyler—"

"No, you listen! After seeing what those killers did to those women, I'd never forgive myself if anything happened to the woman I loved! Do you understand?"

Kelly stared at him and said softly, "...Yes, I do..."

"Good!" Zeke replied sternly, ignoring what he had just admitted to her. "Come on, Jim." Gaines handed him his rifle and before Kelly could reply, they both turned and headed back towards the fence.

Martha called out, "Be careful, Jim!"

Gaines grinned and put his hand to his hat brim. "Ma'am, you just gave me another reason to come back alive."

"Jim!"

"Right there, Kansas!" Gaines turned and ran after him. They both disappeared into the night.

"We should be with them," said Martha. "Any decent person should do what they can to end this madness."

"Don't worry, hon," Kelly said confidently. "We'll be with them...and not just in spirit..."

CHAPTER EIGHTEEN

THE TRAIL WAS READ BY WHAT LITTLE MOONLIGHT COULD SPILL through the overhanging branches, still lush and full on that late August night. They rode on throughout the night, gamely following the wagon tracks which appeared plainly in the road. With darkness against them, however, they were tracking mostly by instinct.

Their horses were tired, and they lagged a bit as they covered close to twenty miles from the Walker farm.

"Zeke..."

"Yeah?"

"How many miles you think we've been goin'?"

Zeke just shrugged. His muscles still ached from the tumble down the basement steps, as well as several hours in the saddle.

"Zeke...We're going to have to stop."

Zeke shook his head. "We can't be too far from them."

"Right now, that's not the subject."

"What do you mean?"

"I mean that I feel my animal's sweat through the saddle.

We've got to stop, Zeke. And soon. Or we're goin' to be stuck out in the middle of nowhere with two lame horses."

Zeke looked at him grimly. "They've got a few hours on us, Jim. We've got no choice but to catch up and catch up fast."

Gaines stared at him and said bluntly, "She's gonna keep, Zeke. She'll still be there when we arrive."

Zeke glared at him. "You sure of that?"

"Stop and think for a minute," Gaines said earnestly. "If they wanted to kill her, they wouldn't have bothered to take her with them. Look at this trail. They didn't stop, they didn't kick anyone off the wagon. They still have her. But they *will* stop, they've got to! They're probably killin' their own horses. But it's a long way from Arkansas—and a wagon will slow 'em up some. They've got to rest and so do we! Believe me, Zeke, they may not be givin' those women a seven-course meal, but they've got to keep 'em alive, if only to make a deal for them later..."

Zeke winced at that remark. Yet he knew what Gaines had said was the truth and he was silent as the Georgian spoke. Zeke was tired and angry, and it showed all too plainly. Some honest words were needed to be said.

Zeke said wearily, "Let's give it another half mile."

"Quarter mile."

Zeke looked at him and then turned back to the trail.

He shook his head and said, "Southerners..."

They camped deep within a grove of cottonwoods some fifty yards off the trail. Both men sat at their bedrolls, a fire burning before them. Jim Gaines held a newly rolled cigarette and studied the end of it.

"You're a lucky man, Zeke Tyler."

Zeke's eyes narrowed as he watched the Georgian. "How do

you figure that?" he asked grimly. "Have you forgotten why we're out here?"

Gaines took a deep drag stared at him. Then he said lightly, "You're still a lucky man...That Irish gal loves you. I hooked up with her while she was on her way to Warrensburg."

"What was she riding to Warrensburg for?"

"She was lookin' for you, you damn fool!"

Zeke stared at the fire and thought about Kelly. He was already sorry he hadn't embraced her back there at the farm or showed her that he was in any way grateful to see her again.

He said sadly, "I didn't even say how glad I was to see her..."

Gaines said dryly, "After you admitted you loved her, I thought she got the idea."

Zeke's eyes widened. "I said *that?*"

"Don't you remember? When you were warnin' her not to come along?"

"I was still upset by what I'd seen. I guess I was excited."

Gaines stared hard at him through the drifting smoke. "Well, do you love her or don't you?"

"Of course, I do!"

Gaines sat back with a satisfied smile. "Well, now she knows it too."

Zeke looked at his boots absently. "I wanted to tell her in my own way...when all of this was over."

"No time like the present."

"At least she's safe. Away from all this."

Watching him with some amusement, Gaines said, "I wouldn't worry too much about her safety if I was you."

Zeke looked at him. "What's that supposed to mean?"

"It means she's already killed somebody."

"What?"

"Shot a Yankee soldier. Put two balls in him."

Zeke's eyes widened further. "You're making this up."

Gaines raised his right hand. "As God is my witness..."

"I still don't believe you."

"Don't believe me, ask her! Three bluecoats rode up to her on the Warrensburg road and one of them dragged her off her horse. I was watchin' them from back in the trees and I figure this was more than just a 'routine search,' if ya know what I mean. The Yankee was twistin' her arm too. I shot two of them, but your Colleen blasted the sergeant twice. Saved my life too. She kept her eyes on him while I was jabberin' away...She risks her safety for you. She'd follow you to the ends of the earth if she had to. Now if a woman's ready to follow a man that far, if it's not love maybe she just has wanderlust."

Zeke sat perfectly still and stared at his hat on the ground. He noticed the shadows of clouds starting to drift in. Gaines laid back on his bedroll and looked at the sky.

Finally, after a few minutes, Zeke asked, "Where'd you find Martha?"

Gaines replied, "Found her on the road headin' back to the farm. When we asked her about you, she told us the whole story. And the things you said..." He crushed out the cigarette and then folded his hands on his chest as he gazed at the night sky.

Zeke looked at him and said quietly, "I'm sorry about that."

Still watching the sky, the Georgian shrugged and said, "Forget it now. Guess you would call that something you said 'in the heat of the moment', or somethin' like that. I've said some things like that to my folks before I left home...I'm sorry to say..."

"No. I'll always be ashamed about that," said Zeke.

After a moment, Gaines said, "Martha's a sad girl. I doubt she's had any kind of upbringin' with a father and brother like that."

"We all have problems."

"Yeah, but she's alone now."

Zeke looked at him with a wry smile. "Looks like she needs a man from Georgia to look after her."

Gaines looked at him sharply. "Where'd you get that idea from?"

"I was heading back to the horses, but I still heard, 'Jim, be careful.' She didn't tell *me* to be careful."

Gaines looked back to the stars. "She's just bein' kindly."

"Kindly, my foot. She likes you."

"You hush!"

"All right," said Zeke, lying back on his bedroll. "But if I were you, I'd do something about it."

"Yankee, heal thyself!"

Zeke grinned as he clasped his hands behind his head and also stared at the sky. It felt good to smile; it was the first time he had really smiled since Lawrence. Then his mind went to the task ahead and he became serious again. He hoped that his sister would still be alive at the end of this.

They said nothing for several minutes.

Then Gaines broke the silence and said, "Storm clouds." He sounded concerned.

Zeke looked in his direction. He could only see him through the glare of the fire. "What do you mean?"

"If you'd been campin' in the wild for years like I've been, you'd notice. Look up."

Zeke turned back to look at the moon and found dark clouds covering it, blotting out all light and bringing with it a sharp wind. The cold struck Zeke immediately and sent a chill through him. He was disturbed by the speed with which the wind came; it had seemed so warm just a moment before.

Still staring at the sky, Gaines said, "This ain't good, Zeke. Ain't good at all."

"How bad?"

Gaines took a deep breath and his shoulders tensed as he searched the darkness above. "I used to see storms like this when I was passin' through Arkansas and the Carolinas. When I was six, my grandma used to say that they picked folks up right off the ground and took them straight to Heaven...It's gonna be bad, Zeke. And you and me are ridin' right into it."

Zeke raised up on an elbow and he looked at Gaines across the fire. He paused before he finally said the word, almost in a whisper. "Tornado?"

Gaines shrugged, still watching the sky. The clouds drifted away again and gradually the moon appeared.

"Maybe a tornado. Maybe it's a cyclone. Or maybe it's gonna be the kind of wind that knocks an old man's hat off, I don't know. But I'd give it some time tomorrow. That's when it's gonna kick up. And when it does, it's gonna play hell with our trail. It might wipe out their tracks before we can catch up—and that's just the good news. You and me are gonna be out in the open. Even if we found a farmhouse for some shelter, that won't help either. Unless we find a spot to hide below ground, we're buyin' a good chance of bein' blown up into the sky and not hittin' the ground for a week! By then we'll be too dead to worry about it."

"You think Morse's bunch knows that?"

Gaines shrugged again. "I don't know, Kansas. Either way, this is not a good time to take a long ride..."

Zeke looked at him hard. The clouds had parted, and he could see Gaines clearly now.

"Do you want to turn back?"

Gaines turned from looking at the sky and stared at the Kansan. He said earnestly, "When General Sherman kisses my ass."

Zeke grinned at him. Then they both laid back in their

bedrolls and said nothing for hours. That was because, despite their worries, they immediately fell asleep…

When dawn came, the sun shone on the town of Kingston with a brighter glow than usual. Several miles north of town, a lonely waystation stood in the hot sun and cast long shadows across the trails.

A lush forest had once existed where now there was an inter-section with a small house and stable nestled in the middle. One road at the crossing went to the town of Holden. The other road, continuing southeast, went on to Kingston and beyond it, Clinton and dozens of other small towns on the long winding road to Arkansas. The waystation was a swing stop on the stage line to Independence. For years it had been run by a middle-aged German fellow named Holtzmeyer and his teenaged son, Hans.

The stage was not due until much later that day and Holtzmeyer was hoping to sleep late, especially after a night of drinking and card playing over in Kingston. This morning, however, he rose at sunrise. The shades were torn, and the sun's rays lit up Holtzmeyer's room like a beacon. When he sat up and rubbed his eyes, even he thought it was strange.

It was shortly after he sat up that he heard the horses approaching outside. He looked at the clock on the nightstand and saw that it was far too early for the stage or anyone else to travel there. He dressed quickly, without stopping to wash his hands or face.

As he was putting on his shirt, Holtzmeyer passed his son's room. Hans was getting out of bed slowly and stretching.

"What is it, Pa?"

"I don't know, Hans. Someone's outside."

"This early?"

Holtzmeyer just shrugged and started for the front door.

When he went outside, he suddenly turned and saw the two men coming around the side of the house. He looked at them carefully. He didn't like the looks of either of them.

Charlie Morse, with his dark hair and piercing eyes under a crisp black Stetson, looked all too serious. And Mart Janey, with his big, sweaty face and crooked smile, his body tightly wrapped in an undersized shirt and suspenders, looked almost clownish.

Holtzmeyer didn't like their looks at all, especially the one with that awful grin.

"Yes?" he asked. "Can I help you?"

Once the two strangers heard his accented voice, they looked at each other.

Janey laughed.

"This'll be easier than we thought, huh, Charlie?"

Morse remained serious. "And a lot more fun."

Holtzmeyer eyed both of them, not quite understanding their private joke.

"Is there anything you want? I—"

Morse quickly cut him off. His voice showed contempt.

"You alone, Dutchie?"

Holtzmeyer straightened up indignantly and glared at him. He had come to America just a few years ago and wasn't that proficient in English, but he understood very well what 'Dutchie' meant.

"Why don't you men leave?" said Holtzmeyer angrily. "And don't come back!"

Janey laughed.

"He still don't see what's goin' on, does he, Charlie?"

A voice from the house said, "I see what's going on already."

Holtzmeyer quickly turned around and saw his son leaving the house and approaching them with a loaded Colt shotgun.

"Hans!"

"Don't worry, Pa," Hans said, eyeing the other two men.

Mart Janey laughed and said, "Hell, Charlie. Look at the tough little Dutchman."

Hans' eyes narrowed and he turned the gun barrel towards the fat man. "You'll be pulling buckshot out of your belly, my fat friend...Now get on your horses and ride out. *Now!*"

Janey's laughter drifted away slowly, and he put his hands to his eyes, as if wiping away tears. He wandered behind Charlie Morse just as Morse took a step forward.

Hans stood beside his father, pointing the shotgun barrel just inches from Morse's belly.

"I said move!"

Morse's stance seemed to relax then. He looked at Hans with sympathy and said earnestly, "I'm sorry, kid." His hands came up and gestured at the two Germans apologetically. "...We meant no harm."

Suddenly Morse's right hand shot out like a cobra and wrapped itself around the gun barrel, pushing it upward.

At the same time, Morse stepped to his right, revealing Mart Janey with his gun out. Without hesitation, he shot the young German twice in the stomach. Before the hammer of Janey's gun came down a second time, a wide patch of blood appeared across Hans' shirt and he crumpled to the ground with his arms across his stomach.

In horror, Holtzmeyer cried out his son's name. Then he faced Janey and lunged at him. Grinning easily, Janey cocked the hammer of the Navy Colt and fired; then cocked it and fired again, emptying his gun.

Holtzmeyer grabbed his right side, his fingers already covered in blood. His knees then buckled under him and he fell to the ground next to his son. Janey's first shot punctured Holtzmeyer's side, but the second shot misfired with just a flash and a pungent whiff of smoke and powder.

Morse now held the shotgun as both men looked down at the bodies.

Janey chuckled and said, "Stupid Dutchman."

Morse looked around and said, "Quiet as a cave. No one coming out to see what happened. I told you, I passed by this place not long ago. I knew it was just them. And we'll have more than enough time to rest up before the stage gets here."

Holstering his gun, Janey looked down at them and asked, "What about these two?"

"Drag 'em off into the woods. Don't want to get the ladies anymore upset than they already are, do we?"

"The wagon's not far behind us. They must've heard the shots and that old Dutchie yellin'."

"Let those tramps think what they want. But seeing these two on the ground might rile 'em some—especially after Beaucaire's latest move. And we don't want any unnecessary rebellions."

Janey shook his head and said, "I don't believe that Beaucaire. He wants at least two of them girls."

"I think some of them old boys who live in those mansions might want a woman who's a little more experienced at her chores. Beaucaire's just breakin' 'em in for us. Just like breakin' in any good horse..."

Janey laughed and then bent over and started to pull Hans' body away.

When the others finally arrived at the crossroads, the covered wagon was pulled into the barn and the door locked. Of the twelve kidnapped young females, there were now nine left. Two of them had died from malnutrition and were lying in the basement of the Walker farm. Another girl, barely sixteen, was taken off the wagon by Jean Beaucaire a mile before the crossroads. Then he dragged her out in the woods as she kicked and struggled and shot her in the head. He returned to the wagon and merely informed the girls that he had paroled her. The frightened women knew what that meant in bushwhacker talk.

It seemed that Beaucaire had remembered the girl because she had the gall to resist his advances a couple days before. To him, it seemed an appropriate moment to pay her back. He felt that covering her with a black sheet afterwards was a nice touch.

The wagon had then continued down the trail in the direction of the waystation, carefully covered from the rear by Tom Janey with a Spencer rifle. If anyone had attempted to jump from the wagon, Janey would have aimed at the woman's head and fired— and Janey was never known to miss.

Within the confines of the small wagon were several starving women who felt they had no hope. Prominent among them was the youngest, thirteen-year old Ruth Tyler, her face reddened by seemingly endless tears. She already knew that her parents were dead and hoped that through all this madness, her big brother was still alive. In the meantime, her own suffering continued.

Home seemed further away than ever...

CHAPTER NINETEEN

By MID-AFTERNOON, THE WEATHER HAD TAKEN A SUDDEN dramatic turn. The sun that had glowed so brightly was now all but covered by black clouds. It was past two o'clock and it seemed more night than day.

At the waystation, Morse, Beaucaire, Mart Janey and Ben Connelly slept while Tom Janey kept his rifle pointed at the locked doors of the barn. The horses had been removed and tied to a fence circling the rear of the house.

The men had eaten what they could find in the kitchen of the Holtzmeyer house and eaten well. Outside of being given some water, the women, weak and begging for food, had not eaten in thirty hours.

The winds had suddenly picked up speed and the horses moved uncomfortably at the back fence. Leaves blew around the house in a never-ending whirlwind and gusts pounded at the windows, shaking them violently. Despite all this, the men inside slept peacefully.

Inside the barn, the women felt the sudden chill and tried to keep warm as best they could. The quick downturn in the weather, besides their present misery, upset them even more; that is, those women who hadn't passed out from hunger...

The winds blew harshly through the trees a few miles up the trail. With their Stetsons tied down on their heads by chinstraps, the two trackers kept their mounts to a trot so as not to miss any unusual markings on the ground. They squinted their eyes in the mounting wind, noticing that the wagon tracks, though still there, seemed to be disappearing as they spotted them.

"See there?" said Gaines, pointing at the ground. "That's the reason we've been able to follow them as long as we have. Deep wheel tracks in the ground. A wagon with a heavy load. I can hardly see the hoof prints anymore. If not for that wagon, we might've lost them way back there."

Zeke shouted in the wind. "It'll take days before they cross the state line. You think they'll stop soon?"

"They might've stopped already for all we know, but I doubt it. No sign of a camp anywhere on the trail. And if they turned anywhere off the trail to camp in the woods, we would've seen where they turned.

"Good thing I'm not a stranger to this trail. Ol' Herb Talley rode some of us up from Arkansas once. We camped outside Clinton and then came up through Kingston on our way to Lone Jack. There are a couple of stage stops on the way and those places aren't exactly crowded."

"You think they stopped at one."

"They've got to eat. And they could change their horses too."

"And how are they going to explain those women hostages to the station line boss?"

Gaines took his eyes off the tracks and stared at Zeke. He said wryly, "They'll explain it with their guns."

"We better ride!"

After they mounted, they noticed that the winds were picking up speed, blowing dirt and dry leaves into their faces. Eventually, the howling winds started to make talking difficult and the two men found themselves shouting in order to be heard. Desperately, they both pulled their collars up and used their neckerchiefs to keep the blowing debris off their faces. The horses too, gamely fought through the dust and pieces of bark being blown off ancient cottonwoods and hitting their eyes.

Then, a mile and a half later, as they passed a grove of cottonwoods to their right, Zeke stopped and held up his hand.

Gaines stopped and looked at him.

"What is it?"

Zeke pointed into the grove, already darkened by the rapidly moving clouds overhead.

"I'm not sure, but there's something back there."

Gaines followed Zeke's gaze and saw something on the ground about fifty feet away, something crumpled and oblong, partly wrapped in a black sheet, one end of it now flapping in the mounting wind.

They looked at each other, then quickly dismounted. After tying their horses to the nearest trees, they both ran over to the strange object.

When they stopped at the figure, Zeke looked uncertainly at his friend.

"I can do it, Zeke," Gaines said.

"No," Zeke said, a catch in his throat. "I'll do it. I already know it's not her. The figure's too tall."

He crouched down and quickly lifted the sheet.

Gaines winced. Zeke's face was hard and grim as the wind lashed at him. He had witnessed sights like this too often recently, and ironically, he was getting used to them.

"Who was she?" Gaines asked.

Zeke shook his head sadly. "No one would know anyway. The ball took off half her face."

Then Zeke was startled to hear the click of a pistol cylinder and he looked up and saw Jim Gaines checking his ammunition. The Georgian whipped the cylinder back into place and put the gun into his holster. His face was taut under the brim of his tied down Stetson.

"Let's fix 'em," he said.

Zeke rose to his feet and said urgently, "First, we'd better know what we're doin'. We ride in there half-cocked and they'll kill everyone. If they did stop somewhere, we'd better be real quiet when we show up."

"Agreed. Let's go…"

Ben Connelly was seated in a wooden chair in a corner of the main room, tottering on the chair's two back legs, his other leg propped against the dining room wall for balance. He was picking his teeth after the meal he had just finished. Morse was sitting at the long table, wolfing down the eggs Connelly had fixed him.

The women were still locked in the barn, with Tom Janey and his Spencer standing guard outside. Tumbleweeds and dried shrubbery were thrown around the perimeters of the barn and Janey was told to have his matches ready. Morse had ordered the barn burned at the first sighting of a Union patrol.

Beaucaire was seated on the porch with a perfect view of both roads. It would still be a couple hours before a stage arrived and there was now serious thought in Independence of post-poning the trip due to word of the approaching storm. It seemed to be getting colder by the minute. Beaucaire had not brought a coat on this trip and he regretted it now. After all, it was still summer. Who would expect the temperature to drop so fast? He had riding gloves on and a long-sleeved ranch shirt, but he still shivered, huddling in a corner of the porch under the low roof.

Connelly continued to rock in his chair, his long legs bending as he went back and forth, but the creaking noise drove Morse crazy.

He slammed his fork down on the plate.

"Will you stop that!"

Connelly stopped rocking, but kept the chair hovered on two legs. He looked at Morse absently.

"What's wrong with you?" Morse asked harshly.

Connelly didn't answer him. He just turned back and faced the wall, lost in thought.

"I asked you a question, Ben."

"I've been thinkin'."

"Oh? About what, as if I didn't know?" He shoved a forkful of eggs into his mouth.

"We can't do it, Charlie..."

Morse wiped his mouth abruptly and scowled at him.

"Is that so?"

"Yes, Charlie. That is so..."

Morse swallowed his eggs, then said lightly, "We're getting away with it, Ben. We'll be in Arkansas in two days."

"Or we'll be dead today..."

Morse turned from his plate to glare at Connelly. "You're sounding defeatist, Ben. The South doesn't need defeatists. We need *men*." He had said it to insult Connelly, but the tall man in the chair didn't seem to hear him.

"We're gonna come up empty, Charlie...It's there right in front of us, but we're too dumb to see it."

Morse's tone was sarcastic. "And what is this important bit of information?"

"We're bein' followed, Charlie..." For the first time, Connelly turned to look at Morse and saw him sitting at his plate, glaring back at him. Despite the look, he kept talking. "He's comin' after us and we're sittin' here loafin' around and stuffin' our faces while he bears down on us." He shook his head sadly. "It was in front of us all the time and we never suspected a thing. I never suspected..."

Morse's face grew livid in the harsh glare of the nearby lantern and he threw his napkin down angrily.

"Who the hell are you talking about?"

Connelly suddenly leaned forward and the movement dropped the chair to the floor with a loud thud.

"I'll tell you who it is!" Connelly said, his voice rising. "Believe me, Charlie, I was asleep along with the rest of you. But this morning, when we moved the girls into that barn, that blonde-haired girl leaned out of the wagon and begged me to feed the older women. It was when she leaned over right into the sunlight and the light struck those blue eyes of hers, that's when it hit me. It was then and there I knew who she was. I asked her what her name was, but I swear to you, Charlie, I already knew it!"

"So?" Morse said impatiently. "Who was she? Dolly Madison?"

Connelly leaned closer and now his expression was angry. He said plainly, "Her name's Ruth Tyler."

"That supposed to mean something to me?"

"You still don't understand, do you, Charlie? And you had him in your house, looked into those same sad eyes and even hired him! Lookin' back on it, Charlie, I still can't believe how stupid you were..."

Morse abruptly rose from the table and went over to Connelly. With a fast hand, he grabbed Connelly's coat lapel and yanked him to his feet. Connelly's hat fell back to the floor and he instinctively reached up and put his hand on Morse's fist.

"One more word," said Morse, his eyes ablaze, "and I'll break you in two!"

Connelly looked up into Morse's eyes.

Then a smile played around his lips. "There's fear in your eyes, Charlie," he said wryly. "And believe me, you've got good reason to be scared."

Morse's other fist came up and socked Connelly just under the chin. The lanky man went down, falling heavily into the chair and crashing through it. Then he sat up amidst the broken wood around him and felt his jaw. But his eyes remained on Morse and they still held amusement. He even managed to grin at Morse as the other man grew angrier by the second.

Mart Janey ran in from the other room. He had been dozing and when he entered, his Colt was already in his hand. He was wearing a rare serious expression. When he saw Connelly on the ground and Morse standing belligerently over him, he didn't know what to think.

Morse looked down at him, breathing fast. Sweat appeared on his chin and forehead and the fists at his sides were trembling slightly.

Connelly noticed it and said quietly, "You always were scared of somethin' you didn't understand. Always lashin' out at anything you couldn't control...that's why you were such a fireball in Lawrence! All those free-staters you hanged. All those Negroes. You even stayed behind to watch 'em choke on the rope. Hell, even I couldn't watch that! But now you've got someone comin' after you who just won't stop. And when he *does* catch up with you, we'll see who breaks who apart..."

The gun sprung into Morse's palm before he realized it. His hand trembled as he held it.

Janey knew that Morse was a hair away from pulling the trigger. He was keeping it all inside, not verbalizing his rage. Instead he was waiting for the words from Connelly that would prompt him to fire.

"Charlie," said Janey experimentally. "Now, Charlie..."

Connelly, in his own way, was actually enjoying Morse's fear. His face seemed to jeer at the man standing over him.

"Yes, sir, *Colonel* Morse!" said Connelly wryly. "That's the title you always wanted...Takin' Bill Quantrill's place."

"Shut up, Ben!" Janey shouted desperately. Gently he said to Morse, "Don't listen to 'em, Charlie. He doesn't know what he's sayin'. He's a little drunk, that's all...Saw 'em with a bottle before... Now...just put up your sidearm and let 'em be. Come on, Charlie, we need him. Put up your gun..."

"I have news for you, Charlie," said Connelly, acting as if Janey weren't there. "You can cross the state line all the way to hell and he'll still follow you!"

Janey saw the face behind the gun and shouted, "For Christ sakes, Charlie, say something!"

"He can't!" cried Connelly. "The fear's got him! Fear of something coming for him that he doesn't understand. And there's nothing he could do about it." And then, he added quietly, "Not a damn thing."

The gun exploded in the small confines of that corner and echoed around the house, carried outside and was soon muffled by the fast winds building throughout the county.

Beaucaire ran into the house. Tom Janey would've ran in as well, but he had strict orders not to leave the women alone.

As the smoke rose from Morse's gun, Connelly looked to the entrance and saw a sober-faced Beaucaire run in with his gun drawn. Then he looked up into the eyes of the man who killed him.

There was a bleeding hole in Connelly's stomach, but when he looked up and still saw the unreasoning fear in Morse's eyes, he managed to smile. It was the last thing he saw before he slumped to the floor.

Beaucaire and Mart Janey stared at them from across the room, holding drawn guns helplessly.

Janey was the first to speak. "Charlie..."

Morse stared at Connelly's body; his face was grim, and his gun was still pointed down at him. Then slowly he holstered his gun, still staring at the body.

"Charlie," asked Beaucaire, "what brought that on?"

Mart Janey answered for him. "Ben said we were bein' trailed by somebody, but he was full of it. And then he starts ridin' Charlie. I didn't get all of it. I just think he was getting' cold feet, know what I mean? He never looked like he was doin' any of this with his heart in it, you know?...You did right, Charlie, and good riddance to 'em!"

Charlie Morse held himself absolutely still. He was still looking at the floor, trying to relax as the seconds passed.

"Charlie?"

Abruptly Morse said, "Is Tom still outside the barn?"

"Sure, he is, Charlie," answered Mart. "You said you'd kill him if he stepped away, even to relieve himself." Mart grinned at that and then started laughing.

Morse spoke suddenly, the voice tight in his throat.

"Tell him to fire the barn..."

Mart stopped laughing and he and Beaucaire gaped at him.

"What's that?"

"You're jokin', aren't you, Charlie?"

Morse turned and faced them. Mart Janey actually swallowed in fear.

"You heard me..."

"But, Charlie, the money we'll get—"

"Are you deaf?" he shouted at the them. "Fire the barn! Do it!"

The two men stared at their boss, still wondering if they heard wrong.

"Are you sure, Charlie? We—"

"Yeah, I'm sure. Fire that barn. Surround it from all sides! If anyone breaks out of there while it's burning, shoot them!" He looked at them both and unconsciously put his hand on the butt of his gun. "...Is that clear?"

"Clear enough, Charlie," said Mart quietly. "And we'll do it... But why?"

"Let's just say," Morse answered grimly, "I've got my reasons."

Beaucaire finally found his voice. "We're going to have some trouble getting a fire going. The wind is kicking up pretty bad. Tom can hardly keep that loose sagebrush in place outside the barn walls, it keeps blowing away..."

Morse glanced at the lantern hung over the sideboard.

"Take that," he said. "Fling it against the outside wall. Pour kerosene around the outside, that'll help."

"If we take that lantern, you'll be left in the dark."

"I don't care! Take it! Look around and see if you can find more lanterns. All of you toss 'em on all four sides of the barn. While it burns, stand there and wait. Gun anyone who tries to break free. When the bluecoats find the wreckage, there'll be no trace of 'em."

"'Cept their bones..."

"The wind'll take care of that. Blow their bones into the sky... It'll just be a horrible accident that happened inside a tinderbox of a barn."

"You sure you want that, Charlie?"

"I'm sure...Remember, ashes can't talk."

Mart and Beaucaire looked at each other, then turned to look around the house for other lanterns. Mart took the one by the sideboard. Its light moved with his huge bulk as he left the room and long, distorted shadows fell across Morse's face as he stood watching them.

After they went into the other rooms, Charlie Morse sat down. He had lost his appetite and the tension within him did not subside.

He just sat there in the dark, his soul as empty as the gun at his side...

CHAPTER TWENTY

THE BARN WAS SITUATED FURTHER BEHIND THE HOUSE AND TO THE right, with a dense forest of tall cottonwoods surrounding the back. Long branches reached out and literally scraped the outside walls, shifted about by the increasing winds. For the frightened women, the front doors were the only way out.

Tom Janey held onto his hat and put up his collar. He was grossly overweight, and the gusting winds made his breathing labored. Still, he would keep close watch on those doors unless told otherwise. He had pulled a lantern from the barn earlier and kept it on the ground, surrounding it with large stones so the flame wouldn't blow out. It was his only source of heat.

He had his Spencer under his arm and was warming his hands when he heard his twin brother's voice coming from the rear of the house. Tom took deep breaths and slowly walked around the side of the barn. Facing the house, he saw his brother's head sticking out the window. He was glad to see Mart, hoping he was finally relieving him, and he could get out of that blasted wind.

"Am I bein' relieved?"

"You will be soon."

"When?"

Mart Janey paused before shouting again. "You still got that lantern?"

"Yeah, why?"

"We'll join you soon. We're gonna fire the barn!"

"What!"

"That's right, we're gonna fire the barn!"

"What about the money we'll get for 'em?"

Mart shook his head slightly and shrugged. "Charlie said to do it. I figure he must know someone's after us and they're gettin' close."

"Don't make any sense!"

"He's givin' the orders."

Tom just stared at him, disbelieving. Then a full curtain of dust blew between his huge form and the house.

"If this keeps up, we won't need the fire. The wind'll blow every stick of wood off the ground—including that barn!"

"Charlie wants to make sure there's nothin' left of them."

"...All right. He's the boss."

"That's right."

"This is a rotten deal, Mart, and you know it."

Mart looked at his brother and then his eyes searched the sky, squinting through the blowing dust. Then he said, "That Charlie's a wildcat, Tom. You know if you cross him you might as well commit suicide. He'd just about tear us to pieces."

Tom huddled in the cold. "Let's figure a 'cross later. It's damn cold out here!...Listen, I checked around the house before. There's a basement behind the house, clear over on the other side. Found two wooden doors covered in sagebrush. Needed the brush for some kindling and that's when I found 'em."

"Was it locked?"

"Wide open! Dutchie must've kept it as a hiding place in case of trouble...After we fire the barn, the rest of us better get down there. There's some canned food and couple of lanterns...Think the others know about it?"

"I don't know...What're you thinkin'?"

"That maybe you and me and them valuable women could go down there and leave the rest of 'em to their maker."

Mart smiled for the first time since looking out the window. "I like it, Tom. I like it a lot...Talk to you again in fifteen minutes."

"Right."

Mart was about to go back in, but then he stuck his head out the window once more. His shout stopped Tom as he was turning away.

"Oh, Tom."

"What now?"

"Ben Connelly's dead."

"*What?!*"

But his brother had already gone back inside and shut the window after him.

Tom Janey just stood in the winds, a baffled look on his clownish face. Then he shook his head and turned back to the barn. He walked back around the side and returned to his original post as the winds mounted again. He peered over at the lantern behind the stones on the ground. Bending over slightly he put his rifle on the ground and then reached out toward the flame, hoping to warm his hands.

That's when the movement in the shrubbery caused him to stop in mid-bend. The howl of the wind followed this sound immediately. He paused and thought about it. *Just the wind.*

Suddenly in the distance the sound of tearing wood and earth shattered the howling winds and hovered in the air. Then a sharp crash to the ground followed.

Tom Janey stood erect and stared at the forest behind him. He spotted a huge cloud of dirt and leaves flying up a hundred yards from the barn.

A tree had fallen to the ground, blown over by the powerful winds. A big tree too.

Tom Janey had seen what a tornado could do down in his native Louisiana. He had seen a building made of wood and adobe sitting right in its path blow apart as if a cannon had been fired at it.

He and Mart better snatch those women away quick. And then after the storm, the two brothers will take the women out to the surface—where there'll be no survivors—and the Janeys will go into business for themselves. Mart will come back in fifteen minutes and—

Then he heard it again. A swishing of branches—they weren't blown rhythmically as if by the wind—they were pushed aside by someone.

But he still wasn't sure. Who would be out there during all this ruckus? The gathering clouds had thrown darkness around the area, and when Janey looked around, his eyes couldn't distinguish one object from another.

Quickly he bent over again and this time picked up the lantern. He held it in front of him cautiously, his other hand halfway around the wick to prevent it from going out. He raised it experimentally and watched the trees before him.

There. The movement was heard again. It was instantly followed by something more easily recognized.

A hammer being pulled back on a long gun.

Tom Janey turned immediately to his left and was shocked to see old man Holtzmeyer standing there, his side and torso covered with blood and pointing the Colt rifle right at him.

Holtzmeyer was breathing fast and barely standing on his feet.

He was exactly eight feet away from Janey and his expression was macabre.

"You killed my son!" was all he said as an introduction.

Tom Janey stared at him and swallowed nervously. He had heard that two Dutchmen were killed before he, Beaucaire and Connelly had pulled up with the wagon. Yet he hadn't seen their bodies disposed of and the sudden appearance of Holtzmeyer scared him.

"What?"

"You killed my son!" shouted Holtzmeyer, with all his waning strength.

Tom Janey nervously watched the barrel of his rifle and said, "Who are you? I ain't never seen you before!"

"You coward!" Holtzmeyer screamed in the wind. "You deny it?"

"I ain't never seen you *or* your boy! I don't know what the hell you're talkin' about!"

"With my own eyes I saw you kill him—as I'm going to kill you!"

With his rifle lying harmlessly on the ground, Tom Janey was truly helpless. With the German's rifle only a few feet from him and pointed at his belly, he knew he had no chance to draw his Navy Colt.

Panic took hold of him suddenly. He had always maimed and killed men, women and children and always had a good laugh afterwards. But suddenly this old Dutchie came out of nowhere and—

"Wait a minute!" shouted Tom shrilly. "It wasn't me! You want my brother!"

For the first time, the old German actually smiled through his pain. He shook his head.

"It took everything I had in me...lying out there in the woods where you and your friend threw me—and where you threw my poor son! I refused to die—until I had a chance to come for you..."

Sweat formed on Janey's forehead despite the mounting cold.

"Listen to me!" he shouted. "It *wasn't* me! It was my brother. We're twins. Listen to me! You've got to listen! I'll—I'll even take you to him. He's the one you want to kill."

The rifle leveled.

Janey saw it and his whole body trembled. "Listen to me. I didn't kill your son! It was Mart! Please, for the love of God!"

Tears were forming in Janey's eyes and fearfully he lifted the lantern in a vain attempt at protection.

Holtzmeyer was breathing hard and his strength ebbed fast. He knew his time was growing short.

"Please!" Janey kept repeating. "It wasn't me!"

Holtzmeyer's eyes narrowed into keen little slits and he stepped back weakly.

The rifle barrel exploded, and a sharp flash cut into the darkness.

Janey held up the lantern and the rifle ball flew into the wick, shattering it into a thousand burning slivers. Yet the ball's rapid flight didn't stop there. It crashed into the wick, inciting the kerosene within and continued on its journey, pulling the lantern's flame along with it like some macabre magnet.

It all happened in a second. The shattering of the wick, then finally the sheet of fire and metal piercing Tom Janey's stomach and, added to the kerosene, igniting into a ball of flame. It happened so fast, there was barely enough time for Janey to react—except to stand there and burn alive.

Janey screamed, less from the impact of the bullet than the flames rising all over his body and quickly eating him away with its unbearable heat. The fire rose quickly and his torso, then his chest and finally his head were engulfed in flames so intense that he was no longer a man, but a human torch, writhing in agony—his only claim to having been a man was his scream. And soon even this died away as the flames burned on and consumed him totally.

With no life left within him, the burning hulk that used to be Tom Janey writhed once more, then whirled around and fell in the gathered brush at the foot of the barn's wall.

The brush quickly caught fire. Soon the flames, rising in the wind, grew higher. With the winds carrying it, the flames spread and started to burn the other walls as well.

Holtzmeyer stood and watched briefly, not realizing that women were within the barn's walls. All he knew was that he had avenged his son's death. His head lowered and the last thing he saw was the dead grass beneath him. He dropped the rifle, keeled over and was dead before his body hit the ground.

Mart Janey and Jean Beaucaire were outside the house and holding lanterns high when they heard the shot and the scream.

They looked at each other and then ran toward the barn, careful not to jar the lanterns.

They both stopped when they saw the flames rising around the barn.

Within, the women were pounding on the doors, screaming for help as smoke rose up in huge black clouds.

Beaucaire said loudly, "I guess Tom fired the barn without us."

Mart worriedly said, "That was *him* screamin'! Where the hell is he?"

"I don't know," said Beaucaire, "but you better get to Charlie and let him know what happened. I'll check on Tom. He probably singed himself in the fire."

"All right," said Mart, doubling back for the house.

Beaucaire watched him run around the side of the house, then turned to look at the barn.

Beaucaire stood in the winds and was thinking about it all. It would be a shame to kill *all* those women. He could do as he pleased with them—and still make some kind of profit off them if he could get them away from Charlie Morse and still get over the state line. But if that was to occur, he couldn't let them burn alive. He couldn't handle all of them, but at least he could the grab the younger ones.

Brandishing his rifle, he went over to the barn doors and with his other hand, shoved the wooden bolt up and out of the two notches. He laid the board against the smoldering wall and then pulled open the door.

He was greeted with a cloud of dense smoke and a wave of heat struck him almost immediately.

The women all ran for the open doors. There were six of them in their early twenties, one in her thirties, one girl of fifteen and Ruth Tyler, the youngest. Their torn dresses were blackened and filthy, and one or two of them were screaming as they came into the open.

Just then Beaucaire raised his rifle and pointed it at them.

"Hold it!" he shouted. They all stopped at the sight of the rifle. A few of them embraced each other fearfully.

"Please let us out!"

"I'll let you out!" Beaucaire said, smiling. He pointed at two of the older women. "You! And You! Back into the barn! The rest come with me!"

"No!" Ruth cried.

"You're crazy!"

Beaucaire fired at the ground in front of one of the women. The women screamed and jumped back. The ball almost took off a woman's little toe.

"You two!" he said to the oldest woman there. "Get back inside or die right here!"

Behind the women the heat of the barn intensified. It was

dangerous just to stand there, much less go back inside. Their attention was riveted on Beaucaire, the look in his eyes wild enough to imply he'd do anything. He pulled back the hammer of the rifle and aimed it at Ruth. "Do it! Or she dies!"

Suddenly a shell from a spencer carbine hit the ground at Beaucaire's feet and flew away, kicking up dirt. Everyone turned and looked at the figure standing before the trees, his carbine aimed at Beaucaire's chest.

"I've got a better idea, Beaucaire!" Jim Gaines shouted in the wind. "Why don't *you* go back in the barn? And close the door after you."

Beaucaire stared at the Georgian, his rifle now harmlessly pointed skyward. The winds swirled around them and fed the growing flames.

Trying to sound calm, Beaucaire said, "Aw, now, Jim...We don't have to be like this. Look at these women. There's plenty for both of us—"

His answer was another shot, fired this time at his right foot. Had he not stepped back, Beaucaire would have lost all his toes.

Gaines' face was taut with fury under the wide brim of his hat.

"I said, get inside that barn!"

"But it is burning!" Beaucaire's voice betrayed panic.

"No foolin'!" answered the southerner, raising his rifle.

The women had been watching this, almost fascinated by their rescuer and witnessing a possible comeuppance to the man who had tormented them the most. But then the heat from the barn increased and they started to move away.

Seeing the danger, Gaines shouted, "You women clear out of there! I'll hold him!"

They didn't have to be told twice, but when they all scattered and ran, two of the women crossed in front of Gaines' line of fire. Seeing this, Beaucaire quickly ran toward the back of the house.

"Damn," uttered Gaines, still trying to aim. Finally, after the women scattered in all directions, Gaines moved forward and chased after the fleeing man.

From inside the house, Morse heard the various gunshots and screams, but oddly showed no concern. At first, he figured it was just the barn being fired and the women trying to make a run for it through the burning walls and timber, only to be shot down in the attempt.

But a strange feeling came over him that something was wrong.

He just sat in the dining area, trying to be calm at the end of that long table. In all that had happened, it never occurred to him to check his ammunition. In his mounting fear, he had forgotten to count his shots and that his last one was used to kill Ben Connelly.

The half-eaten food before him sat cold on his plate.

Feeling some strange sense of foreboding, he just sat at the head of the table. A host without guests. And now possibly a gang leader without a gang.

He was alone in the darkness.

Waiting.

He knew it wouldn't be long before he arrived...

CHAPTER TWENTY-ONE

RUTH TYLER RAN BEHIND THE HOUSE AND CIRCLED SOME BUSHES near the rear fence. She crouched behind them briefly and looked around. The winds were blowing fiercely, and she kept her body low to prevent her from being literally picked up and carried away by the gusts. Glancing to her right, she saw that the way was clear, and she rose carefully.

She was tired and hungry. The clothes she had worn days ago in Lawrence were now ragged and torn. She stank from days without a bath and she felt weak from hunger, yet the possibility of freedom made her strong again.

But when Ruth looked at her surroundings she didn't know where she was or what was happening. She knew one thing: She didn't want to be recaptured and forced back into any barn, wagon or basement. Or worse, whatever that crazy French fellow had in mind.

And who was that good-looking young man with the southern accent; the one they called Jim? Where did he come from?

Then a sadness came over her all at once and tears started to form. Her parents were dead, this much she knew. But she had to keep her head, those men might be nearby. Quickly she sniffed back the tears and wiped her eyes with the torn sleeve of her dress. She had to find her way out of there—her and the rest of those women and that good-looking southern boy.

Making her decision, Ruth turned and ran around the back of the house. Then she stopped short at what she saw. Her heart leapt in her chest as she stared.

A few yards ahead, two heavy wooden doors were in the ground. They had been thrown open and revealed the dank basement underneath.

Frightened now, she turned and fled back towards the fence opposite the trees behind the house. She climbed through it and went down a narrow path into the underbrush. Had she not been gripped by panic she would have noticed the corral further down the fence line and the frightened horses tied there.

She ran back further into the trees, breathing faster as her excitement grew. Fear guided her now and sweat formed beneath her ragged clothes as she ran. The winds pounded at her, with leaves and bark flying at her in a never-ending whirlwind, blinding her and scratching her face and bare arms. She screamed as the gusts picked up speed.

Then, as she came to a small clearing, a wind came and literally lifted Ruth off her feet. She cried out as her body was lifted three feet off the ground and pushed forward towards a row of bushes ahead of her. Waving her arms, she could not control her flight, which lasted only seconds.

Ruth threw her arms in front of her face just before she landed in the dense shrubbery. Sitting up, she found herself wedged between two bushes. Her body ached as she moved to crawl out from under them.

Then she heard a noise made her look up.

"Well, well, hello!"

Beaucaire was standing a dozen feet in front of her. His hat had been blown off and his hair blew wildly in the mounting winds. Still holding his rifle, he stood awkwardly and swayed, holding one arm in front of him for protection against the elements.

He kept his gaze on the little blonde-haired girl in front of him.

Ruth stared at him in fear, the memory of that basement all too vivid.

"Come on!" Beaucaire called out. "I'll take you to somewhere safe."

Ruth was trembling and tears formed in her eyes, yet she managed to shake her head.

"It will be all right!" he shouted through the howling winds. "I won't hurt you!"

Ruth shook her head again. She had not forgotten that this man had abused the other women and had also taken Sheila Farnsworth out into the woods and shot her in the head when she refused his advances.

A smile formed on Beaucaire's lips and he eyed her hungrily. He shifted his stance and put down his rifle, leaning it against a tree.

Ruth was trapped in the bushes, her frightened gaze locked on him. Beaucaire's arms were reaching out and his steady eyes saw nothing but her. His smile widened with every step he took.

Ruth found herself screaming at the sight.

The strong wind had ebbed and now sounds became clearer around them. That was when Beaucaire heard it; a footstep, a movement, and then a voice choked in rage.

The voice was familiar—as was the Irish brogue behind it.

"You lay a finger on that child and I'll blow you straight to hell!"

Beaucaire stopped, trying to keep his figure erect as the winds pushed against his body and swayed him. With some effort, he turned around and found himself standing a good ten feet away from Kelly Ryan. She was pointing his own rifle straight at him.

"You!"

Kelly said nothing, but the anger in her face spoke volumes. As she glared at him, she tried to keep her balance and steady the rifle.

"What are you doing here!" Beaucaire shouted.

Still keeping her eyes on the Frenchman, she spoke to Ruth. "Cover your eyes, lass! Turn away!"

Huddled in the bushes, Ruth obediently closed her eyes tightly and turned her head as well. She had never seen this Irish girl before, but if she was saving her life, she would do anything she wanted.

Beaucaire glanced back at Ruth, then faced Kelly again. "You won't kill me."

"Oh?"

"No, you won't." He staggered towards her in the wind. "You're not the type to kill a man, especially one you're attracted to..."

Kelly's rage grew as he approached. The wind shifted and her long brown hair blew in her face. Holding the rifle pistol-style, she quickly pushed back her hair with her other hand. Then with the same hand she reached out and wrapped her arm around the nearest tree.

"Don't worry," said Beaucaire as he advanced. "I like 'em older anyway..."

The winds shoved Kelly forward, but her hold on the tree kept her from falling.

"You see?" shouted Beaucaire. "The wind will blow you off your feet!" He glanced back at Ruth, then faced Kelly. "The wind will ruin you aim. I am directly in front of the girl. If you fire at me, you might hit her!"

Kelly still aimed the rifle, but she didn't want her shot to hit the girl. The wind then slammed into her and pushed her to the right as if someone had punched her in the side.

Beaucaire's hands came up and he lunged as another powerful gust came and pushed Kelly's rifle downward and to the left.

She fired.

Beaucaire's eyes widened in shock and the hands that reached out for Kelly quickly went down to his midsection.

In horror, he realized that it was no longer there...

Blood sprang from his mouth and his legs folded under him. His frightened eyes looked up at Kelly.

She watched him briefly and then, crouching slightly to steady herself against the wind, she held the rifle with both hands and raised the barrel in a tight aim.

Beaucaire tried to form a word, a quick and short utterance which might do him some good.

"Don't! Ple—"

Kelly aimed at close range, her beautiful blue eyes now bottomless holes with hate behind them.

Through her teeth, she hissed, "Rot in hell, killer!"

She fired. The ball came out of the barrel and flew all of two feet before striking Jean Beaucaire and tearing off half his face. Now devoid of life, the body pitched forward and fell into the dirt, its blood darkening the leaves.

Kelly gradually calmed down and looked up at the frightened girl pinned under the bushes, still with her eyes closed.

Quickly Kelly tossed the rifle aside and ran up to her. Crouching down to her, she carefully reached over and helped Ruth out from under the bushes.

"It's all right, darlin'," Kelly said gently, "he'll never bother you again."

Bursting into tears, Ruth looked into Kelly's sympathetic face and then threw her arms tightly around her neck. She was never as happy to see anyone in her life.

"There now," Kelly said, "we've got to get you somewhere safe before this blasted wind carries both of us away."

Ruth pulled herself away slightly and put her hands gently on Kelly's face. "Who are you?"

"My name's Kelly..."

Ruth looked gratefully at the Irish girl and said, "My name's Ruth..."

Kelly's face froze and she stared at the girl's face, the features getting more familiar to her as she recognized them.

Ruth saw the look and it frightened her a little. She asked, "What's wrong?"

Tears started to form in Kelly's eyes, and she smiled at the girl. Then she pulled Ruth close to her and hugged her tighter than she'd ever hugged anyone. Ruth didn't understand why Kelly was being so emotional, but she didn't care. She was happy that after days of suffering and starvation, someone this nice was caring for her.

"I'm glad to meet you, Ruth," Kelly said tearfully. She lightly kissed the girl's forehead and then turned around. Gingerly Kelly picked up the rifle, then stood erect awkwardly, lifting the not-so-little girl in her arms.

Tenaciously she fought through the wind. There was a basement back there with its doors wide open. Kelly walked back in that direction, holding onto Ruth with every step.

Kelly went through a broken section of the fence and was back on the property grounds. She held the rifle in her other arm pistol-fashion, and her eyes searched the area for anyone who might give them trouble.

Kelly wasn't sure what had prompted Ruth's escape and she didn't much care. No one was going to harm this girl ever again.

No one...

CHAPTER TWENTY-TWO

KELLY HELD RUTH TIGHTLY IN HER ARM AND RAN. BESIDES holding onto the weak girl, Kelly also had to contend with the high winds. The air around her was brisk and by the time they emerged from the woods, Kelly was gasping for breath.

Ruth asked, "Are you all right, Kelly?"

"I will be soon, darlin'."

"It's all right, Kelly. I can walk by myself."

"No, Ruth, look at you! You're white as a sheet and you're so thin! It's obvious the brutes hadn't fed you."

"No, not much."

"Look, darlin', there's a basement over there."

"No!"

"It's all right, hon, I swear!"

"They put us in a basement!"

Kelly looked into the girl's eyes and said sternly, "Listen to me, Ruth! Those men will never bother you again. I'll make sure of that! But we have to get out of this storm and the basement is our only hope. Don't worry, hon, I'll be down there with you." She scanned the grounds. "I just hope we can get the others down there as well."

Suddenly Ruth started crying again and put her head on Kelly's shoulder.

"Don't worry, hon. We'll be safe soon."

"I miss my brother."

Kelly's face became still and she gently lifted Ruth's chin. She said, "He's here, Ruth."

"He's here?"

Kelly nodded.

As she wiped her eyes, Ruth asked, "Where?"

"I'm sure he's around here somewhere. I've got to find him and get him down in that basement as well."

Awkwardly Kelly ran for the basement doors. Just then a figure climbed to the top step and saw them. When Kelly saw the person, she stopped in her tracks and instinctively started to raise the rifle.

Ruth put her hand on the barrel and said, "It's all right, Kelly. That's Jenny!"

Jenny was the fifteen-year old. Her unwashed red hair blew in the wind as she beckoned them over. As they got closer, Kelly also saw that her blouse was torn at the shoulder, revealing an ugly bruise. Her clothes stank and were also marked with ashes.

Jenny said, "Ruth, thank God you're alive!"

Then she looked at Kelly with questioning eyes.

Kelly saw the look and said quickly, "Kelly Kathleen Ryan, formerly of Cork, it's a pleasure to meet you. Now we'd best get down those stairs!"

"Yes!"

"Where are the others?"

"Down below!" Jenny shouted. "That girl, Martha, found us and led us down here."

"Where is she?"

"I don't know. She said she was looking for someone named Jim."

"That figures." She put Ruth down next to Jenny. "Take her. I've got to find them."

"No!" Ruth cried out. She was pulling Kelly by the arm.

Jenny suddenly screamed. She was looking off past them.

As if a silent alarm went off between them, they all plunged down the open doorway as Mart Janey fired his rifle. But waves of sand blew up before him and his aim was high. Kelly was the last one down and a ball slammed into one of the basement doors just as she was closing it after her. The shot had just missed her left wrist.

With all the women now safely down below, Mart screamed in frustration. He was planning to hide in the basement during the storm. Now with Kelly down there and armed with a rifle, he had no way of trying those doors without being shot at.

Mart Janey ran back towards the house. He realized that the house was also in danger of blowing away, but the winds hadn't picked up to that level yet. There was still a chance he might have some shelter there.

Then, when he got within thirty feet of the house, he saw someone at the back window. He was wearing a light-colored shirt and had a brown Stetson tied to his chin. The figure looked familiar.

Tyler!

Zeke was lifting up the window just as Mart Janey stooped and lifted his rifle. All the running in that powerful wind was making him gasp for breath. His huge chest heaved, and he was sucking air. He had to get inside.

But first, a quick kill.

The winds swept through the crossroads and shook all structures in its path. The barn was an inferno, with large chunks of burning wood broken off their foundations and hurling through the air, like flaming missiles.

The sky itself was still dark gray and the whirlpool of cold air gathering in the trees behind the house, suddenly scattered in all directions.

Mart Janey crouched. Sweat appeared briefly and he grunted with the effort, but this was worth it. His muscles aching, Janey raised the rifle. The barrel was right on his target.

The circle of cool air then snapped suddenly and flew north like a shot. The force of it whipped through the fence fronting the house, littering the grounds with splintered wood, and kept going until it struck the house with full impact.

A huge thud echoed through the area and then the sounds of tearing wood and shattering glass. The wooden roof over the front porch tore from the house and fell to the ground with a thunderous crash. It no sooner hit the ground then it broke apart and its pieces flew in all directions.

Inside the house, the front window amazingly did not shatter, but instead cracked down the middle, forming a huge jagged line in the glass.

Charlie Morse looked up and saw it. He breathed heavily and left his chair, drawing himself back into a corner.

He wondered what was keeping his men.

Nevertheless, he was not about to run. Not from the winds, not from God Almighty, and certainly not from Ruth Tyler's big brother.

He realized it now. And through all the chaos outside, it gave him a strange peace of mind, knowing he was going to settle it once and for all...

At the back window, the walls shook, and Zeke felt the impact as his hands rested on the sill.

At that moment, Mart Janey fired just as another blast shook the house. With his hands still on the sill, the impact made the walls shudder and suddenly threw Zeke off.

As he rolled to the ground, Zeke glanced up and saw the window shatter into a hundred slivers. Zeke quickly covered his head as the glass rained down on him. He knew immediately that the winds did not shatter the window.

Pulling out the Dragoon Colt, Zeke cocked the hammer and looked towards the clearing. He saw Mart Janey, on his hands and knees, awkwardly swaying in the winds.

With his thick fingers grasping the cold ground, Janey pushed himself halfway to his feet. With Janey's body now off the ground, Zeke sighted along the barrel of the Dragoon and fired.

The bullet pierced Janey's right shoulder. Ordinarily the shot would have just wounded Janey, but instead the bullet traveled straight down and cut through his lung, finally settling there.

Mart Janey tried to stand but couldn't find the strength. He rose partly on his knees and swayed like a wounded bear. Just then the winds sent an icy blast through the grounds and hit Janey with full force. He was now sucking oxygen desperately. He gasped loudly and suddenly he felt a tightening of his windpipe, abruptly cutting off what little air he could breathe. He tried to rise, but his brain couldn't command his legs anymore.

Zeke watched in horror as Mart Janey's face lost all its color and turned completely white. Janey's eyes were large in their sockets and his huge head dropped to his chest heavily. Then his massive body pitched forward and hit the ground with a thud.

Zeke watched him briefly, knowing Janey would never rise again.

He holstered his gun and slowly got to his feet, keeping close to the ground. He looked at the barn, its burning pieces blowing off into the trees.

Zeke realized that the women could have been inside the barn, but by the time he had arrived it was an inferno. He hoped to God that they were in the house. He had not heard any screams from within the house when the winds struck, but it was the only place left to search. He had not found the basement doors at the other side of the house.

In the back of his mind was something he didn't want to face, but knew he had to eventually. His sister was dead. Just as in Lawrence, he was too late.

The thought filled him with rage and he quickly got up and turned his attention to the house. The howling of the winds increased and soon all that could be heard was the creaking of the house, already shaking on its foundations and the high-pitched squeal of cool air rushing by.

Zeke quickly climbed through the open window.

He looked around the bedroom. It was dark, with awkward shadows cast against the dirty floor. Every piece of bric-a-brac in the room was now shattered, with pieces of furniture and crockery lying about.

The bedroom door was open.

He knew that someone else was in the house. He had heard movement coming from the waystation's dining area. Quietly he pulled out his gun and moved out of the bedroom. He felt along the walls of the darkened hallway, slowly approaching the front of the house. After a few moments, Zeke appeared in the open doorway of the dining area and saw the faded light coming in through the cracked window. With the Colt before him, he moved into the room.

But once he cleared the doorway, a Navy Colt was pushed into his back. He felt the cold metal pushing its way between his shoulder blades and gave a thought to whirling around and firing his own weapon.

He felt that reckless.

And then sanity took hold and he did nothing.

Charlie Morse barked, "Drop it!"

Zeke hesitated.

Morse pushed the gun barrel deeper, hurting Zeke's back. Abruptly Zeke dropped the gun.

No sooner had the Dragoon pistol hit the floor than Morse yanked Zeke around to face him.   Then he shoved the Kansan against the wall, the impact knocking a picture of some 18th century ironclad to the floor noisily.

Zeke's wide hat brim, tied low, cast a shadow over his eyes as Morse tried to study his face.

"Look up!" he commanded.

Zeke looked up and the two men saw each other for the first time since Lone Jack.   Hatred welled up in the Kansan and once again his vision seemed to shake uncontrollably.   He glared at Morse, his rage showing clearly in the semi-darkness.

Stepping back to get a good look at him, Morse said, "Connelly was right.   You're coming for that little girl…"

Zeke breathed heavily and his throat was suddenly dry.   When he spoke, his voice didn't sound like his own.   "Where is she?" he asked thickly.

"*DEAD!*" Morse answered, and for the first time in their encounter, gave a little smile.   He elaborated mercilessly, "She burned alive in the barn along with the others."

Zeke almost braced himself against the wall, his fast breathing the only discernable sound in the room.   He looked and felt like a cornered animal being challenged by a hunter with a loaded rifle, provoking him to pounce so he can shoot him with a clear conscience.

Zeke was not a suicidal person, but he *had* to destroy this man, one way or the other.

Morse continued gravely, "She's as dead as you're gonna be..."

CHAPTER TWENTY-THREE

THEY HAD ONE LANTERN IN THE BASEMENT. IT HAD ALREADY blown out before, but Kelly had found matches on a nearby shelf and re-lit it.

They all looked at their strange surroundings.

At first the women had been reluctant to go down there, but Martha Walker had been convincing. Martha had searched all over for a refuge for the women, and when she found them running into the woods after their encounter with Beaucaire, she gathered them together and led them back to the basement. They were shivering and hungry and, ignoring her own chattering teeth and freezing toes, she brandished her rifle before her and resolved to protect them until she could get them safely underground. And only when they were safe would she search for Jim.

It was the least she could do to atone for her father and brother...

After the women had told Kelly what Martha had done, she hoped that her three friends still on the surface would be able to find shelter. Trapped down below, she felt powerless. They had found small cans of food on the shelves and a cooking pit dig into the earth at the far end of the basement, so the women would have something to eat at last—yet it didn't cheer Kelly too much.

She was hoping against hope that there would be three more mouths to feed...

Ruth had eaten little, insisting that the older women eat first, but Kelly made sure that she ate her fill.

Suddenly exhausted, Kelly dropped onto an old wooden stool in the corner, still grasping her rifle. She was worried about the others, but these women were her first-priority. She must stay and protect them.

After a while, Ruth walked up and climbed onto her lap. She embraced Kelly and said quietly, "I'm glad you came..."

Kelly smiled at her. "So am I, dear...So am I."

Ruth's eyes went up to Kelly's face. She idly put her hand on Kelly's cheek and stroked it gently.

"Thank you, darlin'..."

"...How do you know Zeke?"

Kelly took Ruth's hand and kissed it gently. She looked down at her face and said quietly, "We met while he was looking for you..."

Ruth then searched the Irish girl's face curiously.

Kelly noticed the look and good-naturedly asked, "Now what would you be thinkin'?"

Ruth paused, studying her fingers briefly. Then she looked up and suddenly asked, "Are you his girl?"

Kelly quickly blushed.

Then she smiled weakly and stroked Ruth's hair.

Kelly finally replied, "Yes, Ruth...If he'll have me, I'll be his girl —always."

Ruth happily embraced her. "I'm glad!" she said. "We need to have a family again."

Kelly leaned her head on Ruth's and smiled. Well, she had the little sister's approval. Now all she needed was for her brother to be alive.

Her eyes went to the ceiling and listened for any sounds of life. She thought she had heard gunshots before, but the only noise she could be certain of was that infernal howling...

Silently she prayed, hoping Ruth wouldn't look up and see her mouth the words...

The winds increased again and struck the house from the east, shaking it to its foundations. The wall Zeke was pressed against trembled suddenly and he heard the sound of wooden crossbeams bending above them. Zeke's eyes glimpsed the ceiling and he knew immediately that one more gust might be all it would take to send it crashing down on both of them.

"What's the matter, Tyler? Scared?" Morse was smiling.

Zeke looked him in the eye and said, "If I take you with me, it'll be worth dyin'..."

As the turbulence outside increased, the ceiling above them creaked louder, followed by the sounds of thick wood tearing apart.

It was then that Morse pulled the trigger.

Zeke was prepared to lunge at that moment until he saw Morse cock the hammer back and pull the trigger again and again, only to be greeted with empty clicks.

Icy cold drifted through the room, but neither man noticed.

Morse looked at his empty gun but didn't seem too surprised. He had not reloaded it. And in the quick seconds he stood there, he vaguely remembered taking up Beacaire's challenge to show who was a better shot. Had he not fired so many balls at a used skillet hung over a tree branch somewhere in the woods, Zeke Tyler would be dead.

Or more likely, had he not fired that last ball into Ben Connelly's stomach…

For the first time, Zeke's eyes held amusement as he watched the man and his empty little gun.

Yet Morse did not attempt to run. He just glared at the Kansan, tension rising within him.

The howling winds struck the outside walls and the building's timbers shook with a startling fury. Above them, the tearing of wood sounded eerie in the darkness.

Stepping back further, Morse asked quietly, "Why don't you pick up your gun?"

Zeke replied, just as quietly, "I don't need a gun to kill you."

Then the crossbeam directly above them suddenly snapped and half the ceiling fell in under its weight.

Zeke dove into Morse, plowing into the other man's stomach with such force the two men landed in a corner right near the front window. A large chunk of the ceiling hanging dangerously over the very spot the two men had stood. Splinters and dust rose in angry clouds that filled the room. The clouds swept towards the two grappling men on the floor and covered them both with soot.

Had they not been busy fighting each other, they could have easily turned back and gazed through the hole above, only to see the swirling winds finally taking grotesque form. The winds were spinning miles into the sky, its ugly blackness studded with the debris it was sucking off the ground as it spiraled further and further up into the stratosphere.

Though its epicenter was many miles from the crossroads waystation, the twister was picking up speed as it traveled across land, effortlessly uprooting trees and causing every structure in its path to explode and shatter on contact.

The winds blew into the ruined house and struck the two men, swirling dirt and debris all around them.

They rose slowly, arms locked around each other as they fell back against the long table that was amazingly still standing. Zeke's hat had fallen off in the corner and now his head was fully exposed to the cold that poured into the room. But Zeke was not thinking of the cold as Morse pushed his head against the table's edge. Then, as if it were the most natural thing in the world, Morse put his fingers around the Kansan's throat.

His face inflamed with hatred Morse squeezed tighter as Zeke attempted to push him off. As he stared down at his victim, Morse was reminded of his strength. His mind went back to that day in Nashville, in a busy saloon not far from the capitol building. It was years ago, and he had not thought of him since then. That Negro he had accused of cheating at cards. He had no idea whether the man was guilty or not, but it felt good to strangle him anyway. Being that it was in Tennessee, no one in the saloon interfered with him. Then he had tossed the body aside as if he were a bag of rubbish and let him hit the hard, wooden floor, cards and chips falling onto the man's face.

There were no cards or chips to fall on Zeke Tyler when he was through, but the pleasure of the kill was more than enough for him.

Morse leaned into him even more and increased the pressure around his throat. Coupled with the thin air around him, Zeke felt as if he might black out.

Desperately he reached up with his left hand and dug into Morse's face. The killer was blinded temporarily but kept up the pressure on his enemy's throat.

Taking a different tack, Zeke took his hand off Morse's face and his fist shot upward, striking his enemy's nose with full force. As expected, Morse's head fell back as blood gushed from the now smashed nose. Using his right hand again, Zeke followed with a punch to Morse's left eye that knocked the killer off him and caused him to fall back against the cracked window.

Zeke sat up and briefly felt his throat. His breathing was harsh, and slowly air made its way back into his lungs. It hurt him at first, but he willed himself to breathe deeply, despite the icy chill in the air.

At the rear of the house, the walls suddenly broke from their foundations with a deafening roar and pushed into what had once been the bedroom. Seen through the gaping hole in the roof, the twister seemed to grow in size and its proximity to the house increased.

Morse put his hand up to his shattered nose and as he touched it, the pain felt like needles going through his head. Angrily he faced the Kansan just as he was coming off the table.

For Zeke, all concerns for his safety were gone. He lived for only one thing and that was to make sure Charlie Morse did not live to murder anyone else's little sister.

With renewed energy, Zeke came off the table and threw himself against Charlie Morse with everything he had.

Morse could have easily side-stepped him, but he had no intention of doing so. His hands were out in front of him ready to receive the attack as it came. When Zeke struck him, the momentum of the lunge carried them both through the weakened glass. The window shattered and they hovered in the air for a second before they plunged into the front yard. As they hit the ground amidst a shower of broken glass, an explosion sounded from the rear of the house. It shook the ground they were struggling on, the tremor thundering in their ears.

The rear of the house, including the bedroom and hallway that Zeke had entered through, were now gone. A place where people had lived less than 48 hours ago was now thrown up into the sky, never to return.

The two young men were now rolling savagely in the dirt, the empty corral just a few yards in their path.

Finally, they stopped a few yards before the corral's fence. They were giving each other slashing blows, their faces becoming bloody masks under fists that wouldn't stop. Their shirts were tearing apart as the winds cut through them; the bodies exposed through the tears covered with bruises.

Far behind them, the frame supporting the front of the house finally broke apart and the rest of the structure fell with a horrible crash, its walls shattering into huge chunks of wood and debris before it even hit the ground. The winds then cut through what remained of the building like a giant knife.

Now with the house no longer in the way, the winds that were on the cusp of the twister, blew fast throughout the front yard.

Zeke and Morse struggled to their feet. Tears brought on by the cold were forming in their eyes and they were gripping each other's throats as they rose. Had they stayed close to the ground they might have avoided the winds coming at them from the north. Instead it struck the two men with maximum impact.

Before either man could react, the gusts literally swept them off their feet and their bodies flew across the yard. They were off the ground for only seconds, but it was long enough to carry them towards the corral. Once they struck the fence, the weathered old log shattered and they landed heavily in the corral, its soft earth having turned rock solid against the mounting cold.

They rolled over and Morse ended up above the Kansan, putting one hand on Zeke's throat and using the other hand in a strained effort to crush his head against the frozen ground. Morse's hand was pure muscle and its grip was covering Zeke's mouth and eyes and pushing against his nose. Zeke reached up painfully, his flailing hand finally catching a piece of what used to be Morse's shirt collar. He closed his fingers around it and yanked the piece of cloth down towards him, pulling Morse's head down as well. Zeke then hurled his other fist at the bloody nose and knocked the killer aside.

Then he rolled over, briefly putting a hand on his face and trying to catch his breath. The pause gave Zeke time to push himself up off the ground. Not giving his opponent a chance to rise, he reached out and pulled Morse to his feet by the hair. His left hand swung hard at Morse's jaw, causing the killer to bite down and almost sever his tongue. Blood streamed from his mouth as he tried to recover.

But Zeke wouldn't give him a chance. He hit Morse with his right hand, a slashing blow that closed Morse's left eye for good and opened further the wound to his nose. Then the winds shot through the corral and struck both of them at once. It wasn't strong enough to lift them off their feet, but it did knock them to the ground. Now several feet apart, they both rolled over weakly.

Zeke pushed himself off the ground and came to his feet. His hands were bloody and every bit of him was throbbing in pain, but his rage never left him. This time he stood back and allowed Morse to expend precious energy to rise on his own.

Tiredly Morse rose to his feet, staggering once he stood to his full height. But as soon as the killer put up his fists, Zeke was upon him.

He struck Morse again and again, each blow hard against Morse's body, each driving punch mutilating Morse's face beyond recognition. The energy suddenly drained out of Morse like running water. His eyes were now closed completely, and blood was dripping down his torn shirt as he staggered back. Yet he was still on his feet, stubbornly refusing to fall, taking Zeke's punches as the Kansan kept swinging.

Morse staggered back to a large cottonwood and fell against it as Zeke kept up the assault. The winds came again, and small branches rained down on the two men as they fought, only now the fight was clearly one-sided. Finally, what little strength Morse had, disappeared completely and a final punch knocked him to the ground. His body rolled several feet away as Zeke watched him.

The Kansan was dizzy from the fight and his breathing was labored as he stood wearily in the cold. Suddenly the winds picked up again and struck Zeke hard in the side, as if someone had punched him, and he fell heavily against the tree behind him. Suddenly feeling another mounting wind pulling him off his feet, Zeke reached up and instinctively wrapped his arms around the trunk.

He didn't know why, but something caused him to look back at Morse. With his eyes squinting painfully against the winds, he saw Morse slowly push himself off the ground.

But before Zeke could move, the winds suddenly increased to a velocity faster than anything he had experienced up to that point. He threw himself on the ground and used all his strength to hold onto the tree, his arms straining, and his back stretched almost to the breaking point.

Gradually Zeke found the strength to crane his neck around and look at Morse. The air around was no longer breathable oxygen, but instead a deep vacuum. Zeke gasped, frantically trying to draw air into his lungs. He quickly realized he had to find pockets of air close to the ground. With some difficulty, he finally pressed his head against the tree's base.

He still kept his eyes on Morse.

Unable to see, Morse rose halfway and then suddenly was lifted off the ground and his body blown back by several yards.

Now Zeke looked up from the ground and clearly saw what was destroying the land around them. The twister spun into the sky, black and ominous, looking bigger than anything he had ever seen. Zeke had never been scared of anything or anyone in his life, but for the first time, fear took hold of him and he trembled at the sight. He wanted to shut his eyes to it, to wish it away, leaving nothing more frightening than a slight breeze to remember it by.

But it didn't go away; it only grew in diameter.

Then Zeke turned his attention back to Morse and the sight caused him to shudder.

Charlie Morse, he of the would-be successor to William Clarke Quantrill and proud murderer in his own right, found himself being lifted higher and higher off the ground. Zeke's head craned upwards to watch.

Finally, Zeke couldn't see him anymore.

Then suddenly Morse's scream hovered in the air and caused Zeke to look up again. He searched the skies and finally spotted Morse's body going around and around, spiraling upwards, arms and legs flailing uselessly like some broken doll's. The winds spun him faster and faster, lifting him further, his figure losing all detail and becoming a silhouette, then a shadow and finally just a small black dot hurtling into space.

Zeke winced when he finally lost sight of him. Then he looked down, keeping his head and body close to the ground as the winds increased their speed.

The gusts blew easily through his torn shirt and chilled him. Slowly he tried, with his arms still wrapped tightly around the tree, to crawl around to the other side of the trunk, away from the open, to shield himself back among the grove of trees. Fighting the gusts, he crawled around the base, every muscle already aching from the fight.

Branches swayed fiercely in the winds, more than a few breaking off and falling to the ground around him. Now within the shadows of the cottonwoods, he started to hear a sound that was becoming all-too familiar—the sound of a structure tearing from its foundations.

The sounds coming from back in the woods grew louder by the second. Zeke could barely turn his head, but curiosity and self-preservation got the best of him and he painfully made efforts to look behind him.

He turned just in time to see a huge cottonwood bend towards him menacingly. His eyes widened in fear and he instinctively huddled closer to the trunk. Finally, the sounds of centuries' old wood ripping apart was followed by that of a juggernaut rushing through the air, slamming the thick branches of other trees out of its way as it descended to earth. Zeke saw it clearly—it was falling towards him.

Its trunk grew bigger and bigger as it fell towards him. Zeke quickly put his head down, hunching his shoulders in an effort to cover it from the impact. He did it just in time. As the cottonwood fell, huge branches broke off in its decent and fell on Zeke, almost burying him.

Then it slammed into the earth, the tremor shaking Zeke's body as he fought to hold himself still. Dirt and debris flew into the air in huge clouds as Zeke cautiously peered through his shielding arm. The dead tree had landed less than ten yards away. Reflecting on this, Zeke finally found the breath to exhale gratefully.

But then Zeke's body stiffened in the chilly air and only reminded him of his plight. His face was marked by bruises and his knuckles were caked in now drying blood, his shirt in tatters and his trousers almost in the same condition. He shivered uncontrollably as he lay under a sea of broken tree branches, some as much as a twenty feet long and a foot thick. He had let go of the tree trunk. The fallen branches above him were acting as a barrier to the winds. Releasing the trunk, the blood in his arms and shoulders started to flow again. With a blanket of broken wood and shrubbery wedging itself above him, he slowly found a pocket of air and breathed deeply, his head still close to the ground.

Gradually he put his arms down and looked up. Above him, he saw nothing but branches and piles of leaves. The sky was completely gone from his line of vision. Under his blanket of branches, he still felt the winds above, but much less now. Zeke took in huge swallows of air gratefully, even if it did smell of old wood. At this point, his bare shoulders and chest were roughly scratched by the pointed ends of the branches. He didn't know whether he was going to have the strength to dig himself out of the pile of torn wood, but one thing was certain: He was better off lying there than dealing with the storm still raging above.

Zeke was considering all this when the unthinkable happened. Another sound of tearing wood filled his ears—this time uncomfortably close. It took him but half a minute to realize exactly where the sound was coming from.

It was the tree right above him, the one he had held onto so desperately just minutes before. It was breaking somewhere at its midway point and it was breaking fast. Zeke instinctively pushed closer to the ground, his heart beating rapidly as he heard the roar above. If the tree fell directly on top of him, it would have no trouble getting through the pile of broken tree branches and crushing him.

It was the closest Zeke had ever come to panic—but he had nowhere to go, no way to protect himself. Warily, he reflected that he had spoken too soon when he thought he was safe. *I'm not out of the woods yet*, he figured wryly.

The trunk above him was tearing itself into pieces and the sounds thundered in his ears. Scared and in pain, Zeke was still clear-headed enough to know that the smaller the figure, the less chance there would be for a concussion or a life-threatening bone fracture. He had read something in adventure books that came back to him now. It was about explorers who faced the danger of avalanches, were even buried in them and lived.

He drew his tall frame close, his knees coming up to his chest as tightly as possible. He became a human ball, flattened against the cold ground. His head was as far down his chest as it would go, his hands above him tightly covering his skull.

He waited anxiously.

The tearing sounds stopped suddenly.

Then after a minute, the uncomfortable silence was rudely broken by the sounds of branches hurtling into other branches and then breaking off as the cottonwood continued its descent.

Then its journey ended abruptly.

And with the impact, the blanket of wood above Zeke suddenly pushed down on him and something that felt like it weighed a ton pressed down on his arm, and in turn, against his skull. It immediately hit Zeke with a searing pain and then a blinding flash sprang up before his tightly closed eyes.

Then the pain quickly subsided, and Zeke laid absolutely still, for all purposes, dead to the world...

CHAPTER TWENTY-FOUR

I<small>T WAS THE RUSTLING BRANCHES THAT CAUSED HIM TO OPEN HIS</small> eyes. He half-opened them experimentally; then he opened them all the way.

There seemed to be solid wood all around him. His first thought was that he was in a coffin. Then his eyes gradually gave details to his surroundings and he made out branches and limbs, just as before. He felt as if he had slept for fifty years, his achy body slowly responding to the press of the branches against him.

Then his heart leapt at the sounds coming from above. He lied still, gently breathing his small pocket of oxygen and patiently listened to the sounds, trying to make them out.

There was no mistaking them. He was listening to footsteps on the branches above him. Then the sounds of branches being moved away, some snapping apart as they were being quickly tossed aside.

Writhing under the branches, Zeke put his hands on his shoulders and then his legs. Gently he felt his limbs and joints. Now that he was conscious again, the throbbing pains returned, and he winced as he tried to turn.

As the branches were being moved away, he gradually heard muffled voices—apparently of all kinds—some higher-pitched, some deeper. Then the voices started to take on some familiarity, of various accents from various places.

He looked straight above him and saw piles of branches being pulled away, gradually expanding his line of vision. And as the broken and now rotted wood was being pulled away, his eyes glimpsed a sight he never thought he'd see again.

The morning sun came to him and practically blinded him with its rays. But it was there—and he was glad to see it. He blinked his eyes, painfully making them adjust.

And with the sun came warmth, a sudden burst of late summer heat.

One voice was close, right above him in fact, with answering voices sounding farther away, the words gradually becoming clear in the dawn air.

Then the silhouette of a head with a wide-brimmed hat appeared and looked down on him. At first, Zeke couldn't identify him; the sun was directly behind the man. Yet as soon as he spoke, he knew who it was.

"Son of a bitch!" exclaimed Jim Gaines. Then, suddenly contrite, he turned his head and spoke to someone behind him. "Sorry, ladies!" he called out with a slight tip of his hat.

Zeke heard a few female voices saying something like, "Don't worry about it!"

Then Gaines turned back to him and pushed his hat back on his head. He said quietly, "Welcome back, Kansas..."

Zeke swallowed and looked up at him gratefully. "Glad to see you, Reb..."

Gaines bent over quickly and used his big hands to dig through the branches, clawing at them again and again, yanking away every piece of wood in his sight until finally there was a hole big enough for Zeke to climb through.

"Any broken bones? Can ya stand?"

"I'll soon find out," Zeke replied. "Anyway, I don't like it down here."

"Don't blame you," said Gaines, holding his hand.

It was painful, but Zeke found the strength to reach up with his right hand, steadying himself with his left, and climbed up. Gaines quickly wrapped his other arm around Zeke's waist and lifted him up slowly. When Zeke stood to his full height, he trembled slightly and then staggered, but Gaines quickly caught him.

"It's all right," Zeke said shakily, adjusting his stance. Gaines gradually allowed him to stand by himself as Zeke looked at the ground. They were standing on a fallen tree.

Then Zeke looked at the devastated land and a tremendous sadness overcame him.

He looked at Gaines and almost choked as he said, "We were too late, Jim…"

All the rescued women were standing several yards behind him, watching him and trying to control their joy.

Gaines looked at him now, a smirk on his face.

He said laconically, "Turn around, you idiot."

Zeke slowly turned around and was stunned to see them—all of them—including the one he had pursued for so long. He got down off the pile of branches as quickly as he could and suddenly found the strength to move faster. Tears were running down Ruth's cheeks as she ran towards him.

Zeke went down to his knees in the dirt and when she got to him, she threw her arms around her brother's head and kissed him repeatedly. He responded in kind, embracing her tightly. Zeke was crying uncontrollably, all the pent-up emotion of the past few days coming out.

As she sniffed back her tears, she looked at her brother. She was not crying so much now, and she watched him with a kind of wonder.

It was the first time she had ever seen him cry.

Ruth gently ran her hand back through his hair and said quietly, "It's all right, Zeke...Please, don't cry..."

He finally looked up at her, his eyes reddened by tears. Slowly he gathered himself, still not believing she was actually alive and standing in front of him.

Then he looked at her again, as if seeing her for the first time. He saw the rags she wore and experimentally touched her thin, dangling arms.

"Have you eaten anything?"

Ruth nodded, smiling for the first time. He had long missed that smile.

She said simply, "Kelly fed me."

Zeke looked at her and his eyes came alive at the name. It then occurred to him that he hadn't noticed the others standing some distance away, these people who were giving the siblings their time alone.

Zeke looked up and saw Kelly wiping her eyes as she watched them. In all this time, she still held onto her rifle.

He then smiled at Ruth. "One moment, bunny-head..."

"Go right ahead!" she said, knowing what he was going to do.

He came to his feet and moved quickly over to Kelly. When he came to her, she let the rifle drop to the ground and they embraced tightly. Ruth grinned when she saw them kiss longingly.

Then Zeke turned around and looked at everyone. When he spotted Martha with the women, he looked back at Jim Gaines.

Gaines answered, "Yep, they followed us. We told them to

stay put and they followed us anyway. And from what Ruth told us, it was a good thing too. Kelly saved her life."

Zeke turned to her, but the Irish girl looked at her shoes, blushing suddenly.

"We're beholden to all of you," said Jenny.

"God, yes," said one of the other women, putting her hand on Zeke's arm and squeezing it gratefully. Unfortunately, to Zeke, the gesture made him wince.

Martha said, "As soon as we got here, Kelly and I split up. She searched the woods and I found the basement. After she got everyone down there, I went back to search for Jim."

Kelly asked good-naturedly, "And where were you two all night while the storm was raging?"

Martha looked at Gaines affectionately. "Jim is pretty good at finding havens—from storms and posses, it seems." Now it was Jim Gaines' turn to blush as Martha continued. "He knew the land, and it wasn't long before we found a shelter in the hills not far from here. We wedged ourselves in under a shelf of rock, with barely six inches of room between us..." She looked at him again as he tried to hide his eyes in the shadow of his hat brim. "We were huddled like that all night..."

"Hmm," said Zeke, trying to hide his amusement, "how awful for you..."

It was an hour before Zeke and Jim Gaines found their first horse, a gelding in a pasture not far from the wreckage of the waystation. They both moved towards him slowly, speaking soothingly to the frightened animal until they could get close enough to grab him.

Zeke asked, "Can you ride bareback?"

The Georgian grinned at him. "Since I was four." He steadied the shy gelding and quickly threw himself up onto the horse's back. Then he looked down at Zeke from his new vantage point and suddenly saw him in a new light.

"Hell, Kansas! You got that way from more than just the storm!"

Zeke looked up at him and said quietly, "...I had a little talk with Charlie Morse."

Gaines understood. "I figured you wouldn't quit until you gave him a piece of your mind. I'm just sorry I wasn't there to see it. Must've been quite a show..."

Zeke absently felt his jaw and said, "Yeah..."

"Who won?"

"Well...I'm still alive."

Gaines nodded again. "I figured that would happen too... Where's his body?"

Zeke was quiet for a moment, the memory still fresh. Gaines noticed it.

Finally, Zeke said, "You want to know where his body is? Just look up."

Gaines' eyes went heavenward briefly. Then a chill went through him as he thought about it.

Another horse was found soon afterwards, and Zeke was able to ride to the nearest fort. Once there, he was able to report everything that happened to the fort's commander. In the meantime, Gaines was able to ride into Holden for supplies, including some clothes for Zeke and the women and a much-needed wagon.

After Zeke returned with an army patrol, the women were taken back to the fort. It was another week before they would be settled back in their hometowns—mostly in Kansas—but not in their own homes. They were now gone. Their families were gone as well, though a few relatives were still alive to greet them on their return. But it was the townsfolk, devastated by their own losses, who would take the women in and give them homes again.

A few days later, the four of them separated at the Fort Scott Road in Kansas.

Kelly asked Gaines, "Where will you go now?"

Gaines looked at Martha as she sat her horse in the road and smiled at him, her red hair glistening in the sun.

"We were thinking of California," he said.

Zeke looked at him, then Martha. He was just getting used to his crisp new clothes. "*We* were, huh?" he said, smirking at them.

Gaines leaned towards Zeke and said confidentially, "She's all alone...You know...Got no one to take care of her..."

Zeke said quietly, "The same could be said for you..."

"Now, now," said Gaines, frowning at him. "Keep up that kind of talk and we won't write."

Zeke nodded, still grinning.

"That address still good that you gave us?"

"As far as I know. We're headed there now."

Kelly asked, "Tell me, Mister Gaines, who do you think will win the war now, the north or the south?"

Jim Gaines answered, "I don't give a hang!" Then he leaned forward and shook Zeke's hand. Quietly he said, "Our side won, didn't it, Kansas?"

Clasping his hand, Zeke replied, "That's right, Reb. Our side won..."

It was two days later when Helen Dawson looked up from her wash and heard the horses and wagon pulling up in front of their home. Hank Dawson saw his wife run anxiously to the door and quickly got up.

On his way to the door, he found his daughter and took her aside. "Remember the idea I was talking to your mother about?"

Louisa nodded, smiling.

"Well, I think it's gonna happen sooner than you think."

"Yes, Pa!"

"And, Louisa?"

"Yes?"

"Bring your sister outside with you."

When Hank Dawson showed up on his front porch, he found his wife tearfully embracing Zeke, then Kelly. Suddenly Helen saw the little blonde girl they had brought with them and stared at her, almost in wonder.

Zeke had already broached the idea to Ruth, and though it scared her at first, eventually she was comforted by all the nice things Zeke had said about the Dawsons.

When Helen knelt down to Ruth, she was surprised when the girl threw her arms around her neck suddenly. Helen pressed her close.

"It's been a long time since a mother's hugged you, hasn't it?"

"Yes," Ruth answered, touching Helen's face. "...Mommy."

Hank gave his wife a look and said, "Well?"

Tears came to Helen as she embraced the girl. "Yes. Oh, yes!" She kissed Ruth and then cried on her shoulder.

After a moment, she stood up and turned back to the porch. Louisa stood there watching, her hand gently squeezing Penelope's.

Smiling weakly as she sniffed back tears, Helen said, "Girls, this is your new sister."

The girls came up to Ruth and with little hesitation, both embraced her.

Hank Dawson came off the porch and put his arm around his wife. As they faced Zeke and Kelly, Hank said, "You know, Zeke. One thing bothers me."

"What's that, sir?"

"Well, we got all of Kelly's letters about what's been goin' on, so we know Penny is her sister. Only now, Ruth is part of our family as well...Now my question is this: If Kelly is Penny's sister and you're Ruth's brother, though mind you, you and Kelly have *not* been adopted by us—what does that make you and Kelly in relation to each other? Confusing, isn't it?"

Kelly looked at Zeke and smiled as he put his arm around her. The Dawsons quickly noticed this new familiarity and waited hopefully.

"Don't worry, folks," Zeke said, holding her close. "I won't complicate your lives any further. But *someone's* got to give the bride away..."

A philosopher had once said that when families were devastated by war, humanity always found a way to confound the warmongers and create new families to carry on.

Almost two years later, in June 1865, as William Clarke Quantrill died a slow death of bullet wounds in a Kentucky hospital, the Tylers' little boy turned eight months old...

A LOOK AT: THE MCDERMOTT FIFTY

BY BOB HERZBERG

Ruthless cattle baron Tad McDermott and his partners have hired a band of fifty killers to wipe out newly-arrived homesteaders and their families. When rancher George Bingham is murdered, his son, Jerry, travels from New York to find out who's responsible. Joined by feisty homesteader Jill Carmody, Bingham soon discovers a web of corruption and systematic murder that has made a mockery of the law and endangers the opening of the frontier. And there'll be hell to pay, and blood to spill....

AVAILABLE NOW

ABOUT THE AUTHOR

BOB HERZBERG was born in Brooklyn, N.Y. in 1956. He had graduated from Erasmus Hall High School and went on to take a variety of jobs, from truck driver to warehouse manager to salesman. He always wanted to act in plays and do comedy and soon started performing in community theaters and colleges around New York. By the 1990s, Bob had performed standup comedy, improv and murder mystery/dinner theater at clubs in both N.Y. and Hollywood. Around the same time, he wrote and co-starred in *The Melnicks* series on local TV, which had been aired on both coasts. In 2006, he started writing western novels and mysteries. He is a member of Western Writers of America, International Thriller Writers and the Dramatists' Guild. In the past six years he has had four books published: *Shooting Scripts, From Pulp Western to Film*, which is about western authors and the films made from their works; *The FBI & the Movies*, which focuses on films with FBI characters and the Bureau's influence on these productions; *Savages & Saints: the Changing Image of American Indian in Westerns*, which details the Indian Wars and the films made about them; and *The Left Side of the Screen* which focuses on Communists and Liberals in Hollywood during the years 1929-2009. In 2008, he appeared on TV-Land's *Myths & Scandals* in a sequence about the FBI; in 2013, he appeared as a commentator on the 20th anniversary Blu-ray edition of *The Fugitive*. Bob latest, *Revolutionary Mexico on Film, 1914-2014,* will be released in 2015. He's been happily married to the lovely actress/poet Colleen Hayden. One day they hope to live out west.